He didn't ev...
his glass a...
his hand

Patrick felt no pain as a jagged edge sliced the flesh between his thumb and forefinger. He was transfixed by the face of an angel.

"Kathleen...my God—"

"Hello, Patrick," Kathleen said coolly. She nodded at his hand. "You'd better take care of that. Bloodstains are the very devil to get out."

Puzzled, her host looked from one to the other. "I thought you two should meet, but I see you already know each other. I suppose you know that Miss Collins was a passenger on the *Irish Queen*." Wade turned to Kathleen. "The experience must have been terrible. But my son-in-law understands better than most. He lost the girl he was engaged to on that very ship."

"Son-in-law?" Kathleen repeated blankly.

"Patrick is married to my daughter, Caroline."

Dear Reader,

I think you will find this Superromance very unusual, because the real story of the O'Connors begins in 1926 with Kathleen and Patrick.

I've always felt a particular affinity with the era known as the Roaring Twenties. My mother lived and loved then, marrying her childhood sweetheart. I grew up listening to stories of flappers and the Charleston, Rudolph Valentino, Gershwin, parties galore and, beneath it all, the lack of options for women, except what they seized for themselves.

In that respect, Kathleen Collins O'Connor could have been a woman of the nineties. In developing her character, I saw Kathleen as the vanguard for the women whose stars shine brightest today—those who juggle careers and families, or those who comfortably choose one or the other and do what they do well and happily. Kathleen is strong and practical, resilient in the face of tragedy and heartbreak, and determined to take charge of her own life.

The truth is, Kathleen could easily be any one of my readers. She is a woman who seizes opportunity, yet she is most vulnerable in matters of the heart. For Patrick, her only love, she compromised all. When you read their story, it is my sincerest wish that they will be as unforgettable to you as they have been to me.

Karen Young

Karen Young

THE PROMISE

Harlequin Books

TORONTO • NEW YORK • LONDON
AMSTERDAM • PARIS • SYDNEY • HAMBURG
STOCKHOLM • ATHENS • TOKYO • MILAN
MADRID • WARSAW • BUDAPEST • AUCKLAND

ISBN 0-373-70610-3

THE PROMISE

ABOUT THE AUTHOR

Award-winning author Karen Young usually draws on real-life experiences to write her novels, but *The Promise* is a different kind of story, a story that began in a different time and place.

This final book in the O'Connor trilogy is actually the first—it's about Patrick and Kathleen and their love...a love that wouldn't die. Theirs is a story so unforgettable, readers won't be able to put it down until the very last page. "I love romance," Karen says. "I love writing about it and I love reading about it." *The Promise* is romance at its best.

Karen and her husband, Paul, live in Thibodaux, Louisiana. They have three children and three grandchildren.

Books by Karen Young

HARLEQUIN SUPERROMANCE

PROLOGUE

Savannah, Georgia—1994

IT WAS ONE OF HER favorite places, the rose garden. At this time of year, it was a riot of color, sun warmed and aromatic. Pausing at the sundial, she stood still, her gaze resting on a favorite bloom here and there, savoring the beauty, the peace. The garden was hers. If she could claim a hobby, she supposed it would be this. Choosing an appealing variety, then planting, nurturing, waiting while it matured, watching it flower, everything coming in its proper time, all in wondrous, intricate harmony with nature.

Smiling softly, she watched a dragonfly settle on the face of the sundial and remembered the day the sundial had appeared in her garden. A gift of time, he had promised, of all their forevers. More than sixty years... She put out a hand and touched the carved bronze, just the smallest butterfly caress, and through a murky mist, another hand, masculine and strong, dark, so familiar and oh, so dear, seemed to appear and cover hers.

How ironic that her granddaughter Shannon had just found the diary she thought she'd lost, the diary that began the story of her star-crossed love. She took out a faded sepia photograph of her father in his clerical garb, but it was the photograph underneath that made her catch her breath.

Patrick O'Connor, the man she loved. The picture was taken the day before he'd sailed away from Kilkenny, Ireland, to make his fortune in America.

That night Kathleen's Dream Sight had foretold disaster, but not for Patrick O'Connor. Patrick, whose eyes were as blue as the sky and full of celestial fire. She had only to close her eyes to see him again, to remember his last, fateful night in Ireland....

As she studied the features of the man she loved, Kathleen's expression turned misty. "Oh, you were something, Patrick O'Connor. If I close my eyes, I can see you now..."

"AMERICA! YOU'VE FINALLY saved the money for your passage? Oh, Patrick."

Patrick touched her mouth with one finger. "Not just me, love. Us. We're going to America." He flashed his beautiful smile. "To New York, to be exact. Where opportunities are as thick as the leaves on the trees. I'll find a job, a good job." A grim note entered his voice. "One that pays more than starvation wages, one with a future, one where a man is treated with respect and rewarded for his work with advancement beyond anything he ever dared dream. Then I'll send for you, *mavourneen*. We can marry and there'll be none who can say it shouldn't be."

Kathleen rubbed her cheek against his palm, her green eyes glowing as she visualized the reality of his words. "How long will it be, Patrick? We've waited a lifetime, it seems."

"No longer than absolutely necessary, love." He pulled her close and placed a kiss on her temple. "I plan to purchase your ticket with my first wages, and then I'll be looking for a place for us—our own place."

"Oh, that sounds wonderful, doesn't it, Patrick?"

His arms tightened. "Aye, it does. God knows, we've been patient."

"I wish..."

Patrick caught her face between his hands and kissed her deeply, almost desperately. "I wish it, too, love."

"I will miss you so much," she whispered, trembling as the strength melted from her knees. "Patrick..."

He silenced her with a finger against her lips. "I have something for you," he said, slipping his hand inside his shirt pocket.

"Oh, Patrick, a ring!" Eagerly she extended her hand, her eyes bright with tears as he placed the thin gold band on her finger, then lifted it to his mouth and kissed it. His gaze locked with hers, he whispered, "With this ring, I make you mine, Kathleen Collins."

Kathleen felt as though her heart would burst. Knowing that if she spoke, she would cry, she simply nodded.

"Will you wear it until we're together again, *mavourneen?*"

"I will," she whispered. "Every minute of every day. I'll put it on a ribbon and wear it next to my heart."

"I wish we were truly married," he said, his expression suddenly bleak. "God, I will work like a Trojan to have you with me. I promise you that, Kathleen."

She cupped his jaw tenderly in one hand. "I know you will."

He turned his mouth into her palm and kissed it, then studied her face as though memorizing every detail. "Promise you'll wait for me."

"Until forever, if I must."

"And I promise the same."

They stood for a moment, simply looking at each other. The long separation stretched before them endlessly. Patrick knew that to be alone with her this night was dangerous. "Now, I must see you back to..."

"No!" In the moonlight, the blue of his eyes looked like liquid silver. No man in all of Ireland had eyes as beautiful as Patrick, she thought, marveling that he had chosen her! Had he not been the son of a penniless farmer, they would have long since been able to proclaim their love to the whole world. "I don't know how I shall bear it, Patrick, until we're together again. I ache for you now, for something that I don't even understand. It seems so cruel."

"Kathleen . . ."

She moved closer, intending a last desperate embrace. When her breasts brushed his chest, Patrick groaned and caught her up tightly, his stance altering instinctively to fit her snugly into the cleft of his thighs. Even through the rough material of his pants, she could feel the heat and hardness of him.

Oh, this was wrong! She knew it, and yet . . . It felt so right, so good. Patrick's hands swept from her waist down to her buttocks, anchoring her seductively against him. At her gasp, he groaned and opened his mouth over hers, giving her another deep kiss.

"Patrick, I love you!" she cried when he let her draw breath.

"I love you, too." It was a hoarse, guttural murmur. His mouth was at the hollow of her throat, kissing, biting, licking. She whimpered, nearly wild with wanting him. Her breasts ached, tingled, throbbed. She rubbed against him, and with a groan, he plunged his hand into the bodice of her dress. Kathleen's eyes closed in sweet ecstasy. How could anything that felt so wonderful be otherwise?

But it was. It was wrong. They must stop. "Patrick—"

With a wild blast of profanity, Patrick buried his face in her neck. "I know. God, I know, sweetheart. We have to stop."

"I don't want to."

He laughed, one brief, unfunny sound. "And neither do I. Ah, Kathleen." His eyes burned into her as he watched her attempt to pull her dress together. Just then, clouds obscured the moon. Looking at him, she saw only the clean, beautiful outline of his features, his firm, square jaw, his flinty cheekbones, the thick, dark sweep of his hair. How could she bear to let him go?

With both hands bracketing her waist, Patrick closed his eyes and shuddered. "Kathleen, you are so beautiful. I will take this picture with me all the way to America, and when I'm alone waiting for you, I'll close my eyes and it will be almost as good as being here."

She swallowed a soft, hiccuping sob and Patrick bent and kissed her. It was meant to be quick, but he had not counted on her impulsive response and the still-pulsing desire that had almost swamped them both only a minute before. His hands held fast as body moved against body in fierce, wordless need. It was a wild, undisciplined embrace, a voluptuous melding of mouths and tongues and taste. His body began to rock rhythmically against her softness, the instinctive male movement destined to lead to the ultimate embrace. Even in her innocence, Kathleen recognized it, and in the heat of her desire there was nothing left in her to resist. He was so warm and vibrant, so hard where she was soft, and she felt as though her legs could no longer hold her up.

And then suddenly she was not standing. She was lying on the ground with Patrick's body anchoring her, and the fine rein he'd used to control his passion was gone. Her own caution burned away in the fire. She wrapped her arms around his shoulders and eagerly met his descending mouth. Patrick fumbled with the folds of her skirt and undergarments until there was no barrier to the feel of his flesh against hers. Murmuring a mixture of oaths and endearments, he stroked the soft inner skin of her thighs until she was shifting restlessly, whimpering in need.

And then wild, unrestrained sensation washed through her as his fingers found the soft, moist folds that shielded her virginity. Dazed and greedy, she gave herself up to blind pleasure as Patrick stroked and caressed in a sure, steady, erotic rhythm until she thought she would surely scream with the avalanche of sensation flooding her body. Then he was suddenly in his place between her thighs. She shifted at a touch from his palms, opening to him in wordless welcome.

Even at the first blunt, warm probe of his arousal she felt no fear, only a feverish urgency. She wanted this. She wanted Patrick. Burying her face in his shoulder, she lifted her hips to ease his passage. With his hands beneath her buttocks, his expression rapt as though he, too, was lost in a fevered dream, Patrick thrust once and buried himself deeply in her.

Kathleen sighed, barely noticing the sharp sting of penetration. Above her, Patrick drew in his breath, trying to hold back. Sensing his body's desperate need to thrust, and wanting it as much as he, Kathleen sank her hands into his buttocks and arched, driven by instinct to seek some compelling, far-off goal.

Patrick could hold back no longer. He began to move, slowly at first, then with increasing urgency as Kathleen fell naturally into the rhythm he set, matching each downward stroke with her own thrusts. For both, there was only driving need and the deep pleasure to be found in each other. Faster and faster Patrick plunged while a tension, a coiled . . . something . . . built tighter and tighter inside Kathleen. Holding fast to him, nails scoring his skin, she thrashed, straining . . . There was something . . .

Reaching the summit, Patrick was rigid for an instant, and then, as he felt Kathleen's abrupt, startled catapult into ecstasy, he gave a hoarse shout and erupted in his own shattering fulfillment.

For several long, heartwrenching moments, Kathleen lay dreamily replete. As she stroked his heaving shoulders and kissed his heated flesh, Kathleen gazed enraptured at the moon above and renewed her vow to love Patrick O'Connor through eternity.

CHAPTER ONE

New York—1926

Today, my baby died. He was a fine male child, or so they tell me, but I will never know for I was beyond knowing anything the last twelve hours of my labor. Long and hard and harsh it was, painful beyond anything I ever expected. But this! Truly it is a punishment more cruel than even I deserve. Ah, my heart aches for just one look, a chance to gaze upon his tiny face, to touch his sweet cheek. My soul cries out to know what all mothers crave. Was he beautiful? Was he perfect? All I know is that he seemed well formed and he had a cap of dark hair. But his eyes! Were they green like my own? Or did he have the look of the O'Connors? Were his eyes vivid and blue like Patrick's?

KATHLEEN'S PEN WAVERED over the opened page of her journal and her eyes filled. With an impatient sniff, she dashed the tears away and blinked hard and fast until she focused clearly again. In the seven months since she'd left Ireland, she had cried enough tears to overflow the banks of the River Shannon. A woman in her dire circumstances couldn't afford the luxury of tears.

She laid down her pen and gazed at the worn curtains that blocked sunlight from the single window in the tiny, airless room. Gone was the rainbow optimism that had buoyed her spirits through the sad days after leaving Kilkenny and everything familiar to board the ill-fated *Irish Queen*, the steamer that had set out from Ireland. With Patrick's promises ringing in her ears and her heart full of love and naive trust, she had been bound at last for New York! Her stepmother had predicted many times that her impetuous nature would get her into trouble one day. As indeed it had. But nothing short of death could have kept her from going to Patrick.

Why had she not heeded the warning in her Dream Sight? Death's specter had been real and chilling that night. But not her baby! She pressed a fist to her trembling lips. Never her precious baby.

Was she to blame? Was it a punishment? Should she have been less preoccupied with getting to Patrick the fastest, quickest way possible and more concerned about the welfare of her unborn child on a steamer like the *Irish Queen?*

Conditions aboard the dilapidated ship had been deplorable. It had taken only minutes after boarding to realize that, but there was no turning back. Her bridges had been burned. With her stepmother's scorn scorching her ears and her father's sad eyes tearing at her heart, she'd had no choice. From that moment, all that mattered was getting to Patrick. And soon. Then, almost before the shores of Ireland had disappeared, she had succumbed to violent seasickness.

And now her baby was dead.

Had it been the unrelenting nausea those first days or had she been exposed to something on the ship that had transmitted itself to her unborn child? The cabin had been filthy and the washrooms beyond description. She had been able to scrub them clean finally, but only after the nausea had passed. That had been after lying on her cot for days and days.

And the food! God knows, the food had been terrible. At home, such dishes would have been tossed out, fit only for animals. Had her undernourished body failed to give her baby everything necessary to survive on its own? But forcing herself to eat had been next to impossible. If not for Brigit...

Brigit Murray had occupied the cot next to hers. Although passive and shy, she was a good sailor. She had also guessed Kathleen's condition after only a day or two at sea. It had been Brigit who'd suggested dry crackers and tea in the mornings and Brigit who'd held the detested sick pan when nothing could ward off Kathleen's nausea. Although their circumstances were very different, their friendship grew. Who could have guessed how their lives were destined to intertwine?

Their backgrounds were worlds apart. Kathleen learned that Brigit's passage on the *Irish Queen* had been paid by a wealthy family in New York. Contract labor, it was called. The practice of securing the services of maids, governesses and laborers for periods of up to three years at scandalously low wages was well known, but Kathleen had never realized how degrading it was in reality. It distressed her that circumstances forced Brigit and other good people who needed honest work to sign away years of their lives for the chance of a new life in America.

How naive she'd been, how ill prepared to face the devastating consequences of her decision to turn away from her home, her father and her half-sister and follow Patrick across the Atlantic to this cruel and harsh land. If she had it to do over again, surely she would be more prudent. Surely she would see beyond Patrick's dazzling description of a place he'd never seen, a place about which he could have had no more knowledge than she. If she could turn back the clock, if she could have a second chance, she would heed her Dream Sight. She had never before ignored a message so vivid. She had seen the voyage, seen the accident. She had not, however, seen the conditions under which she'd be traveling. . . .

Life aboard the *Irish Queen* was disgusting. It had been days before her nausea had abated enough for her to take a look around, and what she saw shocked her. First-class passengers were treated royally, while those berthed in the lower decks were treated like cattle. Theft was rampant, making it necessary to keep a keen watch out. Already a pretty hatpin that Brigit treasured had been stolen. Kathleen suggested they keep their belongings in her trunk, which was made of sturdy metal and had a strong lock. She also wrapped her journal and a few cherished photographs along with Brigit's labor contract to a family by the name of Drummond in waterproof oilskin, just in case. Brigit paled and crossed herself as she watched Kathleen safeguard their meager valuables. But that was not the worst of it.

The storm struck in New York harbor on the final day of the voyage. Kathleen knew instantly that the message she had received in her Dream Sight before she left Ireland was coming to pass. She even braced for the collision with a much larger ship before it actually happened. When it did, everything became a nightmare of fear and chaos.

The *Irish Queen* went down quickly. As in her Dream Sight, there was water and panic and stark terror. Within seconds, Kathleen and Brigit were separated, and even though Kathleen had managed to find Brigit a life jacket days before, she was deathly afraid for her friend, who could not swim. The oilskin packet containing her journal and Brigit's contract was securely fastened around Kathleen's waist, but what were things when life itself was at stake?

Until the moment she was cast into the roiling sea, Kathleen had not truly accepted the reality of the baby nestled in her womb. Suddenly it became the single most important force in the universe. She must survive, for only then would her baby live. Clinging desperately to a piece of floating wood that long, long night, Kathleen thought of Patrick and felt strengthened. She had written him about the baby, and although she had not heard from him before boarding the steamer, she knew he would rejoice that the loving they had shared had produced a child. She clung to that thought as tenaciously as she clung to her piece of wood, hour after endless hour.

As her makeshift raft rode the storm-tossed waves, sounds of the disaster diminished. Would she be lost forever? Overlooked by rescuers until she was lifeless and blue with cold? Exhausted and sobbing, Kathleen hung on, her salty tears mixing with the saltwater of the sea.

A sullen, gray dawn was breaking when at last she heard voices and the scrape and pull of oars. Materializing out of the mist was the shape of a boat. She saw it, but with her lips so cold and stiff and her voice no more than a croak, she could not call out a warning. Pain exploded in her head as the bow struck her, and then she knew no more.

KATHLEEN WAS SO CONFUSED. Time passed in a blur of sickbed impressions—coughing that racked her body and strained her lungs, fever that sent her into wild, hot delirium, broth forced down her throat. She did not know where she was, and was too weak to care. Voices came at her like harpies dancing around a corpse. Was she a corpse?

Am I dead?

A door slammed and pain burst in her head, splintering into pinpoints of white-hot agony, wringing from her a weak whimper.

"Well, looks like she's coming around."

"Humph! Thirteen days. It's about time."

"Probably won't ever be able to think straight. I never saw anybody survive a lick on the head like that one."

Someone came closer to the bed. Glass clinked against crockery. Water was poured. Kathleen flinched as the pitcher was replaced with a solid thunk. But, oh, she was thirsty.

"Brigit! Brigit Murray! Wake up, girl!"

Kathleen struggled through a murky curtain of confusion and pain. She should open her eyes, but the effort would hurt. She focused on the thought of water, trying to swallow, but her tongue was too thick, her throat too raw.

"I'll try to get her to take a little." A new voice. Gentle, with the lilt of Ireland. Some of her anxiety quieted.

A sudden sharp clap of hands sounded nearby and fresh pain exploded in Kathleen's head. "Lizzie, you stay with her and see if she'll come all the way round." This voice was harsh and authoritative.

"Yes, ma'am."

"You two! Get back to your duties. There's been enough time wasted gawking at this girl. Pearl, to the kitchen! Annie, get back to the flatiron. I expect Mr. Drummond's shirts to be finished before noon."

Murmurs and a flurry of rustling skirts and shuffling feet followed and then the door closed with a firm thump. Kathleen winced again.

"Brigit, Brigit Murray..." It was Lizzie of the soft voice. "Are you awake?" Kathleen searched her muddled brain, aware of something wrong, but unable to work it out. As she groped, a feeling of dread grew. What was this terrible feeling? What had happened? Where was she? Helplessly, she felt tears well up and trickle from the corners of her eyes.

"Ah, there, there, now. You'll be fine, Brigit. No need for tears, dear. You survived a terrible disaster and that was no small miracle, I can tell you. I never had any use for boats myself. After this, I'm even staying away from the ferry to Long Island."

Terrible disaster. The words penetrated Kathleen's brain. The storm. The collision with another ship. A huge ship. Chaos and panic. And Brigit... Brigit who could not swim. She realized suddenly that they thought she was Brigit Murray.

Her eyes fluttered open. "Brigit..." she whispered, trying to tell them.

"Here, love, I know you must be thirsty."

Gratefully, Kathleen allowed the girl to prop her up and hold a glass to her lips. She swallowed tepid water, almost choking as it trickled down the back of her swollen throat.

"Thank...thank you," she managed to say; then, as her vision cleared, she looked at the girl called Lizzie. "Where am I?"

"Why, you're at the Drummonds' on Park Avenue in New York City, love. Dragged from the ocean limp and wet and your skull near cracked open from being run down by the boat that found you." The girl's tone dropped. "You've been very lucky, Brigit Murray."

"But I'm not—"

"Thirty-four drowned in the disaster, according to the papers. All Irish, all immigrants."

Kathleen blinked in horror, almost unable to take it in. Confusion and pain slowed her understanding, but it seemed the unthinkable had really happened.

Oh, please, let Brigit be one of the survivors. She licked her cracked lips. "Where is Brigit?"

Lizzie gave her a tolerant smile. "What kind of question is that, now?"

With an effort, Kathleen caught the girl's hand and held on. "Please . . . tell me, did Brigit survive?"

Lizzie's smile faded into a look of concern. "Don't you remember your own name, love?"

"Oh, don't you understand? I'm not Brigit Murray. She was my shipmate. Can you please tell me what happened to her?"

With her head to one side, Lizzie studied her. "I'll bet that blow on the head has you confused, love. We found the papers on your body, tied around your waist all right and tight."

She leaned close and patted Kathleen's hand soothingly. "But you don't need to be worrying about it right now. What you need to do is rest awhile. This place is not too bad, the Drummonds', you know? Most of us being contracted, you'd think we wouldn't get much in the way of treatment when we get sick, but that just goes to show you can never tell. When you're stronger you'll recall everything just as it happened. See if you don't."

"I recall everything now," Kathleen told her, even though pain was hammering both temples with such intensity she was almost blind. Still, before she rested, she must let them know. Patrick must be told. "My name is Kathleen Collins," she whispered.

"Kath—" With a little start, Lizzie laughed.

"My shipmate was named Brigit Murray," Kathleen insisted. The ache in her head intensified. Pinpoints of light obscured Lizzie's expression. Her features seemed distorted, while her body and the room and all its contents receded, shifting and shimmering until there was no substance or reality to anything.

"Now, now, love, how could that be . . ."

Kathleen clung to the sound of Lizzie's words, but the throbbing in her temples was excruciating. Noise bloomed in her ears like the roar of a freight train.

"I'm Kathleen," she whispered, desperately hanging on to the thought. "Please believe me. I'm Kathleen Collins, and I came to America to be with my fiancé, Patrick O'Connor. Find him. Please find Patrick. Tell him I need him."

KATHLEEN HATED THE SMALL, airless room. She hated the Drummond mansion. She hated the endless, dreary household tasks and the hateful, carping voice of Amelia Parsons, the housekeeper. She hated Herbert Parsons, Amelia's sharp-nosed, swaggering son, whose persistent staring unnerved her. But because she was penniless and desperate, she was powerless to change anything. Most of all, she hated that.

Brigit Murray, it was finally discovered, had been one of the unfortunate victims who'd perished on the *Irish Queen*. Once Kathleen explained how Brigit's contract came to be strapped to her body with her journal, the misunderstanding over Kathleen's identity had been cleared up. Amelia Parsons had quickly offered her Brigit's position. Kathleen had refused after expressing her gratitude for the medical care and food and shelter she'd received from the Drummonds. She'd explained that Patrick would come for her if they would be so kind as to contact him. Within the hour, Herbert Parsons had returned from the offices of the Leland Shipping Lines, where Patrick had said he'd found employment, and related with a knowing smirk that no Patrick O'Connor was on the payroll there.

Kathleen spent the next few days in anxious, confused uncertainty. She was not strong enough to travel to the Leland offices herself, nor did she have the money to hire transportation. In a fever of impatience, she carried out the small tasks assigned to her by Amelia Parsons, waiting for the moment she could find out what had happened to Patrick.

It was a week after she'd awakened in the New York mansion and nearly three weeks since the fateful accident that she finally had an opportunity to go to the address of Leland Shipping.

The shipyard was a confusion of men and equipment, and Kathleen picked her way through cables and crates, keeping her gaze on the tall Leland Towers building that faced the water off the Sixth Street dock. She knew Patrick would not have approved of her being in such surroundings alone, but there were many things she had been forced to do since coming to America that Patrick would not have approved of. Thank heaven her father would never know of them.

At the thought of William Collins, she swallowed against a lump in her throat. How he had counseled against her decision to follow Patrick to New York. He had pointed out the many hazards and warned that Irish immigrants without specific training often wound up in dire straits. But with Patrick's promises buoying her confidence, she'd brushed aside his concerns. When his objections became too vehement, she had finally been forced to say why she must go to Patrick. She had not wanted to tell him of her pregnancy. In truth, it had almost broken him. What would he say if he could see her now?

As for her stepmother... Frances Collins's vicious condemnation would always live in her memory. Kathleen knew that Frances would feel no sympathy for her plight. In fact, she would very likely delight in reminding her of the wages of sin.

Kathleen placed a hand over her abdomen. She could never think of this child with anything but love, but she must find Patrick, and soon. She was more than three months along in her pregnancy, and her concern for the baby grew with each day. The outlook for an unmarried woman in her circumstances was bleak indeed. There was a good explanation for Patrick's disappearance, she was sure of it.

The administrative offices of Leland Shipping were doing a brisk business. Women were seated behind typewriters and men behind desks as Kathleen entered. Several youths walked around with packages and mail. She put out a hand when one would have rushed by her.

"Please, could you help me? I'm looking for the payroll clerk."

"Goodson, that'll be," the boy said, pointing to a door. "Through there, first desk on the left."

Ignoring curious looks, she wove her way through the occupants of the big, open room and stopped at a door. Etched glass obscured the view, but she could see movement inside. Drawing a deep breath, she turned the knob.

A slight man wearing a green-visored cap looked up.

"Mr. Goodson?"

Balding, bespectacled, slightly anemic-looking, Freddy Goodson was exactly as Kathleen would have pictured a payroll clerk. He carefully marked his place on the ledger sheet in front of him before speaking. "Yes?"

"I was told you are the payroll clerk for this company," she explained, wishing she could sit. After her illness and several days under the pitiless supervision of Amelia Parsons, not to mention the long streetcar ride she'd just endured, she was longing to rest a bit.

"Officer," Goodson corrected her, looking her up and down with an expression that made her wish she'd changed from her work uniform. Unfortunately, everything except what the Drummonds had issued to her was in her trunk at the bottom of New York harbor. "I'm the payroll officer for the Leland Lines, yes."

"I need some information, please."

He frowned as though he smelled something unpleasant. "What kind of information?"

"It's about an employee named Patrick O'Connor."

"There's no Patrick O'Connor employed here."

She blinked, put off by the blunt reply. The man's attitude was intimidating, but Kathleen reminded herself that he was her last resort. She could not afford to be cowed by him, no matter how curt and unforthcoming he was. He was a petty tyrant in a little kingdom, but she reminded herself what was at stake for her and her baby. "There must be some mistake, Mr. Goodson. Perhaps if you looked in your records . . . just to be certain, you see."

Leaning back, Goodson steepled his fingers beneath his chin. "I don't have to check in my records to be sure that there is no Patrick O'Connor working here. I know it."

Kathleen frowned, for some reason not accepting his remark at face value. Were her questions about Patrick inappropriate in some way? She released a soft sigh. "May I sit down?"

With a bored look, he waved at a hard-bottomed chair. Kathleen sank into it gratefully and made another attempt. "Perhaps I should explain—"

"Explanations are not necessary, miss. There will still be no Patrick O'Connor on my payroll."

"You haven't even looked!" she said, feeling exasperated and oddly apprehensive. Fatigue suddenly overwhelmed her, and she had an unsettling urge to cry. She would not. Could not. She had come here for a purpose and she wouldn't let him put her off with his rude, overbearing manner. A bully could only intimidate a person who allowed it. She took a breath. "I have a letter from my fiancé,

Patrick O'Connor, written about six weeks ago, telling me he had a job with the Leland Shipping Lines."

"It was true at that time," Goodson said grudgingly. "O'Connor worked out of the Sixth Street wharf. Judson was his foreman. He resigned a week ago."

Her relief was so great that she dismissed his irksome attitude. "Oh, thank heaven. I knew I could not have mistaken what he told me. You can't imagine... Oh, but why did he resign?"

"My dear young woman, I'm sure I haven't any idea."

"Surely he left a forwarding address? He was expecting me. He got me the tickets on the *Irish Queen*."

At the mention of the ill-fated ship, Goodson managed a pained look. "Most unfortunate, that. I'm happy to see you survived the accident."

"Thank you."

"And it's very irritating being interrupted this way chasing an employee who worked for us only briefly. First Drummond's flunky and now you," he grumbled.

"You must mean Mr. Drummond's chauffeur, Herbert Parsons."

"I don't recall his name," Goodson said stiffly, "but it seems to me this entire tempest in a teapot could have been resolved then and there. O'Connor was still on the facility and I told the chauffeur that. Why didn't he ask the man straight out?"

Kathleen looked stunned. "What are you saying?"

"Are you deaf as well as stupid, girl! Parsons, as you call him, asked about O'Connor and I told him exactly what I've told you. If he had business with O'Connor, he could have stated it to the man in person. I recall the details explicitly because O'Connor had just resigned and I was cutting his final check. For reasons of his own, Parsons left without talking to O'Connor."

"You say he...Parsons...made no effort to speak to Patrick?" Kathleen whispered, her hand over her heart.

"Haven't I just said so?" He suddenly looked impatient. "And now you will have to excuse me. I'm extremely busy this morning."

She could not fall apart in front of this horrid little man, Kathleen reminded herself through a haze of pain. Blinking back tears, she pulled herself together. There were still questions Goodson might answer about Patrick, if only he would.

"Mr. Goodson, do you have a forwarding address?"

"No."

Kathleen hung on doggedly to her patience. "Well, then, did he say anything about why he was leaving? Is there any message for me? My name is Kathleen Collins. We're engaged to be married. Surely, he must have said something."

"Kathleen Collins..." Goodson murmured, then rose from his chair and went to a cabinet against the wall. Pulling open a drawer, he withdrew an envelope folder and untied it as he returned to his chair. "O'Connor didn't mention you when he left, but a letter did come for you addressed in his care a few days later. It's here somewhere."

Letters and various types of mail spilled out on his desktop. "Ah, here it is. It's addressed, as you see, in care of O'Connor at Leland Lines. I assume someone from your former home knew of your fiancé's employment with Leland."

"Yes," Kathleen said faintly. Taking the letter from Goodson, she saw that it was from her stepmother. She slipped it into her pocket. She could see that Goodson was frankly curious, but she would not read it in front of him.

"About Patrick, Mr. Goodson..."

"Yes. I do recall the day he gave notice." His expression turned sly. "There was some talk among the men."

"Talk? What kind of talk?"

"He was approached by a man on the docks that day, a wealthy businessman." He studied her pale features, enjoying the impact of his words. "He gave notice that very day and he hasn't been seen on the docks since."

Kathleen's hand went to her abdomen. "But I don't understand. Patrick wouldn't... He couldn't..."

Goodson studied his fingernails before raising his eyes to hers. "The gentleman to whom he spoke wasn't alone." She looked at him helplessly.

"He was accompanied by his daughter."

She was still confused. "I don't see—"

"She was young and beautiful, Miss Collins. She made no secret of her interest in O'Connor." A born gossip, he watched eagerly as she took in the significance of his words.

Shock held Kathleen rigid. Never in all her efforts to solve the mystery of Patrick's disappearance had she thought of another woman. Fear rushed through her in a torrent. With her thoughts in a whirl, she tried to concentrate as Goodson droned on.

"The gentleman's wealth is well known, of course, although he's situated somewhere down south. Shipbuilding, I believe, not shipping. The name escapes me at the moment. Actually, Judson, the foreman, told me he regretted losing O'Connor. He was a hard worker. Might have made foreman himself one day." He chuckled maliciously. "Then again, maybe he's fixed for life with—" Looking up, he caught her eye and smirked.

Kathleen rose slowly. "Thank you for your time, Mr. Goodson. And for passing on to me the letter from my family."

"See here, Miss Collins. Don't take it so hard, hmm? Your fiancé had an eye to the main chance, I'm afraid, and what's done is done. Take some advice. Forget him. You'll be better off. There are other fish in the sea." He eyed her appreciatively. "Perhaps I could offer you some... consolation."

Kathleen clenched her fists to keep from throwing her small purse at him.

"I say, you look a little pale." Goodson rose to his feet. "Would you like—"

"Nothing, thank you," she said coldly. "I'll find my own way out."

He sank back in his chair. "Well, then..."

"Goodbye, Mr. Goodson."

Outside, Kathleen leaned weakly against the brick wall of Leland Towers and prayed the rushing sound in her ears would subside. With a hand pressed to her heart, she watched unseeing as traffic ebbed and flowed on the street. A horse-drawn ice wagon trundled past and the old man driving it glanced curiously at her. She dropped her hand and smoothed her skirt. She must get back to Park Avenue somehow.

Brushing at her skirt, she felt the crinkle of the letter in her pocket. With little curiosity, she withdrew it. Ordinarily, she would wonder why her stepmother was writing to her, but today... With unsteady fingers, she opened it.

Kathleen,
I don't suppose a wicked, shameless girl such as you deserves to know this, but your father died today. It was his heart, of course. You will have guessed that since it was you who broke it. He could never look any of his parishioners in the face after you left. Are you satisfied?

With a broken whimper, Kathleen dropped the letter. Despair and grief welled up in her chest. Her father, gone.

How could she bear this loss on top of everything else? The roaring in her ears was back. Like a black cloud, it swamped her senses. Dizzily, she groped for a handhold, but her fingers scraped only brick and mortar. She could not faint here. That odious little man Goodson might look out and see her. He would love it if she toppled over in full sight of every employee at Leland. Sinking to her knees in spite of herself, Kathleen waited for her head to clear.

"Here now, lucky it is the old dragon sent me instead of Herbert to find you, ain't it?"

Kathleen blinked away the bright dots and flashes and peered up dazedly at Lizzie. "Lizzie? How—"

"Never you mind how, my girl," Lizzie said briskly. "Just let me get an arm around you and try to stand you on your feet here." She helped Kathleen upright, then urged her gently back against the wall while she collected the small string purse that had dropped to the ground.

"This yours, too?" At Kathleen's nod, she picked up the letter that had fluttered to the edge of the curb.

"I was jumping off the trolley just as you crumpled like a rag doll," Lizzie said, brushing here and there, straightening a cuff, murmuring over a scratch on Kathleen's palm. "Did you bump anything when you fell?"

Swallowing, her senses still whirling, Kathleen murmured, "No, I don't think so."

"Then, nothing's broken?"

Only my heart. "No, nothing."

"Humph. It's a wonder."

"I must have—" Kathleen put a hand to her forehead. "I don't know why I suddenly seemed to—"

"Faint?"

"Lose control."

Lizzie folded the letter and slipped it back into the envelope. Then, looking around the area, she said, "I'm thinking your precious Patrick wouldn't want you out walking in this part of town, love.''

"Patrick is no longer precious to me, Lizzie."

Lizzie gave her a shrewd look. "Oh? What about your wonderful future together? What about your marriage plans?"

"There will be no future. There will be no marriage."

"And why not, pray? It's all you've talked about for all the time I've known you, Kathleen. You slip away from the Drummonds' house and wind up on the docks and I find you in a swoon on the sidewalk outside the offices of the famous Leland Lines where your darling Patrick is supposed to be working, and you tell me it's all been a joke?"

"Not a joke, just a mistake. A... horrible mistake."

Lizzie studied her for a long moment. "And the baby," she said quietly. "Is he a mistake, too?"

Kathleen's eyes closed, her pain so intense she truly wondered if she would ever be whole again. She was not aware that anyone knew of her pregnancy, not even Lizzie. What a fool she was to think she could escape the disgrace.

With a sympathetic sound, Lizzie wrapped her arm around Kathleen's shoulder and gave her a squeeze. "Ah, don't take on so, love. Nobody suspects except me, and that's only because I share a room with you. With my mother giving birth no less than eight times, I know the signs."

Kathleen drew in a shaky breath. "What am I going to do, Lizzie?"

"Well..." Lizzie stared out over the waterfront as though a message might be found on the horizon. "Can we say all final like that you won't be hearin' from Patrick O'Connor ever again?"

Kathleen nodded, and when she'd cleared the tears from her throat, told her what she'd learned from the payroll clerk.

Lizzie sighed, shaking her head. Then her eyes fell on the letter. "What about your family, your da?"

"I have just learned that my father has died. Even if I could somehow earn the money for my passage back to Ireland, my stepmother would not welcome me." Kathleen ran a palm over the still tiny bulge of her stomach. "She made her feelings clear before I left."

"I can imagine," Lizzie muttered.

Kathleen stood a little straighter and lifted her chin. "I am not ashamed of my baby," she said in a low, intense tone. "He is not to blame for the circumstances I'm in. I don't know what I'm going to do, Lizzie, but I can't just stand out here in the street waiting for someone to come along and wave a magic wand and solve my problems for me."

With a blink, Lizzie gave her another approving squeeze. "That's the ticket, love."

Kathleen took the letter and tore it into pieces. "I don't have many options. I do know that weeping and wailing and fainting won't fix anything. I'll just have to go back to the Drummonds' and see Mrs. Parsons. She was willing to keep me on in Brigit's place as long as I was a hardworking Irish immigrant. Let's pray she doesn't consider an out-of-wedlock pregnancy too scandalous."

"We'll definitely pray."

"I'll throw myself on her mercy."

Lizzie, for once, was silent. Both knew there was little mercy in Amelia Parsons's heart.

"But right now I won't have to do anything," Kathleen said, falling into step beside Lizzie, "because what Mrs. Parsons doesn't know won't hurt her."

CHAPTER TWO

QUICKLY AND EFFICIENTLY, Kathleen whisked the crumbs from the huge table into a small silver pan. With a twitch here and a flick there, she straightened the linen-and-lace tablecloth, made of the finest fabric to be found in Ireland, then stepped back to be sure the elaborate floral center-piece was placed just so. Margaret Drummond prided herself on the elegance and style of her dinner parties, and tonight's was no exception. The guests, New York's elite, had sat down to an array of delectable dishes that would not soon be forgotten. Afterward, with Lizzie's help, Kathleen had cleared away the costly crystal, china and silver. Now, rubbing her back, she surveyed the table and the dining room, checking to see that nothing was out of place. The last thing she needed tonight was one of Amelia Parsons's scolds.

So far, she had managed to keep on the good side of the housekeeper. With only herself to depend on, Kathleen had set out to prove that she could do as good a day's work as any other contracted worker. Of her personal circum-stances, she had told the woman as little as she could get by with. If Mrs. Parsons wondered what had happened to her plans to marry or to the man who'd promised to marry her, she didn't ask. Kathleen was grateful for that, at least.

With a sigh, she moved to the double French doors that separated the dining room from the main salon. With her hand on the antique knob, she stood for a moment, watching the guests who were every bit as elegant and glittering as their surroundings.

One woman with cropped hair, in a dress of black sequins that ended well above her knees, bent close to a male guest so that he could light her cigarette. Another woman joined them, her dress equally short and even more provocative. It was a mass of iridescent white beads that shimmered with every movement of her body. And when she turned, Kathleen almost gasped. The dress was entirely backless! Studying the way the dress molded itself to the woman's feminine curves, Kathleen wondered what circumstances could ever induce her to wear such a creation and could not come up with one. The irony of her thoughts made her smile. In her condition, she wouldn't be able to wear the flapper style even if she could afford to buy it. At six-and-a-half months into her pregnancy, she'd altered her uniforms twice to try to conceal her thickening waistline. Still, it was simply a matter of time before her secret was out. When that happened, no doubt there would be another awkward interview with Amelia Parsons.

"Oh, there you are . . . ah, Katherine, isn't it?"

With a start, Kathleen whirled to face Margaret Drummond.

"No, ma'am. It's Kathleen." Her employer's dress was more modest than those of many of her guests. Dove gray crepe with an intricate working of multicolored beads at the neckline, it was beautifully styled. In Paris, no doubt. Kathleen knew that was where Mrs. Drummond shopped for most of her party frocks.

Margaret Drummond's nod was distracted. She looked beyond Kathleen to the kitchen area. "Something must have happened to delay Mrs. Parsons," she said irritably. "I sent her after a section of today's paper which my husband needs in his study."

"In his study?"

If Mrs. Drummond noticed that Kathleen had no business questioning a request from Mr. Drummond, she let it pass. "I don't know why Edward must hole up in that stuffy, smelly place while I'm having a party. It's Maxwell Rutledge, of course. When he gets with Max, he just seems— Well, no matter. They want the morning paper for some inexplicable reason. Mrs. Parsons is obviously having difficulty finding it."

"I know where it is, Mrs. Drummond," Kathleen said. "I'll get it."

"Good, good. Just take it in there, please." She gestured vaguely at the door on the left, then, her mission accomplished, she drifted back toward her guests in the salon. "I can't bear the horrid odor of those cigars they smoke," she said, her words trailing in her wake.

Kathleen closed the French doors and then hurried to the hallway off the kitchen and dashed up the backstairs, heading for her room. Inside, she tossed the pillows off the dilapidated settee that sat in the corner of the room she shared with Lizzie and which they wryly referred to as their "salon." On the settee was a collection of newspapers, which Kathleen devoured daily.

One of the advantages of working in the Drummond mansion was the wealth of reading material available. Edward Drummond subscribed to all of New York's dailies as well as several magazines and newspapers from other major cities. To Kathleen, encouraged by her father to develop her lively intelligence, anything newsworthy was interesting reading. She was especially interested in the editorials and she sometimes amused herself by rewriting them. Or rebutting them.

Snatching up the *Tribune,* she hastily checked the date and then dashed out of the dreary little room.

With her heart racing, she knocked once on the door of the study, which swung open a few inches. She heard the men inside debating the editorial that had run in the *Tribune* that day. She remembered it as being a thoughtful analysis of the future of aviation in America and the world.

"The earth will be a smaller place once transatlantic flight is a reality," Maxwell Rutledge was saying.

"It'll never happen," Drummond countered, puffing at his cigar. "A foolhardy endeavor if I ever heard one."

Kathleen agreed with Mr. Rutledge, who owned and published the *Tribune*. Although he was not the editor, his byline was often on articles she found interesting. "Excuse me, Mr. Drummond?" She said tentatively.

"Eh? What d'you want, girl?" Rearing back in his chair, Drummond frowned at her.

Kathleen walked toward him holding the paper. "I brought you today's *Tribune*. Mrs. Drummond said you wanted it."

He grunted as he took it, shaking it out and focusing through his bifocals. Rutledge, who was younger and needed no spectacles, caught Kathleen's eye and smiled. It startled her because Rutledge was not a man who smiled readily, although he had a kind face. She'd noticed that about him before, as well as the hint of sadness that marked him somehow. His responsibilities were great, she guessed, but there was also something about him that made her think he hadn't always been rich and happy. Most of Edward Drummond's associates flaunted power and wealth with an arrogance that overrode any finer human qualities. Rutledge seemed different.

From behind the paper, Drummond spoke suddenly. "Get us some more brandy—" He stopped, folding the paper aside. "What's your name, girl?"

"Kathleen, sir."

"Brandy, Kathleen. A new bottle, there's a good girl. We're parched, eh, Max?"

"If you say so, Edward."

"I'll just be a minute, sir," Kathleen said. She collected the used glasses from the desktop and walked coolly from the room. Even though she had been hired to serve, it still rankled, and she refused to scurry around like a puppy who lived only to please his master.

Depositing the used glasses in the kitchen, she looked around for Mrs. Parsons to tell her that Mr. Drummond had the newspaper, but she was nowhere in sight. She shrugged, then found the brandy and clean snifters to serve it in and headed back to the study.

The moment she entered, both men looked at her, really looked at her. As a domestic in the mansion, she was so accustomed to moving around unnoticed that she sometimes felt invisible. She stopped short, making the crystal on the tray tinkle musically.

"Kathleen, right?" It was Rutledge who spoke. There was a hint of a smile in his tone.

"Yes, sir." She glanced at her employer, who was puffing away on his cigar. With a closer look, Kathleen decided he didn't appear angry. But what—

Rutledge leaned over the desk and picked up the *Tribune*. With a smile, he waved a piece of paper that Kathleen recognized with a look of dismay. "I've noted your editorial remarks, Kathleen. And your rebuttal to the article on labor unions that ran Wednesday, if memory serves me."

She had forgotten that, just for a lark, she'd grabbed her pen and changed a word or phrase here and there in the aviation editorial. Then, after listening to Lizzie tell of her sister's experiences working in a shoe factory for near slave wages, she'd written a blistering opinion condemning greedy businessmen and a government that seemed to look the other way too often.

"Don't look so stricken, Kathleen," Maxwell Rutledge said, still smiling. "You put forth some interesting thoughts on the labor union issue."

"I'll have no rabble-rousing among the staff here, girl," Edward Drummond blustered, his features obscured in smoky haze.

"No, sir," she stated. "Of course not. That editorial was just an exercise, something I do for the fun of it." She glanced at the owner of the *Tribune*. "The same goes for editing your work, Mr. Rutledge. It's just an amusement, something to pass the time. I beg your pardon if you found it offensive."

"Not at all, Kathleen. I found it refreshing."

"Kathleen, whatever are you doing in here?"

For once, the sound of Amelia Parsons's voice was not unwelcome. Kathleen quickly set the tray with the brandy and snifters on the desk and turned to leave.

"We ran out of brandy," Drummond said. "I sent Kathleen to fetch another bottle."

With a shrewd look at all three, the housekeeper nodded. Then her gaze fell on the newspaper. "Is that the *Tribune*, sir?"

It was Rutledge who answered. "Yes, it turned up."

"Then we'll leave you gentlemen to enjoy yourselves. Come along, Kathleen."

In the hall, Kathleen was sure she would have to explain to the housekeeper how she had managed to locate the *Tribune*, but Margaret Drummond appeared and asked Mrs. Parsons to attend to another small emergency. As the two women left, Kathleen breathed a sigh of relief. Edward Drummond and Maxwell Rutledge might have found her dabbling in journalism amusing, but she had an idea Mrs. Drummond and Amelia Parsons would not.

"My, my, you're having a busy night, aren't you, sweet Kathleen?" She jumped at the sound of Herbert Parsons's voice close behind her.

She never felt comfortable around the chauffeur, especially since she'd confronted him about his inquiries regarding Patrick at Leland Shipping. He'd denied everything, of course, and after all, what did it really matter now? Patrick was gone.

"Cat got your tongue, hmm?" Herbert leaned against the wall and folded his arms across his chest, watching her closely. "I've been wondering how much longer you were going to be holed up with the old man and Rutledge."

She stared at him, familiar with that crocodile smile of his. An insult was an insult, whether it was delivered with a smile or not. "Really, Mr. Parsons, I'm just doing my job, no matter what you may imagine," she said, her tone as discouraging as she could make it.

"Mr. Parsons," he repeated, shaking his head. "Must be a dozen times I've told you I don't want to be Mr. Parsons to you, Kathleen."

Too bad for you. Kathleen bent quickly to scoop up a jeweled button that lay next to the baseboard. "I must return this button to the lady who lost it," she told him, turning to go.

He caught her arm. "So, what was going on in there?"

"I was sent to fetch brandy for Mr. Drummond," she said coldly, freeing herself with a twist of her body.

He studied her skeptically for a few moments. "You know, you're the prettiest thing to come down the pike since I don't know when, Kathleen. I've had my eye on you ever since you got here, did you know that?"

She did know, all too well. She wished he would fix his attention on one of the other maids.

"I wouldn't want you to mess up," he said.

"Is there a problem with my work?"

"Well . . . my ma has no complaints."

She gave him a frigid look that would have discouraged a more intelligent man. "Then I fail to see the difficulty."

"Ah, that's what I like. That tone, that little touch of class. 'I fail to see the difficulty,' " he mimicked. "Snooty-sounding and sort of untouchable. Yeah, real classy."

Shifting a little closer, he propped a hand on the wall beside Kathleen. She told herself there was no reason to feel crowded. What could happen with a dozen guests not twenty feet away in the next room?

"Yessiree, you're something, Kathleen, you know that?"

She took a breath. "Mr. Parsons—"

"And it came to me that you're just too pretty and too smart to be anybody's maid, even the Drummonds'." He trailed a finger down her cheek.

"I don't mind the work," she lied, turning her face. "It's my job."

"Your job can be better, a whole lot better. One little kiss and I'll see to it."

Glancing up, Kathleen got no further than his prominent Adam's apple. She swallowed to keep her revulsion from showing. She needed her work at the mansion. One word to his mother and Kathleen would be out in the street. Oh, God, what was she going to do?

"Umm, I can just hear that little brain of yours ticking, sweet Kathleen. Thinking it over, are you?"

She closed her eyes. "Not really, Mr. Parsons. I—"

"Mr. Parsons . . ." Wagging his head, he chided her. "Now, there you go again. Like I said, love, *you* can call me

Herb, but the rest of the world will call me mister. You can count on that.''

When her expression failed to change, he leaned against the wall again with an expansive air.

"Of course, you can't know how things really are," he continued, "seeing you're stuck in the house. But everyone knows the old man has plans for me. At the club and the factories, folks look alive when I drive up.''

The "club" was an exclusive establishment for men only. Before coming home each evening, Edward Drummond stopped in without fail. The factories were three textile mills, the chief source of Drummond's wealth. Parsons had been Edward Drummond's chauffeur for more than five years. If Mr. Drummond had such big plans for "Herb," he was certainly taking his time getting started.

Apparently she looked unconvinced. Parsons straightened angrily. "I'm not going to be a driver much longer," he told her. "Just you wait.''

"Then I wish you well," she murmured.

"It's true. There's plenty of opportunity for a smart man in Drummond's empire. We've been talking about it. It's just a matter of time before he offers me something.''

"Good luck.''

He regarded her suspiciously. "What's the matter? You don't believe me?''

She certainly didn't. It was ludicrous to think Edward Drummond was seriously considering placing Herbert anywhere in his empire except the garages. He was a fool, a vulgar, ill-educated cretin and she longed to tell him so. But at the moment, it was more important to get away from him without jeopardizing her own position with the Drummonds.

"It sounds very interesting, ah ... Herb. Now, I must be getting this button back to that lady. She'll be wondering—"

He caught her arm in a grip that was surprisingly strong. "You're forgetting something, aren't you?"

Kathleen was still. "Please release me."

He ignored her. "I meant it when I said you're too smart to be a housemaid, Kathleen Collins. You talk real nice, you look *very* nice and you're smart. I can use somebody like you in my plans."

"I have my own plans, sir," she said coldly.

"Oh, yes?" He smiled, showing all of his teeth again. "Well, I don't notice a long line of fellas waiting for your hand in marriage, and what else is there for a girlie like you?"

Although she vowed not to let him see, Kathleen's heart tripped in panic. What was he implying? "I really must go," she said, turning to leave.

He caught her arm again, his expression sly. "You think your little secret isn't out, sugar?"

His gaze dropped deliberately to her stomach. "You don't show much, I'll say that, but it won't be long till you'll be bustin' out all over. I guess you believed that guy who worked at Leland really meant to marry you. Hah, fat chance. He's given you the slip, ain't that right?"

A suffocating, hateful humiliation colored Kathleen's cheeks. Revulsion for Parsons, resentment against Patrick and a sick, impotent fury for her predicament all jumbled together in her breast.

"I was mad as hell at first," Parsons said, seemingly unaware of her seething emotions. "Used merchandise and all that. But it'll all work out. Like I said, I've got plans."

She stared at him, unable to take in what he was saying. Her own thoughts were in chaos. She'd known her condition would be noticed soon, but to learn from this...this toad that her name was probably being snickered over by the staff and the Drummonds and God only knew who else was simply more than she could bear. With a cry, she twisted her arm free and ran for the sanctuary of her dreary little room, In the sudden silence, the small jeweled button went skittering across the polished floor to lie winking under the crystal chandelier.

"EVERYONE KNOWS LIZZIE." With a vicious tug on the sheet, Kathleen lifted the mattress corner and tucked the ends underneath tightly. "If Herbert Parsons knows, everyone else does. He had to have heard it from the staff or...or somebody."

"You're right. He's too puffed up with his own importance to notice your tummy." Lizzie snapped a pillowcase open and reached for a pillow. "Besides, it's not your tummy he's been eyeing ever since you got here."

"I'm six-and-a-half months along, Lizzie. I suppose I'm lucky I've gone this long without causing a scandal."

"You're right there. Lordy! My ma was the size of a whale by the time she was six months."

Kathleen stopped in the act of plumping a pillow and looked worriedly at Lizzie. "Do you think something could be wrong?" Any hint of a threat to her baby pushed Parsons and everyone else to the bottom of her worry list.

"No, no, love. Every woman's different when it comes to carrying a baby. Don't worry. Believe me, I would know if something was wrong."

With one hand at her waist and another smoothing the fine Irish linen on the freshly made bed, Kathleen's expression grew pensive. "I know this sounds selfish, because my baby will surely suffer from not having a name, but I want

him so much, Lizzie. If something happened to him, I don't
think I could bear it."

Lizzie leaned over the bed and patted her hand. "Nothing will happen, love. He'll get here robust as a longshoreman and squalling his head off. You'll see."

"I hope so," Kathleen murmured, her hand going protectively to her stomach.

"What makes you think the baby's a boy?"

"I just know."

"Shh, someone's coming." Lizzie quickly bent and gath-
ered the soiled linen as Kathleen scurried to the dressing table and began restoring order to Margaret Drummond's
impressive assortment of cosmetics. She was dusting a sterling silver dresser set when Amelia Parsons appeared.

"Kathleen!" the housekeeper said abruptly. "I want to
talk to you. See me in my room in five minutes."

"Yes, Mrs. Parsons."

"You, Lizzie! Finish up in here and get to the green room
in the west wing. There are guests coming for the weekend
and I don't want to find a tea towel out of order. Is that
clear?"

"Yes, ma'am," Lizzie said. "I'll get right over there."

"What did I tell you, Lizzie," Kathleen said after Amelia was well away from the room. "She knows."

Lizzie shrugged. "Maybe. But no sense nailing your cof-
fin before it's occupied, my da used to say. Now, chin up!
Don't go in there wearing that blue look. Who knows? The
old dragon might want to elevate you to her assistant. I hear
she's plumb out of patience with her pet Betsy nowadays."

Giggling in spite of herself, Kathleen took up the bundle
of linens again and hurried downstairs. The day she, Kathleen Collins, pregnant, unmarried and penniless, was "ele-
vated" in this household would indeed be a day of miracles.

"I'M VERY DISAPPOINTED in you, Kathleen."

Kathleen stared at her hands in her lap and reminded herself how desperately she needed her job at the Drummond mansion.

"I was shocked that a girl like you with your whole life ahead of you would forget decency and morals and just ruin your life this way. What have you got to say for yourself, Kathleen?"

"I...my fiancé..." She closed her eyes and swallowed past the lump in her throat. There was really no way she could defend Patrick or herself. The important thing was to hang on to her job. "It must appear to you that I have acted rashly, Mrs. Parsons, but I assure you that my...my condition will in no way affect my ability to do my job."

"Rash, you say? Disgraceful is a better word, I think. I'd judged you to be a respectable girl. You can imagine how shocked I was when I learned—"

Then she hadn't guessed, Kathleen thought. Someone told her. Herbert, of course. She should have known he would retaliate when she hadn't succumbed to his nonexistent charm. She rubbed her forehead wearily. Lord, what a muddle.

Amelia pushed on. "I just don't know what the Drummonds will say about this, Kathleen. After taking you in, seeing you had a doctor when you needed one, allowing you to fill the position when that other poor girl drowned. Well..." She shook her head. "I just don't know."

"I need this job badly, Mrs. Parsons." At the thought of being turned out on the street, Kathleen thought her heart might stop. What would she do? Where would she go?

"Of course, there is one way..."

Kathleen held her breath.

"There are agencies," the housekeeper said, looking at a piece of paper in her hand.

"Agencies?" At a loss, Kathleen, too, looked at the paper, but could make nothing of it upside down.

"Yes, these people accept healthy babies and place them—"

"No!" Kathleen shot to her feet. Her heart thudding in her chest, she began edging back toward the door. "I won't give my baby away, Mrs. Parsons. I love him. To the world he may appear to be a mistake, but to me he is precious, more precious than my good name, or even my own life. I could never give him to strangers to raise."

"Sit down, girl," the woman ordered. Then when Kathleen still hesitated, she said again, "Sit, Kathleen! I didn't say you had to make any decision today. Of course it's up to you when all's said and done. Meanwhile, I'll talk to Mrs. Drummond, see whether she sees fit to extend the hand of charity to you."

The hand of charity. Kathleen's cheeks burned while her heart twisted with pain. She wanted nothing so much as to run out of the mansion and never stop until she came to...to what? She had no money, no job if the Drummonds turned her out, no options but to accept that hateful hand of charity. If only...

Her eyes dull, Kathleen watched as Amelia shuffled through more papers before selecting several small tickets clipped together. "I've noticed you seem to have a good education," the woman said.

"My father was the vicar in the village where I was born," Kathleen replied, confused at the change of subject. "He was a scholar. I very fortunately benefited from his knowledge."

Amelia pushed the tickets across the desktop along with a folder bulging with other papers. "My son, Herbert, has been given new responsibilities by Edward Drummond. There is a good bit of paperwork involved—gasoline expenses, repairs." She paused, looking directly into Kathleen's eyes. "Did you have a hand in managing your father's household?"

"I ... I suppose."

"To what extent?"

"My stepmother preferred other interests to running a household."

"Good." Amelia stood up. She didn't smile, but a look of approval crossed her face. Kathleen thought it odd considering the stern lecture she'd just received, but it all fell into place with the housekeeper's next words.

"Herbert was right. It would be hasty to turn you out when he can use your help with his paperwork. Of course you'll have to keep out of sight as much as possible now that anyone can see your ... condition."

She stood abruptly and Kathleen followed suit. "We have an understanding? You will do Herbert's paperwork?"

Kathleen's hesitation was hardly noticeable. "Yes, I'll do Herbert's paperwork." She could not bring herself to say thank you.

"TOLD YOU I WAS GOING places in Drummond's business, didn't I?"

Kathleen carefully filed the sheaf of receipts in a folder and closed the cabinet. Only then did she turn and look at Herbert Parsons. "Yes, you told me. Congratulations."

Parsons leaned against the small desk he'd moved into the garage office especially for Kathleen. "And didn't I say my plans could include you, too?"

Wishing with all her being that she was back serving tables and making beds, Kathleen nodded curtly. "That's what you said."

"So, where's my reward?"

She gave him a chilly look. "What reward?"

"That kiss you owe me, sweetheart."

"I don't owe you any such thing." For three weeks she'd been at Parsons's beck and call, and it had been a mixed curse. On the one hand, she didn't have to work herself into near exhaustion under Amelia Parsons's relentless supervision, but on the other, she had to put up with Herbert's vulgar innuendos and constant attempts to corner her. Didn't the man ever think of anything else? Even the growing evidence of her pregnancy hadn't discouraged him.

Parsons pushed away from the desk and planted himself squarely in front of her. "Still acting like you're too good for the likes of me, eh? Well, you'd better think again, Miss High and Mighty. You're only here because I stepped in. Margaret Drummond ordered my ma to sack you, girlie. So you'd better watch how you look down your nose at me. And you'd better sweeten your attitude, too, or you'll be on the street so fast you won't know what day it is. What'll you do about your brat, then?"

Kathleen's heart pounded, but she held her ground. Herbert Parsons was a bully, and not a very bright one at that. If he succeeded in intimidating her even once, she would have to cope with his disgusting behavior forever.

"You knew I did not welcome your attentions, Mr. Parsons, so don't let us have any quibbling over that." She coolly stepped around him and picked up a ledger from her desk. "This is the main reason you 'stepped in' to keep me from being sacked. You may be an adequate driver, and you may know cars and automobile repair to some extent, but you're unable to handle the paperwork involved in managing Mr. Drummond's garage."

Parsons's mouth twisted in an ugly snarl. "Why you little—"

"Hello, anybody here?"

Both Kathleen and Parsons wheeled at the interruption. With a sigh of relief, she recognized Maxwell Rutledge, currently a guest in the mansion.

"Hello, Mr. Rutledge," she said with only a trace of breathlessness. "Is there something you need?"

He gave her a shrewd look. Had he heard everything? She blushed, imagining what he must think.

"Edward seemed to think there might be a spare vehicle I could use," Rutledge said, his eyes still on her. She felt a new rush of humiliation when he glanced at her ringless left hand. "I need to get to Long Island right away. I shouldn't be long."

Kathleen watched Herbert trying to decide which vehicle to release to Rutledge. "Perhaps you'd like Parsons to drive you," she suggested, jumping at the chance to get him out of her hair.

"I would prefer that," he agreed with a rueful shake of his head. "I'm afraid I haven't quite mastered the knack of all this traffic." He looked at Parsons. "This won't inconvenience you, I hope?"

"Well..."

"Mr. Drummond is busy for the afternoon in the library," Rutledge said easily, "so he won't be needing you himself."

Kathleen watched Parsons as he shrugged into his uniform jacket. His tone was almost insolent as he addressed Rutledge. "You say you're wanting to go right away?"

"Yes... Parsons, is it? If it's not too much bother."

"No bother." Parsons reached for his cap. As the two men left the room, Rutledge glanced over his shoulder at Kathleen. She told herself she must have imagined the brief wink he gave her.

HER LABOR BEGAN that night. At first it was only a dull ache centered somewhere in her lower back. Because it was too soon, she did not suspect what was happening. She was only entering her eighth month.

"Something wrong?" Lizzie asked, rubbing sleepily at her eyes as Kathleen switched on the overhead light.

"No, I'm just a little uncomfortable. Go back to sleep, Lizzie."

"Ah, these last weeks will be a bit uncomfortable," Lizzie murmured sympathetically. "My ma sometimes enjoyed a backrub then, and my da always obliged."

"Your mother had a husband," Kathleen said dryly.

"You're right there, love." Lizzie stirred and stretched, then tossed back the covers. "But he taught me everything he knew, so aren't you the lucky one."

"Oh, Lizzie, what would I do without you?"

"Have the little tyke without a hitch, likely as not."

"I don't see how." And she didn't. Of the few good things that had come of her trip to America, her friendship with Lizzie was the best.

"I'm going to the toilet first," Kathleen said. The bane of her pregnancy, as far as she was concerned, were the endless urges that roused her in the middle of the night.

Her personal needs attended to, she was heading back to her room when she was seized by a sharp, piercing pain that wrung a surprised gasp out of her and nearly sent her to her knees. Lizzie was beside her in seconds.

"What's wrong? What is it, Kathleen? Did you fall?"

Kathleen breathed deeply and slowly, trying to gather herself together enough to get back to her room. "No, I...I think it's time, Lizzie."

"Lord a'mercy! Are you sure?"

"Yes." But her reply was not necessary. With a stricken look at her, Lizzie saw the telltale signs and crossed herself.

Kathleen's gown was stained with pinkish liquid. Her water had broken, an ominous sign. A dry birth was too often a long, excruciatingly hard birth.

Kathleen, too, breathed a prayer for her unborn child. He was so small. That should have filled her with fear, but she felt only a strange sense of satisfaction. It was time, and he would be fine.

Patrick should be here. The thought came and was instantly rejected. What a weakling she was to think of him now that the moment of truth was upon her. With his betrayal, Patrick had forfeited any right to even know about their child. She must remember to tell Lizzie to pay her no mind if she should call his name while in the throes of labor.

CHAPTER THREE

Savannah, Georgia—1926

"Do you, Patrick Ryan O'Connor, take this woman, Caroline Taylor Ferguson, to be your lawfully wedded wife, from this day forward, to have and to hold, in sickness and in health, till death do you part?"

"I do."

"And do you, Caroline Taylor Ferguson, take this man..."

The priest's voice faded as Patrick stared at the huge diamond gracing the finger of the woman he was marrying. Sunshine, pouring through the stunning stained-glass windows of St. John Cathedral, reflected off the diamond and sent a shower of multihued rays over bride and groom alike.

A good sign? Patrick wondered. He would need all the help he could get, marrying a woman he did not love. Would God curse the marriage and him? As he stared at the minister's lips, intoning the ancient words of holy matrimony, he wondered how much more painfully he could be cursed.

Aware suddenly of silence and an air of expectation from both the priest and the bride, he realized that he'd lost the thread of the ceremony. Clearing his throat, the minister repeated, "The ring, sir?"

"Oh, yes..." *Sorry.* He almost murmured the word out loud.

Sorry was not an appropriate response from a groom. What would the priest think? The guests? What would

Caroline think? Slipping two fingers into his vest pocket, he withdrew the elaborate wedding band. As lavish as the engagement ring, it was precisely what Caroline had demanded. Without looking into her eyes, he concentrated on the words coming from the priest.

"With this ring..."

"With this ring..."

"I thee wed..."

"I thee wed."

With the ring poised to slip upon Caroline's finger, he hesitated. Through the haze of the Georgia sun, it was suddenly the hand of another that he held, soft, youthful, long fingered... nails trimmed to a practical length, uncolored and beautifully natural... trembling slightly as vows were exchanged. But the place was Ireland, not Savannah. And the woman was not Caroline.

Kathleen, my only love...

But Kathleen was lost to him forever. With unsteady fingers, he pushed the ring onto Caroline's finger and closed his eyes as pain lodged in his chest. He fought against remembering, but it was too late. Just a crack in the door of his mind and it all crowded in, pushing aside everything except the anguish, swamping him, sucking him under like the waves of the storm-tossed sea that night. That cursed night...

God, the terror. He'd waited desperately on the docks as reports of the *Irish Queen*'s collision with a huge ocean liner were flashed to shore. Once the rescue operation was launched, he'd managed to leap aboard one of the tugs headed to the mouth of New York harbor, the site of the disaster. The rescue effort was hampered by high seas and pelting rain, but the extent of the tragedy was immediately apparent. The *Transatlantic Star* was relatively unscathed, but the *Irish Queen* had capsized. Debris, human and otherwise, littered the angry sea. Miserably inadequate lifeboats fought a losing battle with twenty-foot-high waves.

It was more than twelve hours before the storm blew itself out and then another forty-eight hours before the rescue effort was finally called off. Each time a new corpse was sighted, Patrick, too, died a little. Worst of all, the bodies of some passengers were never recovered. When the final tally was made, Kathleen was listed as missing and presumed dead. It was the worst, the blackest, the most grievous day of his life. Too late he'd learned how overloaded the steamer had been and of its sad state of repair. But most reprehensible was finding out how badly third-class passengers like Kathleen were treated. In a pit of despair, he cursed fate and Leland Shipping. On that day, he put his dreams behind him and focused on another goal. The Leland Company would pay. He would see to it somehow, some way, some day.

He brooded for several days, reading and rereading her letters. Without Kathleen and the bright future they'd planned, he felt as lost and adrift as the debris from the *Irish Queen*. What did he have to live for? Nothing. Less than nothing.

Except for vengeance.

It was one thing to hunger for vengeance and another to actually bring it about, he realized one evening a few days after the tragedy as he sat eating his supper on top of a wooden crate. The way things were now, there was little he could do personally to hurt the Leland Company.

Information, Patrick decided, was the key to his plan. He began learning as much about the company's mode of operation as he could. From former crewmen and longshoremen, he learned much about how the Leland Company consistently managed a profitable bottom line. Most of the Leland ships that transported immigrants were routinely overboarded, and corners were cut on food and in other areas, such as lifeboats and jackets. In the event of an emergency, third-class and steerage passengers in the crowded lower decks were at a disadvantage if it became necessary to board the lifeboats. Still, even if the *Irish Queen* had not been overloaded, the steamer had stood little chance of survival in a storm such as the one encountered the night she sank. Needed repairs had been postponed once too often. Although crews had reported rust and decay in the holds, the reports were ignored by Leland management.

The more Patrick learned about the conditions Kathleen had been forced to endure, the more his own guilt grew. Why hadn't he checked more thoroughly? Leland's reputation was hardly a secret. A few questions here and there would have alerted him. Why had he been blind to the evidence right before his eyes? No Leland ship catering to Irish immigrants was truly safe, and that included the *Irish Queen*. Why hadn't he waited? The answer was seared into his guilty soul. He'd been too impatient, too eager to have Kathleen with him, too caught up in his own selfish needs. The single night they'd consummated their love would forever haunt him. Even though he could never forget the passion he and Kathleen had shared, he knew he would never overcome the crushing guilt of knowing that two precious lives, one only a tiny flicker in Kathleen's womb, had been claimed that night. Because of the callous, criminal operation of Leland Shipping, their child, their baby conceived in love, was lost forever.

Leland would pay.

Tossing aside the core of an apple, he vaulted off the crate, ready to get back to work. A yell to his right drew his attention. A man in a business suit and hat was sauntering down the dock amid crates and supplies waiting to be on-loaded. Overhead, a huge crane maneuvered a wooden platform stacked high with boxes. As Patrick watched, one of the cables lost tension and the entire load shifted. If it broke, the boxes would be lost in the drink and the operator would be held accountable. That was Leland Company policy, no ifs, ands or buts.

Even if the load crushed an unlucky pedestrian.

Patrick shouted and the man looked his way. Too late. With a grating crunch, the cable snapped.

Afterward, Patrick didn't remember making a decision. With a muffled oath, he lunged instinctively, striking the man from behind with his shoulder. Together, they tumbled across the rough planks and slammed into a crate of oranges as the boxes hit the ground near them with a deafening crash.

Patrick got up, shaking his head to clear it. At his feet, the man stirred then put out a hand. Patrick took it and pulled him upright, watching him as he leaned against the orange crate and caught his breath. He was well dressed and wore a diamond stickpin in his tie and a watch fob that, even to Patrick's untutored eye, appeared costly.

"Thanks, I owe you." With his hand extended, he introduced himself. "Wade Ferguson. And you are..."

"Patrick O'Connor." He shook hands. "Are you hurt, sir?"

"No, thanks to you."

"Are you sure? I gave you a pretty solid lick there."

Ferguson smiled. "I'm fine. And thanks again for doing it. You could have been injured yourself." He nodded at the splintered crates not fifteen feet away from them. "The load on that crane must have topped half a ton."

"Yes, sir, I expect so."

"Yes, well...you didn't have to do what you did and I'm grateful. I won't forget it."

"It's nothing."

"Hmm, to you, maybe." He looked around, his gaze taking in the activity on the docks with the air of one who was no stranger to it. "You work for Leland, I take it?"

As much as he hated to admit it, Patrick nodded.

"Longshoreman?"

"Yes, sir."

"O'Connor, eh?"

"That's right."

Looking around, Ferguson found his hat and stepped over to it. Using his sleeve, he rubbed at a smudge on the crown before fitting it carefully on his head. Turning, he gave Patrick another shrewd once-over. "Thanks again, O'Connor."

Watching Ferguson as he threaded his way through the maze along the dockside, Patrick noticed that he took a little more care than before. When the man had disappeared, Patrick located his own cap. At a yell from his foreman, he turned and headed back to the job.

The next day, he was in the act of snagging a bale of cotton with a grappling hook when Judson called his name. Patrick turned and saw Wade Ferguson standing well behind Judson. Close by Ferguson's side was a woman with cropped black hair curling around her face. Her shapely legs were bared by a short dress that ended above her knees. Straightening slowly, he sensed the men around him staring. Even at a distance of fifty feet, Patrick could see that she was beautiful, but he took little notice. It was Ferguson who interested him. After anchoring the grappling hook in the bale, he headed over.

"Hello, Mr. Ferguson."

"O'Connor. Good to see you again." Ferguson shook his hand. "This is my daughter, Caroline."

Looking at her directly, Patrick realized she was younger than he'd thought. "I'm pleased to meet you, Patrick," she said in a breathy southern drawl.

"Ma'am." He nodded politely. She had the modern look that seemed to be all the rage in New York. Her lips were pouty and red, her gaze boldly flirtatious. What was she doing out here? Why would her father expose her to these surroundings? Didn't he know these men weren't gentlemen? They were as likely to say something coarse to a lady as look at her.

"We're on our way home to Georgia, O'Connor," Ferguson said. "My business in New York is concluded. I wanted to talk to you before I left. If you've got time, that is."

Patrick glanced at his foreman whose attention was fixed on Caroline Ferguson. "I usually break about now to eat."

"I counted on that." With a gesture, Ferguson indicated a chauffeured automobile parked on the dock premises. Whoever he was, Ferguson traveled first class. Taking his daughter by the elbow, he turned and began walking toward the Packard. Patrick followed, falling into step beside Ferguson. He wouldn't trail behind any man, not here in America.

"I won't take much time," Ferguson said, getting right to the point. "I know a man who works as hard as you is hungry as a bear, come lunchtime. So I'll just get to it. Do you have any particular reason to stay in New York?"

Patrick leaned against the Packard, his gaze going beyond Ferguson to the gray water of New York harbor. For some reason, he saw Kathleen's face in his mind. She was smiling, with that look in her eyes she always got when they talked about America and their future together. Their dreams. The family they would have...

"O'Connor?"

He fought off the seduction of his memories and looked at Ferguson. His reason for staying in New York? "New York is as good a place as any other, I suppose," he told him. Especially if he wanted to see the Leland Company get what was coming to them.

"I took the liberty of checking a few things," Ferguson said. "I know you've no personal ties here. Your family is still in Ireland, am I right?"

He paused, and when Patrick only nodded, he went on. "And I was told your fiancée was a passenger on the *Irish Queen*. A tragedy, that." He shook his head. "A real tragedy."

"Kathleen," Patrick murmured.

"Eh, what's that?"

"Kathleen," he repeated softly, his gaze drifting to the harbor again. "Her name was Kathleen."

A moment passed as Ferguson studied the younger man's harsh features silhouetted against the gray harbor. "You have my sympathy," he said gruffly. "I know what it's like. I lost my wife, Pamela, over fifteen years ago, but I still—"

Think of her? Love her? Miss her? Feel as if a black hole has replaced your heart? Patrick squinted out across the bleak water. All of that and more. Grief and guilt and loss were always with him. Knowing another man may have felt the same pain did nothing to lessen his own. At Ferguson's next words, he wrenched his thoughts away from the well-worn track to nowhere.

"Under the circumstances, I'm surprised that you stayed on with Leland," the older man said, his curiosity tangible.

"I have my reasons."

"Ah." Ferguson nodded. "So, would those reasons keep you from considering a job offer from me?"

Patrick studied him in silence. "I'm not sure. Why? What did you have in mind?"

"Daddy! Do hurry, please," Caroline interrupted impatiently. "The wind is merciless out here."

"In a minute, baby," Ferguson replied absently. "I don't forget my debts, O'Connor. You saved my life a few days ago and I'd like to show my appreciation. I own Ferguson Shipyards. Are you familiar with it?"

"I've heard the name," Patrick replied slowly, unable to recall details. But from the look of Ferguson, his glittery daughter and the luxurious automobile, his business must be doing all right.

"We build yachts, small sailing craft, some fishing boats," Ferguson said, a note of pride creeping into his voice. "And none finer in the industry, you can check on that. I'm thinking of branching out—U.S. Navy stuff, PT boats."

Patrick knew what a PT boat was—a high-speed motorboat used by the navy to patrol the waters. "Where exactly are you located, Mr. Ferguson?"

"Savannah, Georgia." With no hesitation, he added, "How would you like to come and work for me, O'Connor?"

"Doing what?"

"Whatever it turns out you do best."

Patrick turned and gazed at the horizon. At home in Kilkenny he'd begun apprenticing as a carpenter. He'd only taken the job with Leland to get the bargain price for Kathleen's passage, thinking to find a better job later. He'd stayed to learn the inner workings of the company. He knew enough now to begin thinking of a strategy to bring it down. Whatever he worked out, it would take a long time. Years. Working for a competitor, even one as small as Ferguson, might be the first step in a winning strategy. After all, he had time. All the time in the world.

"What do you say, O'Connor? My company's sound and Savannah's a far better place than New York. I can tell you right off I wouldn't waste you as a longshoreman. I checked you out pretty thoroughly. You're underemployed here. A man with your potential just needs the right opportunity. I'm offering it."

THE CITY OF SAVANNAH was situated eighteen miles up the mouth of the river of the same name. It was beautiful and lush and green. Patrick liked it on sight. He found an upstairs apartment in one of Savannah's old houses and settled in. Unlike many "Yankees," a label placed on anybody in Savannah who was not southern born, he acclimatized right away. Now, after six months, he hardly noticed the sultry climate and mesmerizing humidity.

His rooms overlooked one of the city's unique squares. When Savannah was founded in 1733, it was set out in an orderly grid pattern, and by the middle of the next century, the central city comprised twenty-four squares. When Patrick arrived in June, Chatham Square had been a picture with its bright pink oleanders and gnarled old magnolia trees loaded with huge, creamy, fragrant blossoms. And everywhere, ancient oaks dripped Spanish moss. Sitting there in the evenings, unwinding from a job that had turned out to be hectic and demanding, he often thought how much Kathleen would have delighted in Savannah.

With a grunt, he stood and tossed his thin cigarillo to the ground below, then went inside. He didn't want to start thinking about Kathleen tonight of all nights. Nothing blackened his mood faster, and a bottle of the best Irish whiskey wasn't enough to kill the pain.

Striding to his closet, he took out his suit coat. He had been invited to some kind of social gathering at the home of Wade Ferguson and after six months under Ferguson's direction, he knew better than to be late. He'd been puzzling over the invitation ever since it was issued. Although Ferguson had shown Patrick as much respect in their working relationship as he could ever wish, he wasn't in the habit of including him in his social life. Patrick wondered what was up.

Arriving at Ferguson House just as the lights were turned on to showcase the spectacular gardens, Patrick thought it grand indeed. It was one of the new estates built outside the city proper, and Wade Ferguson had done himself proud, especially considering his humble origins. He'd been penniless but brash and ambitious when he'd arrived in Savannah in 1910. Employed by one of the cotton mercantiles, he'd quickly advanced to managing the warehouse. There he'd met the daughter of a wealthy cotton broker and determined to marry her. After the marriage, he'd persuaded his father-in-law to invest in a rundown boatyard and had successfully parlayed it into one of Savannah's most prosperous businesses.

Yes, Wade Ferguson had certainly done well, Patrick thought, standing at the elegant front door. Before he could lift the brass knocker, the door was pulled open by a black-liveried servant and he was ushered inside.

Surrendering his hat, Patrick looked around. The huge ballroom was packed with elegantly gowned women and men in formal attire. His own suit was black and his shirt brand new and snow-white, but it wasn't in the same class as the garb worn by Ferguson's other guests. Again Patrick wondered at his invitation.

"Patrick! Here you are, sugah. And right on time, too."

"Hello, Miss Ferguson."

Wrinkling her nose, Caroline lifted her champagne glass and sipped. "Oh, you! Always so polite, so formal." She slipped her arm through his and rubbed against him like a cat. "This is a party, honeylove. Relax a little."

"I am relaxed." She was tipsy, he decided.

Stepping back a few inches, she studied him. "Liar."

He chuckled softly. "Well, maybe I'm a little nervous. This is the first time I've been invited to my boss's home."

With a smile playing at her mouth, she sipped more champagne. "I'll bet you're wonderin' why?"

"I confess I am."

"Daddy's got a little surprise planned for you."

Patrick frowned. "What kind of surprise?"

"Now, if I told you that, I'd be a naughty girl, wouldn't I?"

He stared at her in silence, uncertain about her in this mood. Caroline Ferguson was an enigma to him. When he'd first arrived in Savannah, she had made clear their obvious differences. She was the boss's daughter and he was an employee. She had drawn the line very definitely. It had been fine with him. With Kathleen's image still imprinted on his heart, he was indifferent to most women. Besides, Caroline was willful and outrageously indulged by her father. If Wade Ferguson had a weakness, it was his daughter.

"Being naughty is your special thing, isn't it?" If he played along with her, maybe she would give him a hint as to what Ferguson wanted.

Her smile took on a sharper edge. "I'm not sure I like you, Patrick O'Connor."

He wasn't sure he liked her, either, but he wasn't stupid enough to say it out loud. She provoked gossip around town. It was said that she was fast. He wondered if her father knew of her reputation.

"What are you thinkin'?" she demanded suddenly.

"That I'm the only man here without a drink."

"We can fix that, sugah." Tucking her hand under his arm, she began to walk with him toward the bar. "No Irishman can stay sober at a party. What's your pleasure?"

"Whiskey."

She signaled his choice to the black man who was mixing drinks. Apparently the prohibition on liquor didn't faze Wade Ferguson or the circle who attended parties such as this one. After six months in his employ, Patrick knew the man's influence ranged far and wide.

"I suppose bein' Irish explains more than a few things about you," Caroline remarked, her gaze raking him audaciously from head to toe.

"Such as?"

"Well, isn't it obvious, honey? Your taste for whiskey, your penchant for rollin' up your sleeves and workin' right along with the men on the job and your black Irish looks."

He could hardly deny any of it. But coming from Caroline, it felt like an insult. He reached to accept his drink from the bartender.

Caroline sighed. "I don't think I've ever seen such a fascinatin' combination, sugah. Eyes blue as Georgia skies and hair black as sin. I've only got one question."

"And what would that be?" Over her shoulder, he spotted Wade Ferguson standing with a group of business cronies. But Caroline's reply brought his startled gaze back to hers. "What?"

"What I said, honey, was ... do you look this good all over?"

"How much champagne have you had, Miss Ferguson?"

She giggled. "Not nearly enough." She handed her glass to the aged servant behind the bar. "I'll have another one, Ezra."

"Yes'm." Ezra refilled the glass.

"Mmm, delicious. I love champagne. Now, what were we sayin'? And no more scolding about my drinkin'. I get enough of that—"

"O'Connor, there you are."

"Good evening, sir." Patrick shook hands with Wade Ferguson, then with Joe Powell, the company's head bookkeeper. He didn't recognize the other men.

Ferguson made the introductions. One was a naval architect, another an accountant and a man named Whitley, who looked vaguely familiar, was an engineer. Patrick realized why when Ferguson said, "Whitley worked at Leland Shipping. You two might have met."

"I don't think I've had the pleasure," Whitley said with a smile.

Startled, Patrick suddenly placed him. Whitley had stormed down to the docks one day and given Judson hell for overloading the hold of a steamer headed for London. Whitley seemed quiet, but he'd held his own with Judson that day. Patrick had been impressed.

"Naturally you know Ben Sculley—my right-hand man, I guess you'd call him," Ferguson said, nodding to a tall, swarthy, unsmiling man in his late forties. Patrick knew him. He was hard; he played favorites and he was not well liked. Patrick gave him a brief nod.

"We've been talking about you, O'Connor." Ferguson signaled Ezra for a fresh round of drinks. "Let's go into my study, gentlemen. Business before pleasure, that's my motto. Caroline, girl! That's enough champagne for you. Go entertain our guests now. Don't forget you're my hostess, sweetheart."

"Yes, Daddy."

She sounded obedient, but her eyes flashed dangerously. Was he the only one who noticed? Patrick wondered. Daddy's little girl didn't like being chastised or dismissed while men took care of business. But he had no time to wonder about Caroline Ferguson. His boss was headed for his study with the other men on his heels. Clearly Patrick was expected to follow.

As soon as the door closed, Wade Ferguson cut right to the chase. "We want you for the new production manager, O'Connor."

After six months, Patrick knew he hadn't disappointed Ferguson with his performance. But this! He was stunned. "I can think of three men with seniority who won't be happy about this, sir," he said, keeping his tone respectful.

Ferguson held a match to his cigar. "Stokes, Johnson and Lunigan, right?"

"That's right." Not to mention Ben Sculley, he thought, noticing the man's scowl.

"I run my shipyard the way I see fit!" Ferguson snapped. "Stokes is a procrastinator, Johnson hasn't got your way with the men and Lunigan's a hothead. No offense," Ferguson said, puffing up a blue cloud. "I know he's one of your countrymen. But you know he blows up at the drop of a hat. Production would be in a turmoil most of the time with him in charge." Privately, Patrick agreed. Still, his mind whirled at the possibilities. He wanted it. He'd assumed he'd have to work for several years before getting a break like this.

"Well, what do you say, man?"

Patrick put out his hand to clinch the deal.

PATRICK WAS FIRMLY established as the production manager at Ferguson Shipyards within six weeks. The expected grousing and grumbling had soon faded. Even Ben Sculley seemed to have overcome his initial animosity. As Ferguson had noticed, Patrick had a strong connection with his men, a connection based on mutual respect. Men were the heart of any work force, and Patrick never forgot that. Instinctively, he was generous with praise and fair and just in criticism. In Wade Ferguson, he had a fine role model. The more Patrick knew him, the more he respected him.

He'd been in Savannah nearly nine months when he was called to Ferguson's office early one morning. The keel for the first navy PT boat had been laid the week before. In securing the contract from the government, Ferguson had been forced to commit to some tight scheduling. The successful completion of the first milestone was something that Wade Ferguson would appreciate. Patrick hoped he was in for a pat on the back and not an unpleasant surprise.

Ferguson looked up as Patrick entered his office.

"Patrick. Come in, son. Come in."

"I got your message a few minutes ago, sir. I was out in the yard looking for the best place to situate the paint shed."

"Yes, yes. Fine. Have a seat."

Patrick went to the tea cart that occupied a corner of the older man's office and poured himself a cup of tea from a pot that was always fresh and piping hot. A preference for strong tea over coffee was another trait the two men had in common. He sat down.

"It's a chilly day," he said, cupping his hands around the warm mug.

"Yes, February can be nippy, that's a fact. Nothing like New York, though."

Patrick smiled. "No, sir."

"You did a fine job on the keel, Patrick. Congratulations."

"Thank you, sir."

"There's a bonus in it for you, naturally."

Patrick hadn't been aware of that. He savored the moment and as usual thought of Kathleen. Would she be proud? Clearing his throat, he got up and replaced his empty mug on the cart.

"But that's not why I called you today."

Patrick studied Ferguson. He seemed distracted. His eyes were red, as though he hadn't slept well. He was not usually restless, but today he was shuffling papers with hands that were a bit unsteady.

"Is something wrong, sir?"

Ferguson stared at him. "Wrong? No, no. Everything's... Well, maybe just a little... unsettled. I reckon that's as good a word as any."

He stood up suddenly and began to pace behind his desk, something else that was unlike him, Patrick thought.

"You know my Caroline," he said abruptly.

"Yes, sir. Of course."

Ferguson's features softened. "She's very beautiful. I daresay you've noticed." When Patrick nodded with a half smile, Ferguson transferred his gaze to the window. He seemed to be gathering his thoughts. "Her mother died when she was only four. I always regretted that. Pamela was a beauty, too. Every man jack in Savannah would have killed to win her, but she chose me. I always wondered what she would have thought if she could see how well I've done. Her family thought she married down, you know."

Patrick was completely baffled. His conversations with Ferguson had never before crossed the line into personal territory.

"Anyway, if Pamela were here, she might have been a... how shall I say it? A steadying influence on Caroline. She's headstrong and spoiled, you've noticed that. Oh, I know the gossip that circulates about her, but most of it's just that, gossip. But I'll be honest. One thing bothers me more than a little. She's a few years past the age when most young women marry."

"Women seem more independent these days," Patrick remarked neutrally.

"Voting, getting on juries, talking politics," Ferguson grumbled, straying from his subject momentarily. Ferguson cleared his throat. "Yes, well, nothing we can do about the times, don't you know? But back to Caroline, my boy. As I was saying, she's of an age to marry, and some might say I've no business taking a hand in it, but I happen to think otherwise. Yes, sir, I certainly consider it my business to see to my little girl's happiness."

Patrick did not like the feeling he was getting. He stood up and went to the tea cart. Ferguson kept some liquor in the office. He eyed a bottle of top-quality Irish whiskey with longing, but poured himself more tea.

"Do you like Caroline, Patrick?"

He hid behind the mug of tea a second or two. "I don't know her well enough to say yes or no, sir."

"She's aware of you, I can see that."

Since the night he'd first been invited to Ferguson House, she had flirted with him outrageously every chance she got, but Patrick knew it was meaningless. She flirted with every passable-looking man she was near. What was Ferguson getting at?

"Do you find her unattractive?"

"No, sir. Of course not."

"Good, good." He cleared his throat again. "I've been thinking... You're young, Patrick. You have a fine future here at Ferguson Shipyard. A man needs a stable family life, a home. I've got that big place out on Orchard Road. Eighteen blasted rooms and just me and Caroline and the hired help."

"Sir, I'm afraid I—"

"I don't think of you as an employee, Patrick. Haven't for a long time. I got your measure as a man that day in New

York when you shoved me out from under that overloaded platform. I'm happy to say I wasn't wrong. Since then, I've had many opportunities to judge your capabilities and character.''

Patrick took a seat again. He couldn't get over the feeling that Ferguson was waiting to drop a bombshell.

"There isn't a young man I respect more, Patrick."

"Thank you, sir."

"And there isn't a man in Savannah—hell, in the whole state—that I'd prefer to make this offer to, son."

Son?

"I'm offering you my daughter's hand in marriage. There. I've said it." Ferguson took out a handkerchief and wiped his face.

Patrick sat stunned for a full half minute while his thoughts raced. What in hell was going on?

"Mr. Ferguson, this is a great...uh, compliment." He swallowed hard. "And a great surprise, too. But, sir, I'm more than happy working for you. Maybe we'd better just keep it that way."

"Don't turn me down flat, not until you've thought it over a little longer."

"I can't marry your daughter, sir. And you shouldn't even be doing this. This is 1926, sir. Arranged marriages are a thing of the past. Only Caroline has the right to choose the man she'll marry."

"I'm doing this with Caroline's full consent."

Patrick's jaw fell. "You can't mean that!"

"Caroline is ready and willing, Patrick." Ferguson's tone hardened. "She'll be a most fortunate young woman to marry a man of your caliber and I've told her so."

"Still, sir... Ah, with all due respect..."

"There will be some benefit to you, of course," Ferguson said, going back to his desk and picking up the papers.

"This is a contract, all legal and binding, giving you a full partnership in Ferguson Shipyards and naming you to the board of directors. Your new title, once you marry my daughter, will be vice president of manufacturing."

Patrick leaned back slowly, studying Ferguson's face. There was something else going on here, but what was it? Not that he wasn't ambitious, but why was Ferguson offering him this job now? And why would he hand over his only child, his heir, to a nobody? Why, for that matter, would Caroline want to marry him?

The questions mounted in his head, but another look at Ferguson's face told him there would be no real answers. At least not today. He might know the man's reasons in time, but today he would have to answer yes or no on trust.

Instinct told him to stand up and walk away.

"We won't be a small-town outfit for long, Patrick." Ferguson's expression failed to hide his excitement. "We're going to be expanding, my boy. Russ Whitley's connections in New York have proved invaluable."

"What do you mean?" Russ Whitley was one of the former Leland employees. As always when he thought of the giant shipping concern, Patrick's gut tightened. He fought to focus on Ferguson's words.

"Our future's looking rosy, Patrick. We'll be entering into a partnership with the Leland Company!"

There was total silence in the room as Ferguson played his trump card. With unsteady hands, Patrick uncapped the whiskey and poured himself a double shot. It was almost too neat, he thought. A way to get Leland from the inside! Dropped into his lap like a too-ripe plum. Marrying for the wrong reason seemed somehow a betrayal of the love he and Kathleen had shared, but Kathleen was gone. Because of Leland, he had lost his chance for real happiness. Why not seize this opportunity to make Leland pay?

Ferguson got up and poured himself a glass of whiskey, too. "I'll join you if you don't mind," the older man said. "I think we both can use it."

FROM SOMEWHERE IN THE big house, Patrick heard a striking clock. Midnight, and he'd finished nearly half a bottle of the finest, smoothest whiskey money could buy. Wade Ferguson's money. With his arm propped on a bent knee, Patrick stared at nothing in the dark.

He'd done it. Call it opportunity or fate or luck, whatever, he'd done it. Just three weeks after Ferguson made the offer, he had stood before a priest and tied himself to a woman he didn't love—didn't even like very much, to tell the truth—and all because it would ultimately open doors for him. The marriage was his ticket to Leland's inner workings. Information was power. And only the powerful could bring down a company like Leland.

Turning his head, he looked at the door of Ferguson's study and thought he should get up and go to his new bride. He was married to Caroline Ferguson. Caroline O'Connor now. He'd have to get used to the sound of that, he supposed. He stood up and tossed back the rest of the contents of his glass. He didn't feel like a bridegroom. He felt tired. He wished he could just go to sleep, put it all out of his mind. Maybe wake up and find that the clock had been turned back a year or two. But that wasn't possible.

He set the empty glass on Wade Ferguson's desk, then raked a hand over his face. His bride was waiting. He had a duty to perform. And then he could sleep. As he started up the stairs, he had a thought. Could a man sleep knowing he had just possibly sold his soul to the devil?

CHAPTER FOUR

New York, January—1927

Childbirth will remain forever hazy in my memory, although moments during my labor do surface from time to time. I remember Lizzie's agitation when the baby was discovered to be in a breech position. I remember Amelia Parsons harping and complaining throughout. I remember a fierce and heated exchange between Lizzie and Mrs. Parsons, which I learned later was because they banished Lizzie from my side at the moment of birth. Even in my travail, I recall being shocked at Lizzie's impertinence. I remember the midwife forcing an evil-tasting draft down my throat. Drugged and helpless from that moment, I have no clear recollections of the rest. No matter how I struggle to remember it, I cannot recall the moment of birth. Nothing, however, can change the bitter truth. My baby is lost to me forever. Patrick's desertion hurt, but I always knew there was our child to love and care for, to make my life worth living. Waking up and finding that there was no child has been devastating, and the pain will be with me always.

And the dreams. I almost dread the nighttime when my conscious brain shuts down and my subconscious takes over. In the most distressing dream I see a baby and hear hushed, furtive whispers. It is night, a cold,

*moonless night, and drizzling rain. Headlights on a
long, sleek automobile glisten off wet pavement as tires
hiss on a dark, winding road. Then, after a long journey, tall iron gates guarding a huge estate loom ahead.
At a signal, they open, allowing the car to drive
through. Then the doors close, and when the harsh,
metallic clang echoes in the night, I always wake up.*

*Why do I have such a dream? Is it because of my own
recent loss? Was another baby in danger? Then who? I
know no other infants.*

*The other dream I discount as sheer fantasy. In it,
Patrick returns for me and we are together at last.
Happily married.*

*But enough of that. Although my heart will never
come to terms with my loss, I came to terms with my
situation and resumed my duties.*

WINTER SETTLED IN with a vengeance, and it seemed as if
spring would never arrive, but it took more than snow and
ice to deter Margaret Drummond's passion for entertain-
ing. It was at one of her gatherings in March that Kathleen's life was changed forever. The day of the party, Lizzie
became ill and Kathleen was pulled from Herbert Parsons's
domain to fill in.

After dinner, she was sent to get fresh coffee for the men
holed up in Edward Drummond's study. She guessed they
were spiking it with fine Napoleon brandy while smoking
imported Cuban cigars. Balancing the sterling coffeepot and
cups and saucers loaded on a heavy silver tray, she knocked
once briefly and pushed the door open.

With the exception of Maxwell Rutledge, neither Drummond nor his guests gave her more than a fleeting glance as
she served them. Rutledge, as usual, looked directly at her
as he took the china cup.

"Thank you," he said, smiling into her eyes.

Although Rutledge usually acknowledged the services performed for him, his courtesy always caught Kathleen off guard. She gave him a hesitant smile.

"I was surprised to see you in the dining room tonight," he said, speaking in a tone that did not carry to the other men in the room. "I thought you were Parsons's clerk."

She blushed, wondering if that was all he thought.

"Have I offended you, Kathleen? If so, please pardon me."

"No. No, sir, of course you haven't." She wasn't sure just what to make of Maxwell Rutledge. He was always pleasant, even friendly. She was sure he had overheard Herbert Parsons's disgusting innuendos that day in the garage, but he'd never mentioned it. She'd hated feeling embarrassed in front of Maxwell Rutledge, of all people. Hastily, she began collecting used ashtrays, cigar stubs and wineglasses and loaded them on the silver tray.

"You're no longer clerking for Parsons?"

Why was he asking these questions? "Yes... uh, yes, sir. I'm only filling in for Lizzie tonight. She's not well." Actually, Lizzie had taken sick after inhaling some caustic cleaning compound that Amelia Parsons had forced her to use to scour the white tiles in the foyer. Even though Lizzie had told the woman she'd had an allergic reaction once before, Amelia hadn't been moved by the maid's plea. Kathleen felt outraged on Lizzie's behalf and frustrated. Such unjust treatment of maids wasn't unusual at the mansion. Women in general had such poor options. Oh, to be able to control one's own destiny.

"I hope it's nothing serious," Rutledge murmured.

"Thank you. She'll be fine by morning." And whether she was or not, she'd be expected to perform her duties.

"Kathleen!"

She glanced over at her employer, who was rummaging through a stack of papers on his desk. "Yes, Mr. Drummond."

"I'm looking for the morning papers. There was an article..."

"Today's papers are by the side of your desk in that magazine rack, sir." She no longer took them to her room until they were a few days old.

"Yes, yes... Now, Frank, it's articles such as this one in the *Times* that inflame the populace, don't you know? It would be a disaster for me if the workers started to organize in my plants." Working his cigar to the side of his mouth, he straightened and barked at Kathleen, "Where is it, girl? I can't find the blasted thing."

"If you mean that editorial about union violence," Kathleen said, putting aside the silver tray to approach Drummond's desk, "it wasn't today's paper, sir. It was yesterday's. And it wasn't the *Times,* it was the *Mirror.*"

"Well, where is it?" Drummond demanded crankily, strewing newspapers everywhere. "I expect my papers to be right here until I've read them. You haven't tossed them out, have you, girl?"

"Let me see, sir. I think I can locate it." Bending down, she retrieved the papers on the floor and found the offending article. "Yes, here it is. See, it's the *Mirror.*"

"Well, thank God it's not the *Tribune.*" Drummond frowned at Maxwell Rutledge over his bifocals. "But I'm warning you, if you start running this sort of claptrap, I'll cancel."

"The *Tribune* is far too responsible," Kathleen said without thinking. "You're never going to find an article advocating unionizing to the masses. The *Tribune* reports, it doesn't generate news."

As she reached for the tray to leave, she discovered all four men were staring at her. It was only then that she realized what she'd said. She thought of making an apology, but she hadn't really said anything to apologize *for*. Departing hastily seemed the best course, and she took it.

As she closed the door behind her, she almost ran directly into Herbert Parsons. "Oh! I didn't see you."

He was wearing the sly expression she hated. "Too busy cozying up to the big boss, were you?"

"I wasn't cozying up to anybody, Parsons."

"Why do you have that tray? You're not a maid anymore."

"Lizzie's sick. I had to fill in for her tonight."

A sneer came to his face. "That lazy slut! She's probably out on the town somewhere and dumping her chores on you."

"That is absolutely untrue," Kathleen said, struggling to keep her temper. "She's upstairs in our room and she's very sick. If you don't believe me, check with your mother." She turned to leave, but he caught her arm, and she put the tray on a nearby table.

"Hold on, missy. You're getting just a little uppity, aren't you? Now that you're rid of the brat, I guess you think—"

Crack!

The sound of her hand against his cheek was like a shot. Kathleen stared at him, almost as shocked as Parsons. Her reaction had been as quick and elemental as any reflex and straight from her soul. She might have lost her child, but he was as real to her as if he still lived beneath her heart.

"You're going to pay for that, you haughty bitch," Parsons hissed, rage glittering in his eyes. He reached for her, tearing the sleeve and bodice of her dress as she twisted to get away from him. His hands were everywhere, brutal and hurtful. He was slightly built, but strong. Surprisingly strong. Catching a handful of her hair in his fist, he used it to thrust her up against the wall, then crowded close.

"No need to fight me," he grunted, trying to squeeze her breast. "I ain't going to do no more than you've already done with somebody else. You'll like it, doll. You'll see."

"Let me go!" Struggling wildly, Kathleen pushed against his arms to try and hold him off. But he was out of control, excited and breathing heavily. Her stomach rolled sickeningly at the smell of car grease and onions and she arched her neck to avoid his wet mouth. He slapped her viciously across the face, cursing. She cried out, tasting blood.

"Stop! Oh, please, somebody help me... Oh!"

Suddenly Parsons flew backward, leaving her dazed and limp against the wall. Fumbling to pull her torn dress together, Kathleen gaped at the sight of Maxwell Rutledge holding Herbert Parsons by his collar, shaking him like a disobedient dog.

"What in hell do you think you're doing!" Rutledge exclaimed furiously, breathing hard himself. Kathleen hadn't realized what a big man Rutledge was. Her fingers pressed to her lips, she watched him toss Parsons over one of Margaret Drummond's antique chairs, toppling it and breaking a delicate leg. When the chauffeur's head cracked against the hardwood floor, Rutledge looked savagely satisfied.

Hearing the commotion, Edward Drummond opened the study door abruptly. "Here, here, what's going on?"

"Your chauffeur has insulted Miss... ah, Kathleen, Edward. His behavior was contemptible. If I hadn't come out when I did, I hate to think how far he would have gone."

With a dark frown, Drummond turned to Parsons, who had managed to get to his feet. "What is this, Parsons? What have you been doing?"

"Nothing that wasn't invited, Mr. Drummond," Parsons said, throwing Kathleen a vengeful look. "We have an understanding, me and Kathleen."

At Kathleen's gasp, everyone looked at her. "Is that so, Kathleen?" Drummond asked.

"Don't be a fool, Edward!" Maxwell Rutledge snapped. "There is no doubt in my mind that if I hadn't interrupted, Parsons would have forced himself on Kathleen. Look at her!"

Kathleen's shaky hand spread wide over her bodice, which gaped open from the tear that began at her sleeve and slashed across her breast. Her face burning, she tried to smooth her hair, which had escaped the ribbon tying it at the back of her neck. The lush, auburn mass tumbled around her face and down her back. As she huddled against the wall, she realized they were looking at her mouth. Touching it gingerly, her fingers came away bloody.

"He *struck* her!" Rutledge said fiercely.

Parsons began to talk. "Mr. Drummond, this ain't what it seems. I tell you, Kathleen Collins ain't no lady. You know she ain't married, ain't never been married, and she had that brat—"

"Edward!" Rutledge barked. With a forbidding expression, he looked at his host. "Are you just going to stand there while this...weasel insults this young woman?"

"Well..." Drummond rolled his cigar between his lips, looking as though he'd rather be anywhere else.

"I see you are," Rutledge said quietly. Drawing a deep breath, he turned to Kathleen. "Then it seems I must take a hand here. Kathleen..." He put a hand beneath her arm. "Come with me, my dear. I've a proposition to make to you."

New York, March—1927
Something wonderful has happened! I am no longer a

*servant of the Drummonds'. Mr. Maxwell Rutledge has
engaged me as secretary-companion to his wife, Lily,
who is confined to a wheelchair. Even more wondrous, he has paid off my labor contract, and Lizzie's,
as well. I can hardly believe it. Not only am I living in
the house of the owner and publisher of one of New
York's finest newspapers, but Lily Rutledge is an ad-
vocate of women's rights, and as her secretary, I write
her correspondence and am present at her sessions with
her famous, fascinating, interesting friends!*

*My father was fond of a saying: "When one door is
closed, God sees to it that another is opened." I know
this door leads to a new and happier life for Lizzie and
me.*

"I WANT YOU TO GET OUT more, Kathleen," Lily Rutledge
announced one day. "Use the car."

"Thank you, but I don't really need anything," she said.
"I did some shopping yesterday."

Lily laid down her glasses. "I didn't make myself clear.
I'm not suggesting taking time off to shop for necessities. I
thought you might like to sightsee a bit. New York is an exciting, interesting city."

"Perhaps I'll go this weekend, but I don't need to tie up
your driver. I'll go on the streetcar."

"You don't need to wait for the weekend. I'm going to cut
your hours. Lizzie's here to help now, too. You're too young
and pretty to bury yourself in this house with a bunch of
radical-thinking women."

Kathleen laughed. "Those radical-thinking women are
your friends, Lily."

"Yes, and I love them, one and all. But I'd still like to see you spend a bit of each day out of this house."

"Each day! Hardly. This is my job. I love it here. I like your friends. I don't need to spend part of every day driving around aimlessly."

Lily folded her hands in her lap. "Not even as a roving reporter?"

"Roving— Lily, what are you talking about?"

"Your instincts as a writer are pure and strong, Kathleen. I thought you might use your time sightseeing to advantage, as it were. Interesting things happen on the streets. You might stumble on something newsworthy. Who knows, someday you might sell something to Max's paper."

"The *Tribune?*" Kathleen stared at her in astonishment. Only in her wildest dreams had she ever dared hope to see words she'd written in print.

Lily chuckled with satisfaction. "I see that something I said seems to have caught your fancy."

Kathleen jumped up and went over to hug her employer. "Oh, Lily, you are so special, do you know that?"

Leaning back in her wheelchair, Lily looked at Kathleen. "You are the special one, my dear. You're lovely and quick and talented. You deserve a chance to develop your talents to be the person you were meant to be. If that means I do without you a few hours each week, then I'm happy it's in my power to help you."

New York, August—1927
I am a journalist! It is almost too wonderful to be-
lieve. Lily was right. The streets of New York are no
longer anonymous, bustling avenues of strangers ebb-
ing and flowing with whatever errands they are driven
to accomplish. No, the streets of New York are an
evergreen forest of stories just waiting for me to tell. I

refused Lily's offer to be driven around, and although she wrings her hands in secret, she finally acknowledged that no true reporter worth her salt would rely on a chauffeur. Oh, the sights to be seen from the streetcars and the buses in New York!

I have told no one—not even Lily and Max—that my work has been published in Max's own newspaper. Six articles—I can hardly believe it—and all published under a pseudonym: William Collins. My father's name, of course. I think he would have been proud.

ONE NIGHT KATHLEEN AWOKE with the smell of smoke in her room. In a panic, she threw off the bedclothes and ran out into the hall to alert Lily and Max. But once she had left her room, the smoke mysteriously disappeared. Frowning, she retraced her steps. There was nothing. Standing at the foot of her bed, she realized that her Dream Sight was to blame.

Concentrating fiercely, she recalled a burning building and cries for help. Flames leapt high into the sky. Behind the building, the setting sun was as bright as the flames. But where it happened and when were a mystery to her.

She lay awake the rest of the night.

The next afternoon as she stood on Seventh Avenue in the garment district, she again smelled smoke and knew instantly that her dream was about to become reality. Craning her neck, she hardly noticed the pedestrians hurrying around her. Forgotten was her research on the famous fashion houses. With a quick check to see that her pad and pencil were tucked in the side pocket of her shoulder bag, she began to run.

It was past ten o'clock that night when she finally boarded the streetcar that would take her home to Marlboro House.

As the lights of the city slipped by, she quickly wrote an account of the fire as she had witnessed it. A scathing indictment of the management of J. Wagner, the posh fashion house that owned the warehouse, took a while longer. With the ravaged faces of the victims' relatives etched in her mind, Kathleen's pen flew across the page.

At Marlboro House, the door was flung open and Max appeared looking more like a concerned father than her employer. Catching her hand, he pulled her inside.

"Kathleen, we've been worried!"

"I'm sorry, Max." Then, to Lily, who rolled up in her chair looking pale and concerned, "Oh, Lily, you shouldn't do this. You know I can take care of myself."

"It's after 10:00 p.m., child," the older woman said. "We just can't help—"

"I know. Please forgive me." Slipping her shoulder bag off, she laid it on a chair in the vestibule.

"Do I smell smoke?" Max asked, helping her as she took off her coat. "What have you been up to, young lady?"

"Oh, Max, there was a fire near Seventh Avenue. I was just getting off the streetcar when the alarm sounded. It was terrible. People were trapped. Here, I wrote it all down." She grabbed her shoulder bag and pulled out her tablet. "If you hurry down to the *Tribune* you can get it in before deadline for the morning paper. The details are all there, I think," she said, scanning it without noticing the look exchanged by Lily and Max.

"Hold up a minute, Kathleen." Max took the tablet but didn't read what she'd written. "What fire? Seventh Avenue is the garment district. What were you doing there, of all places?" He shot a look at Lily. "I thought you said she was sightseeing at museums and parks and..."

Lily raised her hands, palms up, and looked helpless. Hardly noticing, Max frowned, pulling his thick, dark eyebrows together as he scanned the words Kathleen had written. "This isn't bad," he murmured. "Not bad at all. In fact—"

"Yes...in fact, what, Max?" Kathleen watched his face, holding her breath.

He gave her a perplexed look. "Is this your work alone?"

"Of course!"

"It's excellent, Kathleen. It's a tight, dramatic account of a very serious event. And of course you wrote it. How could I forget the first time I ever saw you, you were rebutting my editorials. And quite eloquently, too, I might add." Reaching behind her, he took his hat from the tree. "But we've no time to discuss your talent as a writer. I need to hurry if I want to make tonight's deadline."

He flipped the paper in the tablet and found the editorial lambasting J. Wagner. "Here now, what's this?"

There were a few minutes of silence as he read. Standing and waiting warily, Kathleen sensed Lily rolling silently to her side. When Lily took her hand, she looked down into the woman's eyes. With a smile, Lily glanced at her husband. "Is it a William Collins piece, Max?"

Kathleen's mouth fell open. "Lily! How did you know?"

Max dropped the tablet to his side and gave them both a keen look. "I know better than to ask whether you wrote this, too, Kathleen. Obviously you did. But would you just answer one question for me? How long have I been harboring a ghostwriter in my house?"

"I'm not a ghostwriter! I sign every one of those articles. William Collins is a perfectly legitimate pseudonym."

"Indeed it is," Lily agreed, squeezing her protégée's hand.

"Every one?" Max repeated. "I know how many have run in the *Tribune,* but how many have you submitted to other newspapers?"

Kathleen was shocked. "None, Max! How can you even suggest such a thing? I work for the *Tribune*."

With his arms crossed, he studied her in silence. Then he smiled, shaking his head. "I'm speechless, Kathleen, but pleased as punch. And patting myself on the back for having the good sense to snatch you away from Edward Drummond. And you do indeed work for the *Tribune*, starting this minute. No, starting about five this afternoon, which, according to your article here, is just about the time the fire started."

"Max, you're offering me a job as a real reporter? But what about Lily? I can't leave Lily."

"You don't have to leave me, darling." Lily held Kathleen's hand to her cheek, smiling softly. "And thank you for even thinking of me when I know you've just been offered your heart's desire."

She looked at her husband. "Max, let's work out a compromise and share Kathleen. She can work for you in the morning at the *Tribune* and me in the afternoon here. And, naturally, she will continue to live at Marlboro."

Kathleen looked hesitantly at Max, who stroking his chin, clearly still trying to take in the fact that he'd been publishing Kathleen's articles for months. "I can't believe I didn't suspect a thing! We've been wondering who this William Collins person was. The articles were timely and interesting, sometimes even scathing. We wanted more, but all we had was a post office address." He shot her a look. "Has the accounting office been paying you satisfactorily?"

She smiled. "Yes, Max."

"Humph... Well, I suppose I shouldn't say this, but you could have gotten a lot more for those articles. Did you know that?"

"Yes, Max."

"Well, why didn't you, girl?" he demanded.

"It was enough to see my name in print."

"Well, now you'll see it regularly and you'll get paid a lot more, too," Max said. Shaking his head, he looked at his wife. "Printer's ink for blood, Lily. Didn't I tell you when I brought her home to you that she would be writing for the *Tribune* one day?"

"You did, Max."

"And of course she'll stay here at Marlboro. This is her home."

Kathleen looked at them, her throat thick with tears. "Thank you, both," she whispered.

She told no one about her dream.

New York, September—1932
Time has a way of slipping by, like a quiet cat in the night. Birth and death make us take notice. For five years, I have been with Max and Lily, treated by both as a daughter. And now it will be only Max and me. Lily died quietly in her sleep, as she would have wished it. I dreamed it, of course, more than a week before it happened, but told no one except Lizzie, who crossed herself and was blessedly subdued for a few days. Max mourns silently. My heart goes out to him.

I am still plagued by two recurring dreams—the wretched one of the infant and the accursed one of Patrick and me living a happy, loving life together. Meantime, real life goes on. I have my job as William Collins, journalist and rabble-rouser. What a flap would ensue if my readership were to discover I'm a woman!

"HERE, DANNY, WILL YOU take this copy to Joe?" Kathleen leaned over her desk and handed the copyboy the article she'd just written. "It's only a couple of minutes before deadline, so don't get sidetracked on your way, okay?"

"Sure, Miss Collins." Tucking the pages in the satchel he carried on one shoulder, he hurried off.

"And thanks, Danny!"

"Sure thing!" he yelled, his shout blending into the noise of the newsroom. One of these days, Kathleen told herself, she was going to find a job where there was an abundance of peace and quiet. Which meant that it probably wouldn't be a newspaper office, she thought, taking in the chaotic activity going on around her. So she probably wouldn't like it.

"What's funny?"

"Max! What're you doing here? You're supposed to be sailing on Tommy Isherwood's yacht somewhere off Cape Cod. What happened?"

"I was bored," he said, taking a seat on the edge of her desk. "I don't know why I thought I'd enjoy something as unexciting as sailing, anyway."

"You didn't, I did. You needed to get away, Max. You've been six months without taking off a single day."

"Six hundred months wouldn't keep me busy enough to stop missing Lily, Kathleen."

She touched his hand, wishing she could take away his grief. "I know. I just thought—"

"It's all right, love." He picked up a paperweight that had been given to her by Lily. "It was worth a try. It just didn't work."

Kathleen knew she would never forget the sight of Max holding Lily, weeping in deep, wrenching despair. A heart attack, according to the doctor. Whatever the cause, their indomitable, wonderful, loving Lily was gone.

"What do you have there?" he asked, cocking his head to get a better look.

"Hmm? Oh, it's the business section, but I haven't had a chance to read much." She raked both hands through her thick hair. "What a day we've had, Max. A train derailed at Grand Central, a jumper on the Brooklyn Bridge and a brawl at a soup kitchen in the Bronx. Welcome home."

He chuckled softly. "Don't tell me. You covered the soup kitchen thing."

"Why would you think that?"

His eyebrows lifted. "What? With your bleeding heart? You're worse than Lily. Sometimes I think she'll be with us always as long as you're around. But tell me, anyway—what happened to cause a brawl among homeless, jobless derelicts?"

"Not derelicts, Max, unfortunates. When a man is out of work, he's frustrated and resentful and scared, wearing a chip on his shoulder the size of plank. Who knows what started it," she mused, her eyes on the newspaper at her elbow. "One minute they were a bunch of hungry men and the next they were fighting like . . . animals."

"Steal a man's pride and rob him of hope and he can feel like an animal," Max said.

"The stock market crash was almost two years ago," she said, idly turning the pages of the business section. "When do you think this depression will be over?"

"No time soon, I'm afraid." Max reached out and stopped her, pointing to a feature article. "Fortunately, some businesses seem to be holding their own. The Leland Company, for one. Partnered up a few years back with a small outfit in Georgia that had a contract with the U.S. Navy. Helluva success story."

At the mention of Leland, Kathleen's expression grew cold. She would never be able to forget the ordeal of the many. "I hope their business practices have improved," she said, scanning the article. "Otherwise, the navy had better look out."

Suddenly she tensed and bent to study the article more closely. "My God, it can't be."

"What is it?" Max looked curiously at the paper.

Her eyes riveted to the newsprint, Kathleen rapidly finished the article and then her eyes flew to the picture that accompanied it. With a choked sound, she crushed the paper in her hands, then leaned back in her chair, her eyes closed.

"Kathleen!" Max started around her desk, then bellowed for someone to bring a glass of water. Reaching her, he ripped the paper from her hands, barely glancing at it, then began rubbing her wrists. "Kathleen, girl, what is it? What's wrong?"

"It's him, Max," she whispered, her lips barely moving.

"Who?" Max returned sharply, genuinely alarmed. "Get me some water here!" he called again just as Danny appeared, wide-eyed, with a glass. Behind him, two or three co-workers looked on in concern.

With a hand to her cheek, Kathleen waved the water away. "I'm all right, Max. It...I was just..." Shaking her head, she fumbled in her pocket for a handkerchief and dabbed at her eyes. "I had a shock, that's all. I'm fine now."

Max looked unconvinced. Around them, all eyes were fixed on Kathleen. She was always in control. Even in the heat of a major breaking news event, her composure rarely slipped.

Which made her emotional collapse even more alarming to Max. "Come, lean on me, love," he said. "Let's get out of the newsroom. You need a bit of privacy."

"Yes." Blankly, Kathleen rose and started to leave with Max. "Wait!" she said, looking around anxiously. "The article, Max. I need . . . I mean . . . I can explain . . ."

"I've got it. Let's get out of here." With an arm around her shoulders and the newsprint in his other hand, Max steered her out the door.

At his office, he ushered her inside and seated her on the sofa. She was still too pale. Walking to a cabinet, he found a glass and splashed a shot of brandy in it. He didn't speak until she'd consumed half of it. "Now, what was that all about?" he asked.

"That article," she began huskily. "I saw someone in the picture that I once knew. It . . . it took me by surprise. I never thought to see him again."

With a heavy frown, Max took the paper and shook it out so that he could read it. Half a dozen men were posed in the photograph accompanying the article, their names listed beneath. "Wade Ferguson?" he asked, looking at her. "You know him?"

She sighed, leaning back against the sofa. "No, Max."

"Russell Whitley?"

"No."

"John Leland? The old man himself? Where on earth did—"

"Max, please!" She covered her eyes with her hand. "I don't know John Leland or any of the others you've named. Patrick O'Connor. I know Patrick O'Connor. Or at least I used to know him."

Max spent a moment studying her before dropping his gaze back to the newspaper. "It says here he's their vice president of manufacturing."

"Amazing," she murmured.

"What?"

"Just..." She shrugged helplessly. "I don't know." Eyes closed, she fought the images that came, but she may as well have tried pushing back the tide. There he was, striding back and forth painting glowing word pictures of the life they'd share in America while she listened enthralled, pledging they would build their future together as soon as she came to him. Promising to marry her, to love her. Forever.

"Kathleen?"

"Patrick O'Connor was the man I once thought I would marry."

"Lord, child." Max sat down beside her on the sofa. Although he and Lily knew of the circumstances of her betrothal in Ireland and her fiancé's disappearance in New York, Kathleen had never told them the man's name. "Are you sure this is the same man?"

"I'm sure, Max."

He glanced at the article. "I don't know what to say, Kathleen. He must have been out of his mind to desert you. You're beautiful and good and smart—"

"And penniless," she said bitterly. "However, it looks as if he managed to land on his feet."

Max frowned. "Things aren't always the way they look, love."

Kathleen lifted the brandy to her lips and swallowed the rest of it. "Well, it doesn't matter much one way or the other now, does it? It was over six years ago. Ancient history." She gave him a smile, unaware of the pain that lurked in her green eyes. "I can't imagine why I reacted the way I did. It was ridiculous, really. I'll have to make up some story to explain it. Everyone in the newsroom must think I—"

"It says the company's in Georgia," Max said, interrupting her babbling. "Savannah, I think."

Kathleen shrugged. It made no difference to her where Patrick lived now. Absolutely none.

Max tugged on his chin, thinking. "Wasn't the *Savannah Sentinel* one of the dailies we acquired when we bought out Henson Publishing last year?"

"Really, Max. You've got to be the only publishing magnate in America who isn't sure which newspapers you own."

"I am sure," he told her, still looking thoughtful. "I just haven't had a chance to give much personal attention to the new acquisitions. With Lily's condition deteriorating the past year, I didn't want to leave New York. And then, once she was gone, I didn't particularly care."

"I know." With her own emotions so raw, just the mention of Lily brought a sheen of tears to her eyes.

Max straightened suddenly. "However, you're quite right. I should take a sharper interest. It's high time we took a firsthand look at the *Savannah Sentinel*."

Her heart did not speed up, Kathleen told herself. "We?"

"Yes, we. You pushed me off on that silly cruise by myself and I nearly expired from boredom. With you along, I won't be bored or lonely."

Kathleen crossed her arms over her middle. "I don't want to see Patrick, Max."

He looked at her. "Don't you?"

"No. I feel nothing but contempt for him. He *deserves* nothing but contempt. Besides, if I saw him again, what good would it do? I'm certainly not going to humiliate myself by asking a lot of uncomfortable questions."

"Then may I ask one?"

She looked at him warily. "I suppose."

"Are you happy, Kathleen?"

She stood up and walked across the spacious office, stopping at the window, and looked at the busy thoroughfare five stories below.

"I'm not unhappy, Max."

"That is not enough. You're young and beautiful and talented. You have much to give and yet you never look at the young men who try to catch your eye. I've seen you crush a thousand egos."

"Hardly."

"All right, a hundred."

"I'm too busy."

"That busy?"

"They're . . . dull."

"Yes, wealthy, attractive, educated, eligible and...dull." He got up and went to stand beside her. "Call me fanciful if you will, Kathleen," he said softly, "but you were meant to see that article. It's fate."

"Oh, Max." Turning, Kathleen leaned against him briefly. He was solid and safe and, apart from Lily, the only person left in the world who loved her.

With a smile, he slipped an arm around her waist. "So...we go to Savannah, hmm?"

"Yes, Max. We go to Savannah."

CHAPTER FIVE

October 1, 1932

Only two weeks in Savannah, dear Journal, and already Max is beginning to look and act the perfect southern gentleman. He has taken to wearing light-colored seersucker suits and a Panama hat. He even closes his office from noon to two each afternoon as many business people do in the deep south. "A nap in the middle of the day is a damn good idea," he says, telling me he thinks we "Yankees" can still learn a thing or two about relaxing and taking life as it comes.

As for me, I find Savannah lush and green and sweltering. Sometimes in the steamy humidity, it seems difficult just to draw a deep breath. Still, it is very beautiful—roses, even in October, and hibiscus and zinnias and chrysanthemums. Yes, there is something about Savannah...

I have not seen Patrick.

"THIS IS CRAZY, MAX. Why are we going to a party at Wade Ferguson's house?" Kathleen tugged the hem of her dress over her knees after getting in the passenger side of Max's new Hudson Straight-Eight.

"Because he invited us, love." With a squeal of the coupe's tires, they were off. "He wants to meet you."

She looked startled. "Me?"

"Well..." Leaning into an upcoming curve, Max took it at hair-raising speed. "Actually, he wants to meet William Collins."

"Max!" She rolled her eyes. "You know how I hate it when you do that. He'll be expecting a man. When are you going to get tired of pulling that stunt?"

"When are you going to start writing as Kathleen Collins?"

She stared out of the window into the dark. "When a woman's opinion begins to mean as much as a man's," she muttered.

"I heard that."

Glancing over at him, she laughed softly. "Sorry." Max Rutledge was the last man she could accuse of chauvinism. If not for him and his newspaper, she might still be a housemaid.

"I'm nervous, Max," she said, pressing a hand to her midriff. "And we both know why."

She would see Patrick tonight.

Wade Ferguson's shipyard was one of Savannah's major businesses. It had taken only an afternoon in the "morgue" at the *Sentinel* to learn what Patrick had been doing in the six years he'd been in Savannah. He was Ferguson's right-hand man, and, according to some, Patrick O'Connor was the reason Ferguson's small enterprise had prospered beyond anyone's expectations.

"Here we are." With a flourish, Max whipped the coupe into the curved driveway of Ferguson's house. It was large and lavish and traditionally southern in design. Studying the pair of outside stairs curving up to the second level of the house, Kathleen was reminded of an antebellum lady with billowing skirts. Tonight she was dressed for a formal affair. Everything was aglitter, the magnificent grounds, the wraparound veranda, the sparkling windows where the twinkle of chandeliers and guests bedecked in their most valuable jewels could be seen.

"Somehow, it makes me think of the Drummond mansion, Max," Kathleen murmured.

"Yes, I had the same thought."

"I hope it's not an omen." Five years was not long enough to erase from her memory that first painful year in New York.

Max reached for her hand to help her out of the car and squeezed it. "The past is over and done with, Kathleen. Let it rest in peace, love."

At the door, they were invited inside by a grizzled, gray-haired servant in black livery. He gave them a big smile as he took Max's hat and Kathleen's emerald satin cape.

Immediately beyond the foyer, the ballroom was choked with guests. A band was crowded into one corner playing something bright and breezy. Some couples danced, others were grouped in small knots here and there. Almost everyone held a cocktail. Across the room, Wade Ferguson spotted them and then detached himself from a group and headed their way.

"Max! I see you made it." He shook hands. "Welcome, welcome. Did you get a drink?"

"Hello, Wade. Not yet, but I will. Beautiful place you've got here."

"Yes, well, I like it. Built it about six years ago, right before Caroline married."

"Caroline?"

"My daughter. You'll meet her later." Wade Ferguson pulled a watch from his pocket and frowned. "She should be here by now. Likes to make an entrance, but no matter." He seemed to notice Kathleen for the first time.

Max nudged her forward with a glint in his eye. "I've brought a guest, Wade, as I promised. This is William Collins."

Ferguson's surprise was almost comic. "Well, now, can you imagine that? A woman. And a very beautiful one. I'm happy to meet you, ah..." He chuckled. "Mr. Collins, what shall I call you?"

"Call me Kathleen," Kathleen said with a smile, liking him instantly. "And please ignore Max. This is his favorite prank."

"Kathleen Collins, our host, Wade Ferguson," Max said, still smiling.

Ferguson was shaking his head. "The joke's on me, all right, little lady. I was planning to ask you to cover the launching of a ship we're building for the U.S. Navy, but I suppose I'll have to find a man..."

"Why?" Kathleen accepted a glass of pink lemonade from a waiter carrying a silver tray.

"Well, now...I mean..."

"You planned to ask me to cover the story when you thought William Collins was a man, is that right?" When he nodded, Kathleen shrugged. "Then I will be happy to oblige, Mr. Ferguson. I promise, I will try to avoid sounding female in the final copy."

Wade Ferguson looked at Max with chagrin. "I guess I asked for that, didn't I?"

Max chuckled. "I guess you did."

"Come along," Ferguson said suddenly, taking Kathleen's arm. "There's someone I want you to meet. He's going to get a kick out of this. Been reading your editorials and quoting them at breakfast." Shaking his head, he laughed. "William Collins, a woman. Can you beat that?"

He headed across the room with Kathleen in tow, leaving Max to follow. Near a grouping of huge potted palms, as far from the band as possible, half a dozen men stood apart. Two, both tall and wide-shouldered, had their backs to the crowd in the ballroom. In typical male fashion, most nursed drinks and puffed on cigars. The air around them was literally blue.

Wrinkling her nose, Kathleen allowed Wade Ferguson to haul her right up to the group. She had no warning, no moment of alarm. So she was caught in frozen shock as Ferguson clamped a hand on the shoulder of the tallest man and turned him around.

"Patrick!" boomed Wade Ferguson. "Look who's here. It's the reporter from the *Sentinel*, William Collins."

Smiling at something Russ Whitley had said, Patrick turned toward them. He glanced first into Wade's face and then at the man beside him. A shrewd, piercing look locked with his. For some reason, Patrick's smile faded. And then he looked into the green eyes of the woman with them.

He didn't even hear the crack of his glass as it splintered in his hand. He felt no pain as a jagged edge sliced the flesh between his thumb and forefinger. He heard none of the murmurs or oaths from his friends. He was transfixed by the face of an angel.

"Your hand!" Wade Ferguson blurted out, staring. "It's bleeding." He fumbled for his handkerchief. "Here, boy, what on earth—"

"Kathleen . . . my God—"

"You look like you've seen a ghost, son," Wade Ferguson said, looking concerned.

Patrick didn't even hear him. "Kathleen, is it really you?"

Looking from one to the other, Ferguson said, "You two have met before?"

"My God, I can't believe it," Patrick said, his eyes burning into hers.

"Hello, Patrick," Kathleen said coolly. She nodded at his hand which was dripping blood onto the expensive carpet. "You'd better take care of that. Bloodstains are the very devil to get out."

Numbly, Patrick wrapped the handkerchief around his palm, unaware of anyone or anything except Kathleen and the wonder of seeing her again. Without thinking, he reached for her. "Come...I mean...there's a place—"

"Patrick!" Obviously puzzled by Patrick's behavior, Ferguson looked at him sharply, his joviality fading.

Max cleared his throat. "I don't believe we've been introduced," he said smoothly. "I'm Maxwell Rutledge. Kathleen and I have recently arrived from New York." With a smile firmly in place, he put out his hand, forcing Patrick to remove his hand from Kathleen's arm.

Still dazed, Patrick shook hands and managed to say something, but his eyes clung to Kathleen. With her dark, fiery hair and glittering green eyes, she was incredibly beautiful. It was *Kathleen,* by God.

"You've been in New York?" he said, his eyes devouring her.

"Yes."

"All this time?"

"Yes, all this time."

Her voice was husky and low, with that same musical sweetness he remembered. He longed to hear more of it. He wanted to sweep her up and run until they were somewhere private and he could tell her...what? That he now had a wife. A child. Tongue-tied and shocked, he simply stared at her as reality washed over him.

"She's William Collins, the reporter," Wade Ferguson put in impatiently. "That's what I've been trying to tell you."

"William Collins." Patrick repeated the name blankly.

"My father's name," Kathleen said. As you well know, her eyes told him.

Ferguson tilted his head to study her closer. "Is that a bit of the Irish I hear in your speech, Kathleen?"

"I was born in Ireland," she said quietly. "I've been in America about six years now."

Rutledge spoke suddenly. "Kathleen's arrival in New York was a bit rocky, but with her talent, it was simply a matter of time until things began coming up roses for her." He smiled down at her. "She's a born journalist."

Talent. Journalist. Kathleen, his Kathleen was a journalist. She was William Collins. Patrick struggled to take it all in. He felt as though he'd been caught up in a tornado, then set down in another place, another land. He realized Ferguson was speaking.

"So you two met in New York. It's a small world, I always say." Not noticing that neither commented, he rambled on. "Of course, it's New York's loss that you both found your way to Savannah. I trust you will be staying here awhile, Miss Collins. As I always say to Patrick, this little town's going to be on the map in a big way one day. Already over a hundred and twenty thousand, yessirree."

"The *Irish Queen*," Patrick said suddenly. "Were you actually on board?"

Her look was cool. "Yes."

One of the men spoke up. "That was the immigrant ship that sank in the harbor a few years back, wasn't it?"

Kathleen's eyes never left Patrick. "Yes."

"The Leland Company took some criticism for that mishap," Wade Ferguson said.

"That mishap," Kathleen said, "took thirty-four lives. I was lucky to survive. The woman who shared a cabin with me drowned because she couldn't swim and what lifeboats there were for third-class passengers were overloaded."

Rooted to the spot, Patrick listened and felt the slash and sting of every word. The very evenness of her tone made her words that much more telling. Blood pounded in his ears and pain crushed his chest. A thousand questions came to mind, but he bit them back. Wiping a hand over his face, he looked around blindly. He felt hot, in need of air.

"The experience must have been terrible," Ferguson said sympathetically. "But my son-in-law understands better than most. He lost the girl he was engaged to on that very ship." He gave Patrick a fond pat on the shoulder.

"Son-in-law?" Kathleen repeated blankly.

"Patrick is married to my daughter, Caroline," Ferguson explained, oblivious to the tension that thrummed all around them. "Five years now, isn't it, Patrick?"

Locked with his, Kathleen's green eyes flashed. Patrick could only nod.

Max Rutledge touched her arm. "Come, Kathleen, there's someone I want you to meet," he said, nudging her away from the group of men.

Helplessly, Patrick watched her walk away. By clamping his jaw tight, he managed not to call out her name, managed not to tear Maxwell Rutledge in half for touching her, for claiming his place by her side. *His,* by God. He watched as she and Rutledge melded into the color and confusion of the ballroom, then sharp, piercing pain forced his attention to his lacerated palm. Muttering something about tending to it, he bolted for the door.

An interminable half hour passed before Kathleen could decently slip away. Sensing Max's concern, she murmured something about powdering her nose, holding on to the false smile she'd worn since the encounter with Patrick. She headed for a tall door off the ballroom that opened on to the veranda, which was cool and quiet and unoccupied, for the most part. Like herself, a few couples had sought a moment of privacy, but she quickly brushed past them, heading for the deepest shadows toward the far end. Only when the sounds of the party gave way to the chirp and buzz of night creatures did she stop.

With her hands resting on the waist-high railing, she lifted her eyes to the stars. It was worse, much worse, than she'd expected, seeing Patrick again. He looked the same, and yet...so different. His eyes were still that incredible blue, but there were little lines at their corners that aged him. Naturally. He was *older*. His shoulders seemed broader, his body stronger, his face harder. And he was married.

She had been prepared for changes, but somehow she had not been prepared to find Patrick married to another woman. In her Dream Sight, they were reunited as one. How could that be if he already had a wife? Her mind stumbled over the reality and her own gullibility. Oh, foolish, foolish! Had she truly believed that accursed dream? Had she been tantalized all these years by stupid, unrealistic Irish blarney?

She lifted her eyes to the night sky. Blurred by her tears, the stars still twinkled, held fast in their unique place in the universe. Like her life, she told herself. Nothing could really change just because the mystery of Patrick's disappearance was finally solved. Destiny, Max called it. She smiled bitterly.

"You'll get chilled out here with no wrap." Patrick's voice was deep and quiet. "I brought your cape."

Stiff and unwelcoming, she allowed him to settle the cape on her shoulders. "There was no need," she said, her tone as cool as the evening. "I needed a breath of fresh air. I was just going back—"

"Wait, Kathleen. Please." He touched her arm through the cape, but she shied away as though stung. "I'm sorry. I have so many questions that—"

"*You* have questions?" She was incredulous. "The time for questions is past, Patrick. I had a few myself, once upon a time, but I quickly learned how useless questions are when there are no answers."

He raked both hands through his hair. "My God, I thought you drowned, Kathleen. I was told... They said..." He gave an anguished groan. "They said your body would probably never turn up."

"Brigit's never did," she said quietly.

"What?"

"I was mistakenly identified as my cabin mate, Brigit Murray."

"Where were you? Where did you go? I went to all the hospitals, just on the chance that you'd been rescued and not identified."

"Since they believed me to be Brigit, I was taken to the people who'd sponsored her to come to New York. She had signed a two-year contract as a domestic for the Drummonds, a family on Fifth Avenue."

"Why didn't they notify anybody when you told them who you were?"

"They did, eventually. I suffered a concussion in the accident and was in and out of consciousness for almost two weeks."

"I was still in New York then!" he burst out. "Why didn't you tell them about me? Why didn't someone come and get me?"

She felt his frustration and rage. "Someone did go to the Leland offices—Parsons, Mr. Drummond's driver. He was told by the payroll clerk—"

"Freddie Goodson." Gripping the porch railing with both hands, he stared straight ahead.

"Yes, Goodson. He was told by Goodson that you'd re-signed. That you'd had a job offer from some wealthy businessman who lived somewhere down south."

"Yes, well..."

"And that he had a beautiful daughter with him." Kathleen released a bitter laugh. "Under the circumstances, I guess you'd call that fate, hmm?"

He said nothing to that, merely turned his head and stared at her. And his eyes...Kathleen's breath caught in her throat at the look in his eyes. Was it regret, despair, guilt, sorrow? Whatever it was, he no longer had the right to express it.

"The baby, Kathleen," he whispered, his tone tormented. "Did you lose the baby?"

She turned from him then, and although her throat was thick with unshed tears, her chin rose a notch. "I wondered if you remembered."

"Remembered! If you only... Kathleen, tell me!"

"I didn't miscarry, no."

Joy flared in his eyes. "Then we have a child. My God, Kath—"

"No!" She closed her eyes and began again. "No, Patrick, we don't have a child."

"But..."

"He... was born prematurely."

He made a choked sound. Standing so close, she could feel his breath stirring her hair. He wanted to touch her, she sensed it. And she, fool that she was, wanted to turn into his arms. But she didn't. Couldn't. Wouldn't. She turned from him and, head back, fixed her eyes on the stars. Funny how they blurred again. She was going to have to get hold of herself before facing all those people.

"Kathleen... tell me what happened to our baby."

"He died, Patrick."

CHAPTER SIX

"I THOUGHT I SAW YOU heading this way, O'Connor." Max spoke from the shadows, and Kathleen drew a relieved breath as she reached to take the hand he held out to her. It closed over hers, warm and reassuring. Max looked directly at Patrick. "Your family is looking for you."

"What?" With Kathleen's words still searing his heart, Maxwell Rutledge's appearance meant little. At any other time, Patrick might have sensed an off note in the older man's tone, but all his attention was focused on Kathleen, on the crushing pain of what he'd just learned.

"I told your father-in-law that I thought I knew where to find you," Max said patiently.

"Yes. Thanks."

Max spoke to Kathleen. "I think it's time for us to leave. What do you think?"

"Yes, I want to go home now, Max."

He nodded, protectively pulling her close. Patrick watched as Kathleen clung to Rutledge's arm and he was awash in another wave of pain. Then he looked into her eyes. "We'll talk later."

Kathleen said nothing, wanting only to escape. Although held fast by Max, she stumbled a little in the deep shadows of the veranda. Patrick, a step behind, shot out a hand to steady her, but his support was the last thing she wanted. Meeting his eyes, she ignored the emotion that burned there.

Party noise greeted them at the main entrance. Kathleen hesitated, hoping the expression on her face didn't reveal the turmoil inside her. Otherwise she would be the talk of the town tomorrow. Why had she thought she could see Patrick and come away with her soul intact? Stepping over the threshold, she came face-to-face with her host. A word of thanks, a quick goodbye and she and Max could be away.

There was a woman with Wade Ferguson, a stylish, blatantly beautiful woman with smoldering dark eyes and ebony hair. Dangling languidly from her fingers was a cigarette in an onyx holder; the other hand held a delicate champagne flute. As she sipped from it, she smiled slowly and provocatively at someone behind Kathleen. Patrick. And in that instant, Kathleen knew. This could be no other than Ferguson's daughter. Patrick's wife.

"Patrick, darlin'!" She blew out a stream of smoke. "Where on earth have you been?"

"Hello, Caroline."

Leaving her father's side, Caroline strolled up to Patrick and gave him a sensual kiss. Then, still intimately close, using two scarlet-tipped fingers, she wiped at the lipstick stain on his mouth. Patrick is mine, the possessive act declared. "Daddy was just thinkin' of sendin' out a search party."

"Funny," Patrick replied, "only ten minutes ago he was saying the same thing to me about you."

Her dark eyes flashed. "Hardly ten minutes. You've been out of pocket longer than that."

"Here, now, you two," Ferguson said suddenly, "what does it matter where you've been or how long? Our guests are wondering about our manners." He smiled at Kathleen and Max. "I want you to meet the rest of my family. Caroline, this is Kathleen Collins, who is sometimes known as William Collins, the journalist. And Maxwell Rutledge, the new owner of the *Sentinel*. My daughter, and Patrick's wife, Caroline O'Connor.''

Caroline's gaze flicked over Kathleen, narrowly assessing, before turning her attention to Max. Smiling, she held out a hand.

"A pleasure, Mrs. O'Connor," Max said, bowing slightly.

Caroline pouted prettily. "Oh, please...it's Caroline. This is not New York. We're all very informal around here."

"Where's Jessy?" Ferguson asked, glancing around the room. "She was here a second ago."

"Daddy! Daddy!" From behind Ferguson, a small, dark-haired girl suddenly materialized and headed directly for Patrick. For the first time that evening, Kathleen caught a glimpse of the man she'd once known. A genuine smile warmed up his remarkable eyes. Opening his arms, he bent and scooped up the child, hugging her as joyfully as she hugged him.

"Hi, Cricket," he whispered and playfully rubbed noses with her.

With a delighted laugh, she leaned back and looked into his face. "I've been looking everywhere for you, Daddy. Did you know that?"

"I'm sorry, I didn't know that, sweetheart. I went to the train station this morning, but I guess I missed you."

"We didn't take the train, Daddy." Her enormous brown eyes sparkled. "We came on a big, big boat!"

Straightening slowly, Patrick looked into Caroline's eyes. "A big boat?"

"Duncan Wheeler's yacht, darlin'." Her smile held a hint of challenge.

"Duncan Wheeler." Patrick's tone revealed nothing, but his jaw was a wedge of granite.

Kathleen was beyond noticing. Her attention was riveted on the child. Patrick's child. Short dark ringlets and huge brown eyes. A snub nose and bright, delightful precociousness. Her heart was a painful knot in her chest. How many times had she pictured the child she and Patrick had conceived? A thousand. A million. But never had she pictured a child of Patrick's that belonged to another woman.

"Meet my granddaughter," Ferguson was saying, pride and affection in his voice. "Jessy, this is Mr. Rutledge and Miss Collins. Say hello, sweetheart."

Shy suddenly, Jessy hid her face in Patrick's neck.

"Jessica! You heard Papa Wade." Caroline's tone was sharp. "You know it displeases me when you act shy."

"She *is* shy," Patrick said quietly, cradling the little girl's head. With his hand stroking her small back, he whispered in her ear. "It's okay, Cricket. Say hello to Papa Wade's guests and then we'll see what Maybelle has in the kitchen. I'll bet she has raisin cakes."

"Oh, for pity's sake, Patrick! You spoil her rotten," Caroline snapped.

"Someone needs to."

The words dropped into the tense silence gripping the circle. The hostility between Patrick and his beautiful wife was so powerful that no one even made an attempt to smooth it over with small talk. Watching with distaste, Kathleen found that her sympathy was all for the child. At a touch from Max, she turned with relief.

"Thank you for having us," he told Ferguson formally.

"My pleasure, my pleasure," Ferguson said heartily.

Kathleen glanced at Patrick but could read nothing in the look he was giving her over his little girl's dark head. What kind of man had he turned into? The Patrick she'd known was nothing like this hard, grim-faced combatant who indulged in ugly little exchanges in public. As she and Max pulled away in the Hudson, leaving the party and its brittle gaiety behind, she reminded herself that her opinion hardly mattered. Patrick's relationship with Caroline was none of her affair.

They were miles away from the Ferguson estate when Max suddenly slammed on the brakes, forcing Kathleen to put out a hand to keep from tumbling sideways against the gearshift.

"Damn black cat," he muttered.

"Did you miss it?" Kathleen asked, turning around in her seat to look.

"Kathleen, I'm sorry," Max said, groping for her hand and squeezing it.

She glanced at his face, knowing he wasn't talking about the cat. Withdrawing her hand, she pulled the folds of the cape over her knees. "It's all right, Max."

"No, I had no right to drag you to that...place. To put you through that scene."

She gave him a faint smile. "Well, I admit I've been to parties that were more fun."

"A person has a right to lay their ghosts to rest in their own way and in their own time. I can't remember why I thought it was a good idea to come to Savannah."

"I'll remind you of that the next time you try bullying me."

"My God, a wife and a child. And such a wife!"

"She's very beautiful," Kathleen murmured.

He stared at her. "Beautiful? She's a barracuda. Did you hear her tone when she spoke to that little girl?"

Kathleen's face was turned to the darkened window. She had, but she didn't want to feel a tug on her heartstrings for little Jessica. "Not really," she lied. "I was too shocked by the fact that he had a child. Fool that I am, I never expected..."

I never expected a wife. Or a child. My God, how could I have thought that finding Patrick would be a good idea?

"Do you want to go back to New York, Kathleen?"

"It's okay, Max. Don't worry, I'm tougher than I look."

Coping with frequent potholes and tight curves, Max couldn't take his eyes from the dark, narrow road, but his skeptical snort told her he was far from convinced. "Then the next time you see him, you won't turn pale as a ghost, hmm?"

"Was I pale?"

"And clinging to my arm like a frightened virgin."

"Hardly that," she said dryly.

"You know what I mean."

She took refuge in staring out into the night again. "I admit it was...difficult." She smiled, shaking her head. "I don't know what I expected. That he would have gone on with his life, I suppose, just as I have. A man's life doesn't consist of work alone. I should have been prepared for his marriage."

And a child. She drew a slightly trembling breath. "But now I know. I can close that chapter in my life. It's behind me. Really. Next time, I—"

She broke off suddenly, realizing she didn't want a next time. It was all well and good to put up a brave front for Max, but her feelings had nearly overwhelmed her tonight. If she saw Patrick again in public, she wasn't certain she could manage to appear indifferent.

"I'm happy to hear it," Max said, taking her at her word, "because Ferguson has lined it up for you to cover the launch of the ship they've just built for the U.S. Navy."

Panic flared. "Oh, I don't think—"

Max looked at her. "You don't think you can do it?"

A moment passed as Kathleen realized that she was trapped. No male reporter would shirk an assignment for emotional reasons. "When exactly is it scheduled?" Maybe she could come up with a good excuse between now and then.

"Saturday morning at ten."

Her head whipped around and she stared at him. "That's the day after tomorrow!"

"Uh-huh. And the way Ferguson tells it, O'Connor is almost single-handedly responsible for turning out a product that the navy will be proud to put out to sea. Your Patrick would make a powerful story."

"He's not my Patrick."

Max immediately apologized. "I'm sorry, love, you're right, of course. Although—" his voice dropped and gentled "—since he believed he'd lost you on the *Irish Queen*, it isn't unreasonable that he married, now, is it?"

No, of course not. Everything that had happened in the years they'd been apart was reasonable and understandable. She should be happy that he'd found his niche, had seized the opportunity handed to him. Wasn't that what they'd dreamed about before ever leaving Ireland? She shouldn't feel cheated that fate had torn them apart. She should wish him happy now that he'd found someone else to love. Nevertheless, pulling her cape closer, she shivered.

PATRICK SHRUGGED OFF his shirt and tossed it aside. Sitting on the side of his bed, he removed his shoes and socks, leaving them where they landed on the floor. The house was quiet. The party was over. His bed was turned down, ready for him alone. The housekeeper always performed that thoughtful little service. She did the same for Caroline in the bedroom across the hall. And for Wade in the east wing of the huge house. And for Jessy in the nursery.

All those beds, but each one lonely. All the silence. All the unhappiness.

Rubbing a hand over his face, he gave in to the thoughts that had plagued him all evening long.

Kathleen was alive!

She was here in Savannah. He had seen her and touched her and she was ten times more beautiful than she'd been six years ago. Kathleen, Kathleen, Kathleen . . .

"Mmm, something extremely weighty must be on your mind, darlin'."

Instantly on guard, Patrick turned to face his wife. Leaning against his door, she watched him, wearing little but a taunting, teasing smile.

Like a cat, he thought, getting slowly to his feet. A well-bred cat, but without the warmth and appeal of a beloved pet. His wife, he had learned, was a totally self-absorbed woman, avaricious and egotistical. She had no interests beyond gratifying her own desires, which were many and, for the most part, expensive.

"We've had our daily confrontation, Caroline," he said evenly. "It's late. I'm ready for bed."

She was silent for a moment, then she laughed softly. In the dim light, the ivory satin of her gown clung to her body. She was a voluptuous woman, her breasts lush and inviting, her hips generous. One shoulder strap had slipped, nearly exposing the nipple of her breast. "You know," she said, pushing away from the door and heading straight for him, "one of the sexiest things about you, dear husband, is the way you turn all cold and controlled in the bedroom."

With her fingers curled slightly, she grasped a handful of his chest hair. Her tone dropped to a husky whisper. "It's absolute heaven when you lose it."

He knew the drill. She was between lovers. She wouldn't even be at home in Savannah if she hadn't broken it off with her latest. Of course, he'd bet money that even now she was setting up the hapless Duncan Wheeler. But it hadn't happened yet. Otherwise she wouldn't be trying a heavy-handed seduction on her husband. Her interest in Patrick had cooled a very long time ago. If she'd ever had any interest.

With a weary sigh, Patrick removed her hand. "Not tonight, Caroline."

She twisted away furiously. "Not tonight, Caroline. Not tomorrow, Caroline. Not next week or next month or next year, Caroline," she hissed, striding across the floor in a rage. She faced him suddenly. "You know, I've been wonderin' somethin', Patrick. About your sex life. Not that I give a damn."

"Keep your voice down, Caroline," he ground out, his jaw clamped like iron. "Jessy's only two doors down."

"I know where my daughter sleeps, you arrogant bastard!"

He picked up a half-finished drink from the table. "And I know where this scene always ends, Caroline. You don't want me, so why come in here and pick a fight with me? Money, I suppose. It's either that or—"

Or her infidelities. That used to be the theme of most of their fights. But he'd stopped caring that his wife was unfaithful a long time ago.

"I bet I know what's really on your mind," Caroline said suddenly.

He swore. "I told you—"

"The redhead."

He went still. "What redhead? What are you talking about?"

She circled him, watching him with shrewd eyes. "The tall, stringy redhead who claims to be a reporter. The one who was all over the new owner of the *Sentinel*," she said silkily. "That redhead, as if you didn't know."

"Miss Collins," he said stiffly. "You know her name as well as I do."

"I don't think so."

"What?"

"I don't think I know her name nearly as well as you do."

Something spread through him, something cold and heavy. Panic. Fear for Kathleen. Caroline had a vindictive streak. She would not stop short of destroying Kathleen if she suspected . . . What? She couldn't suspect anything, because there was nothing. Kathleen was new in Savannah and she would be leaving soon, going back to New York. Sidetracked by his thoughts, he suddenly felt desolate at the thought of her leaving.

"Now, this is interestin', Patrick, very interestin'."

"I'm not in the mood to play games tonight, Caroline," he said.

"It's been a long time since I've seen that control of yours shaken," she said maliciously. "It almost makes me want to get in your pants again."

Only when hell freezes over. Schooling his face to show nothing, he looked at her.

"She's Irish, obviously. Does that give you a thrill?"

He put his drink down on the table with a loud clatter. "Get to the point, Caroline. As I said, it's late and I'm tired."

Tiring of the game, she said, "Did you complain to Daddy about my allowance?"

"Your allowance?" He looked confused. "No."

"You're lyin'! Tonight I was hardly halfway through my first drink when he began scolding me for a few charges I made last month. He never would have done that if you hadn't started carping about money. You have no right, Patrick. It's not your money, it's mine," she said shrilly, tapping her fingers against her breast. "You never would have seen the inside of this house if Daddy hadn't bought you! Bought you!" she screamed. "Do you hear me?"

"The whole county can hear you, Caroline," he said coldly. He caught her arm, ignoring her efforts to free herself. "Now, come over here and sit down." With a firm grip, he drew her toward the couch beneath the window in his bedroom. "And calm down, for pity's sake. When are you going to grow up?"

She flounced to the corner of the couch when he sat down. "I didn't come in here for one of your lectures, Patrick. I want to know why you went to Daddy behind my back. You know I can't manage on what you dole out to me."

Patrick closed his eyes. It was a familiar complaint and one he had no desire to debate at this hour. Caroline went through money with the abandon of a spoiled child in a candy store. When Patrick had finally drawn the line, she had simply turned to her father. Now it appeared that even Wade had set limits.

"I didn't go to Wade, Caroline. It's the first of the month. The bills for your extravagances must have reached his desk. You've brought this on yourself. Even your father's generosity has boundaries, so you needn't look to me. I meant it when I told you I'm no longer responsible when you exceed the amount we agreed on."

"I never agreed to anything, you dictator!" She surged to her feet. "I don't have to take this! You have no right to withhold money from me. Who do you think you are? Livin' on a stupid budget means I can't vacation where I want, I can't dress properly, I can't entertain my friends. I can't do anything on the paltry amount you give me."

"Then I suggest you negotiate something with Wade," Patrick said implacably. "As I've told you before, this well is dry."

He got to his feet, tall and hard and powerfully male. Maybe at one time Wade Ferguson's daughter had intimidated him, but that had been before he'd married her.

He went over to the door and opened it. "After all, you're so fond of telling me what's Wade's is yours. So go see him. And good luck to you."

"I hate you, Patrick O'Connor! I despise and loathe you. I should never have let Daddy talk me into marryin' you!"

"It will be simple enough to end this farce of a marriage," he told her softly. "Just say the word."

She drew a sharp, trembling breath, and when she spoke, the venom in her tone was like acid on metal. "You know he won't let me. For some idiotic reason, he likes you! He thinks you're a good influence. He doesn't care about my feelin's, my needs." Her mouth twisted bitterly. "He's still punishin' me, still old-fashioned enough to think—"

He shot her a look. "To think what?"

But whatever she had started to say, she thought better of it. Not that it mattered to Patrick what she said. Or threatened. All respect and caring had been gone from their marriage for longer than he liked to remember. He watched her wheel around and leave the room and felt nothing.

KATHLEEN HAD THE DREAM again that night. There was the now familiar dark, winding road, the same lashing wind and rain. As the car sped through the night, forks of fierce lightning cast bright, glaring illumination on deeply forested lands. From inside the car, a baby cried. It was the weak, plaintive wail of a newborn.

Tossing, turning, moaning fretfully, Kathleen felt the baby's need as though his connection to her was basic, deeply personal, quintessentially maternal. Then the gate materialized.

And, as always, with the clang of the hateful iron barriers, she woke.

Trembling, she pulled at the covers to try to warm herself, though she knew it was no use. She would not be warm again this night. Nor would she sleep again. There was no use in trying to analyze the dream again, either. The answers were still shrouded in secrecy and . . . evil. Evil not yet ready to be revealed.

Sitting on the side of her bed, she pulled on her robe and rubbed her hands over her face, then through her tangled hair. It was no mystery why she had dreamed tonight. Any event that unsettled her could trigger her Dream Sight. Her reunion with Patrick certainly qualified as an unsettling event. With shaking hands, she fumbled for the handle of her bedside table. Opening it, she withdrew her journal.

With the pain in her heart and tremor in her hands almost under control, she opened it and began to write.

Patrick is married and has a child. I am still trying to take it in.

CHAPTER SEVEN

"WHAT'S THIS?" Kathleen glanced at the note Max tossed on her desk. "'Friday, 6:00 p.m., main office,'" she read aloud.

"It's the interview we promised Ferguson."

Ferguson. Not Patrick. She relaxed slightly, clearing her throat. "Friday," she repeated, then looked at him in dismay. "Not today?"

"Yes, today. The launch is tomorrow at ten, remember?"

"I remember."

"I thought you'd consider that the fun part," Max said, watching her carefully. "From what I picked up at Ferguson's party, a launch ceremony is a patriotic affair—festive and fun, too. Considering the generally dismal state of the economy elsewhere, any event that celebrates work and the men who do it should be an enjoyable assignment."

"You're right, of course," she said, folding the note and tucking it into her tablet. "I'm interested in seeing the boat—" She stopped as he held up a hand.

"The ship, dear. The boat is always referred to as a ship."

Kathleen rolled her eyes. "Whatever. I'm interested in seeing the thing launched. I'll ask Eddie Perkins to go with me to take pictures. He's the *Sentinel*'s best photographer. It'll be a nice spread for the Sunday paper."

Pleased, Max smiled. Kathleen began clearing the top of her desk. "I don't know why Ferguson wanted the interview done today," she complained, stuffing tablet and pencils into a tote. "Couldn't he have set aside a few minutes for me tomorrow morning before the ceremony?"

"Perhaps he's expecting a more comprehensive article," Maxwell said. "He's almost boyishly proud of his company."

Kathleen fixed the fasteners on her tote and looked up. "I'm not sure what he's expecting, but I write what I think, not what he wishes to see in print. I'll acknowledge the phenomenal growth of the shipyard, especially in these hard times, because that kind of success should be applauded. But I intend to mention Ferguson's relationship to Leland Shipping, as well." She looked at Max. "Is that going to upset anybody?"

With his arms crossed on his chest, Max smiled at her. "Would it make any difference if it did?"

She picked up the bag. "Not really."

"Then I won't waste my breath."

"THERE SHE IS, the USS *Marshall Johns,*" Wade Ferguson said, pride evident in his face and in his voice as he looked at the huge, gray ship.

"Yes, there she is," Kathleen murmured. With its masts and engine stacks standing tall in the Savannah sun, the ship was an impressive sight. At least to her inexperienced eye.

Standing beside Ferguson at dockside, she watched the flurry of activity on the ship as it was readied for launch the next day. Men swarmed over the decks, occupied with last-minute tasks. The ship rested on waxed ways. Beneath the hull, strategically placed wooden keel blocks were being systematically removed. By the following morning, Ferguson told her, only a few vital blocks would remain. Then, at the appropriate signal, they would be removed, all other tethers would be loosened and the ceremonial bottle of champagne would be cracked against the hull. The ship would then slide down the ways and hit the water in a dramatic splash.

He painted a picture of the cheering crowd, throats that would thicken with patriotic fervor as the navy band played "Anchors Aweigh," the pride of the rough, tough workmen whose labor had turned sheets of wood and metal and a multitude of cable and pipe and machinery into a swift-sailing, seaworthy vessel.

"Gets to you somehow, doesn't it?" Wade Ferguson said, watching her with a grin.

Kathleen nodded, her eye on Eddie Perkins in the thick of things on the docks, recording the event for posterity with his camera. Taking her tablet from her tote, she flipped it open. She suspected Ferguson had brought her out here to give her a feel for the occasion, hoping to impress her. He'd certainly succeeded.

"It's very...exciting," she said, her pencil poised. "I didn't expect the ship to be so big. How long is it, exactly? And what is its mission? How many years of service can we expect out of it? Ten? Twenty?"

"Well, now," Ferguson puffed at his cigar. "As for its mission, that is to patrol the waters to ensure the safety of Americans. Particulars like its dimensions and durability can be supplied by my son-in-law. There he is now, on the staging. See him?"

Kathleen's pen was still. Following Ferguson's gaze, she spotted Patrick striding the length of staging platform fixed to the side of the ship. He moved along the narrow surface as confidently as though he was walking a city sidewalk. One misstep and he would fall at least forty feet. With her heart in her mouth, she watched until he was clear of the platform and safe on the gangway that led off the ship to the dock. With a shaky hand, she scribbled a useless note on her tablet. When he reached her and Ferguson, she looked up.

"Hello, Patrick."

"Kathleen." His blue eyes were somber as they skimmed her face, then went to his father-in-law. "Morning, Wade."

Ferguson gave him an affectionate clap on the back. "Everything on schedule here, son?"

"As much as can be scheduled. There are always last-minute problems that crop up, but everything seems under control."

"Good, good. In that case, you've got time to answer a few questions for Miss Collins." He removed his cigar, unaware of the quick, wary glance exchanged by Kathleen and Patrick. "She tells me the article will probably run in Sunday's *Sentinel*."

Kathleen drew in her breath. "Oh, I'm sure Mr. O'Connor is too busy to break away right now. Surely somebody else—"

"Not at all, my dear." Ferguson looked at Patrick. "Why don't you take her to your yard office, Patrick? You'll be undisturbed there. I'll tell your foreman to call you if there's anything that can't wait an hour or so."

An hour or so! She didn't want to spend an hour alone with Patrick. She looked around anxiously for Eddie Perkins and nearly groaned out loud as she saw him making his way cautiously up the gangplank.

"Your photographer?" Patrick asked, following her gaze.

"Yes," she said, exasperated. Eddie would risk life and limb for a dramatic photo. Even if she'd stopped him before he took off for the ship, she wouldn't have been able to persuade him to sit in a small office doing nothing while she interviewed Patrick. But it had been worth a try.

"Here, it's this way." Not waiting for her reply, Patrick put his hand beneath her elbow and urged her toward a small building. She looked back at Ferguson, but he was already following Eddie up the gangway, no doubt intending to oversee what was photographed.

Patrick pushed the door open and waited while Kathleen took the single step that brought her into the cramped confines of his office. It looked much as she'd expected. A long table furnished a work surface for paper, plans and specifications, correspondence, notes, memos. Mixed with the paper jumble were coffee cups and overflowing ashtrays, pencils, erasers, clips and various other necessities. No glossy hardwood furniture and desk sets or expensive wall hangings here. Kathleen realized at a glance that this was where the ship was actually conceived, where the plans were drawn, studied and altered before the first plank was cut.

Patrick pulled a chair forward. "You can sit here," he said, brushing off the seat. "I think it's reasonably clean."

"It's not necessary," she said quietly, rummaging in her bag for her writing materials. "I can take notes from any one of a dozen awkward positions."

"I never thought we would feel awkward together, Kathleen."

"Well, things change." There was no point in denying it. "So let's just get through it if you don't mind."

He did mind, Patrick thought. He wanted to savor this time, prolong it until he'd had his fill of looking at her, hearing her voice, watching the play of sunshine from the window in her fiery hair, imagining the feel of her skin, pale and flawless. God, what he wouldn't give to move close enough to breathe in the scent of her.

But he knew she would turn on her heel and walk right out if he gave her an inkling of his thoughts, and so, as she flipped open her notebook, he allowed himself only the luxury of a long, hungry look.

The waterfront breeze had destroyed her hairdo. Strands had worked loose from the once-stylish pile of auburn curls on top of her head and now drifted around her face and neck. She raked them back impatiently, and he was reminded of the way she'd looked lying beneath him with that glorious mane spread wide around her face. He remembered the smell of it . . . roses. Toilet water filched from her stepmother's dressing table.

She was beautiful in apple green linen. Her dress was short, as fashion dictated, with a wide white collar trimmed in lace, which gave her a chaste look. A look almost of innocence.

Talk to me, please, Kathleen. I want to know so much. I want to know everything you've done, every place you've been, every honor you've achieved without me. Have there been lovers, Kathleen?

"Can we please get on with it, Patrick?" she said curtly.

"Of course." Since she would not sit, he took up a position against the wall. "Ask away. What is it you want to know about the USS *Marshall Johns*?

She repeated the questions she'd asked Wade Ferguson along with a dozen others, carefully writing Patrick's replies in her notebook. It came as no surprise to her that he knew the ship as well as if he'd designed it himself. She said so.

"I didn't design it," he told her. "I'm not a naval architect, as you know."

She gave him a direct look. "I know no such thing, Patrick. It has been more than six years since I last saw you. You could have earned a college degree in that time."

"Well, I didn't."

"Who is Marshall Johns?"

He was thrown off for a second. "He was a naval officer in the Civil War, I think."

"Do they always name navy ships after famous military men?"

His mouth quirked with sudden humor. "I don't think he was famous. In fact, he was pretty obscure."

"Then why honor him?"

"His family is very big in politics in Washington," Patrick replied without thinking. Suddenly he remembered that Kathleen was a reporter and he pushed away from the wall, looking at her notes. "Hey, don't print that. I shouldn't have said it."

Kathleen very deliberately crossed out the remark in her notes, then looked up at him. "There, all right?"

"I forget you're a reporter," he said, studying her face hungrily. Although she was more beautiful, she was still the Kathleen of his youth. His first love. His only love. Looking at her, he felt pride and a keen joy in her success.

"How can you bear to work for Leland?" she asked suddenly.

"I don't work for Leland. I work for Wade Ferguson."

"You can't wriggle out of it that way, Patrick," she said accusingly. "I've researched Ferguson's business. He sits on the board of directors of Leland Shipping. There's a partnership between the two dating back five years. And don't bother to tell me you aren't aware of it."

"There was no partnership when I went to work for Wade." That, at least, was true. A full eighteen months had passed between the time he hired on with Ferguson and the partnership with Leland Shipping. Whether he wanted to admit it or not, he was linked with the huge company. Still, it galled him not to be able to explain to Kathleen, of all people.

He looked at her. "Did you expect me to resign on a principle?"

"Considering what you knew about Leland Shipping?" she asked coldly. "Yes."

"And what did I know?"

Kathleen's eyes flashed green fire. "That they deliberately jeopardized the lives of the passengers aboard the *Irish Queen* by failing to make proper repairs, by skimping on life jackets and lifeboats, by overbooking. And the *Irish Queen* was not an exception," she charged hotly. "There are many other incidents of negligence by the company that have resulted in injury and death. I won't even go into the number of Leland workers, mostly laborers, who have suffered because management is more interested in making a profit than in treating their employees decently and fairly."

"Is your research always so complete?" he asked, knowing instinctively that it was. Kathleen would never do anything halfheartedly. She had matured from the sweetly idealistic young girl he'd worshiped to this compelling, passionate woman. She had been desirable then, but she was a thousand times more desirable now.

Just as she was a thousand miles out of his reach.

"My research is accurate," she told him. "I go as far as I need to to get the whole picture."

"I'm sure you do. I would not presume to tell you anything about the way you do your job, Kathleen."

She stared at him. "If that's a roundabout way of saying you aren't aware of the way Leland Shipping does business," she said coldly, "then I simply don't believe it."

"You can't tell me anything about the company that I don't know," he said shortly.

She stared at him as though she'd never seen him before. "I nearly died, Patrick, and that company would have been solely to blame. Does that mean so little to you?"

"How can you even ask that?"

"And what about Brigit Murray? She did not survive, Patrick, along with thirty-three other unlucky souls."

"I know," he said, rubbing the back of his neck wearily. "I'm sorry."

Because Kathleen was a reporter, he could say no more, but how he longed to tell her everything. To share with her the desolation and pain that he had felt when the *Irish Queen* sank. To give her some understanding of the way he'd felt when he believed his future and everything meaningful in his life had gone to the bottom of the sea with that damned ship. "I wish there was something I could say, I wish I could find words that would erase that night from your mind . . . somehow."

"There are no words to work a miracle, Patrick." The finality in her tone cut him to the quick. Seeing the expression in her eyes as she studied him, he supposed he must seem like a stranger to her, considering the principles he had always professed to have. And the truth was, in many ways, he *had* changed.

But one thing was certain. He was going to destroy Leland Shipping, and every rung up the ladder at Ferguson Shipyards brought him closer to his goal.

Kathleen seemed to have forgotten the notebook in her hand. "You should know that I plan to subject Ferguson's company to intense scrutiny, and if my findings aren't flattering, I won't hesitate to expose everything. It's what I do. And if some of the companies I've targeted have been forced to make changes that cost them some profits, their employees have benefited. I happen to think that the welfare of a company's employees should also be a priority."

"I read your editorial in the *Sentinel* last Sunday." He shook his head. "I'm impressed, Kathleen, but not surprised. When I read your words, something about your style, and the substance of your theme, reminded me of

William. I'm surprised I didn't make the connection.'' He blinked and then looked at her. ''William must be bursting with pride. How is he, by the way?''

''My father is dead.''

Patrick frowned. ''I'm sorry, I didn't know. When? How?''

She fixed her eyes on her tablet. ''It was a sudden heart attack,'' she said quietly. ''According to my stepmother, it happened a few days after I boarded the *Irish Queen*.''

She was pale. Watching her, Patrick felt a prickle of unease, as though he should brace himself for...something. ''I always knew William was reluctant to let you go to America. I didn't know it would literally break his heart.''

''It wasn't that,'' Kathleen said, lifting her eyes to his. ''It was disappointment and disgrace that killed him.''

''Disgrace?''

''My pregnancy.''

Oh, God, here it was. His chest burned with guilt and fear and foreboding. ''You told him that you were pregnant?''

''Eventually. I had no choice. He was determined to talk me out of following you to New York. He wanted to believe I would get over my infatuation, I think.'' She closed the cover on her notebook. ''Finally, I realized nothing would convince him except the truth.''

''My God, I didn't know what you were going through. Your letters...'' Patrick's breathing was labored as he stared first at Kathleen, then at the walls, the ceiling. Anywhere but inwardly, where he writhed with remorse and regret. ''I wish—''

He wanted to beg her forgiveness, but there weren't enough words in the universe. God, he'd been the instrument of her downfall and he hadn't known a thing. The cruel downturn his own life had taken was nothing compared with Kathleen's suffering.

"You should have let me share the pain, Kathleen." When she said nothing, he turned from her and looked out the window. "Your sister," he said, watching the activity around the ship. "She's well and happy?"

"I don't know. I haven't heard from her since I left."

He looked back at her. "Not once? In six years?"

"No."

"Why not?"

"It was something my stepmother decided."

"And I'm guessing that you haven't heard from her, either."

"No." Restlessly, she tapped the edge of her notebook against her palm. "Patrick, what does this have to do with anything?"

"They cut you off when your father died." It was not a question.

"Since it was my fault," Kathleen said quietly, "it was understandable."

"It was heartless," he said, wanting to pull her into his arms and promise to make it all up to her, and to keep her safe from all hurt forever. But he had proved undependable in keeping promises made to Kathleen. He groaned and rubbed a hand over his mouth. "God, I feel so responsible, Kathleen."

"Let it go, Patrick," she said wearily. "I have."

Neither said anything for a few moments. From a distance came the low whistle of a freight train. It was a mournful, lonesome sound. Through the window, the noise of the shipyard reminded Patrick of his responsibilities for the launch. "Was there anything else you wanted to know, Kathleen?"

She looked at her notebook. "I think I have everything I need to write a decent article."

"Well, then..." He took a few steps toward the door, then, with his hand on the knob, turned to wait for her.

Kathleen didn't move. She took a deep breath. "How did it happen, Patrick?"

She was not talking about the ship or the launch or his association with Wade, he knew. "My... involvement with Caroline?"

"Your marriage, Patrick. Involvement is something that happens with your lawyer, or your doctor or your boss. You're married to Caroline."

He looked beyond her to the dingy window. "Yes."

"She is very beautiful."

No, she will never be beautiful to me. She's vain and selfish and unfaithful, and those qualities destroy beauty from within. But as long as he was married to Caroline, he could never say those words. His frustration was like a brick wall. Time spent with Kathleen was precious and he didn't want to taint it with talk about the vast emotional wasteland of his marriage.

"Are you happy?"

The look he gave her was anguished. "God, Kathleen..."

She looked down suddenly and began toying with the papers that littered the tabletop. "You must have fallen fast and hard. Her father told us at the party that your... your little girl is five. Your marriage would have to be nearly six years ago."

"Yes."

"You're right," she said when his silence became unendurable. "It's none of my business." She smiled brightly and began stuffing things into her bag. Notebook. Pencils. A gum eraser that didn't belong to her. "So, how do you like Savannah? I find it delightful, to tell the truth. A bit humid, but so close to the ocean, I suppose that's to be expected, isn't it? And the people are very friendly. There really is something about southern hospitality, don't you think?"

"I didn't fall fast and hard."

With her bag held tightly against her midriff, she looked at him, her green eyes wide and wary.

"The last thing on earth I was thinking about was marriage," Patrick said, speaking so low that she had to strain to hear him. "The only woman I ever loved was dead, or so I believed. And I was dead inside, Kathleen. You can believe that or not, but it's true."

He turned, gazing through the window, but taking nothing in. "As I stood at the altar repeating vows to a woman who was virtually a stranger to me, I wondered if I would ever feel anything again." He made a soft, derisive sound. "I did, of course, and as time went on, I wished with all my might that I could be numb again."

At her soft gasp, he looked at her. "And yes, Kathleen, Savannah is a delightful place, although humid as hell, especially in the summertime. But I like it. The first time I ever saw it, I thought of you and knew you would like it, too."

But his words had stolen her power to speak. She simply stared at him.

He crossed his arms over his chest. "So, where are you living? There are some attractive places near the squares in town. You wouldn't be far from the *Sentinel* offices."

After clearing her throat, she found her voice. "We live in a lovely old Greek Revival two blocks off Bull Street on Oglethorpe Square. It was recommended to Max by one of his staff."

"Max."

At something in his tone, her chin went up slightly. "Yes, Maxwell Rutledge. You met him last night at Ferguson's party."

"You live with him?"

She stared directly into his eyes. "Yes, I do."

His jaw clamped down hard before he spoke. "Is that wise?"

"Whether it's wise **or not**, surely my personal decisions are my own concern," Kathleen said icily.

"This is not New York, Kathleen."

"I could hardly mistake Savannah for New York."

"Damn it! People talk. You'll have everyone in Savannah thinking you're some kind of...of..."

"Strumpet?"

"No! I mean—" He left the door and came over to her. "It's just that you're a woman alone, Kathleen. And vulnerable to gossip. You should think about that."

"Max is old enough to be my father," she said evenly.

"But he isn't your father!" he said angrily. Caught up in the argument, he failed to notice the dangerous flash of her eyes. "People are going to think he's your lover!"

"And what do you think, Patrick?"

He didn't know and it was killing him. He opened his mouth to tell her exactly what he thought of any other man as her lover, but nothing came out. He clenched his fists to keep from grabbing her and shaking her until her beautiful auburn hair fell around her shoulders. Until her remarkable green eyes flooded with tears. Until a promise came from her too-kissable mouth that she would sever her relationship with Rutledge that very day.

Turning away with a shrug that was a miracle of control, he reached blindly for the doorknob. Who did he think he was, advising her how to live her life? He'd given up that right years ago. "I can see that with your professional success, you have become a sophisticated woman of the times," he said, yanking savagely at the doorknob.

"Think what you please," she said, sounding remarkably unruffled, but her hands shook slightly as she arranged the strap of her bag on her shoulder. "And now I must run. I have a deadline to meet if this article is to run in Sunday's edition."

"Wait..." he said, putting out a hand to stop her. She dodged his touch, and the bag fell with a thump, spilling the contents all over the floor.

"Oh! Now look what you've done." Kathleen bent down and began gathering her things, angrily stuffing them back into the bag.

Muttering an apology, Patrick went down on one knee to help her, fumbling with a comb, loose hairpins, a scarf. Kathleen scooped up her notebook and pencils, staring blankly at a strange gum eraser before tossing it onto the table. Then she reached for a coin purse at the same time Patrick did. At the touch of his hand, she looked up quickly and their eyes met. With her heart beating like a wild thing, Kathleen looked at him. Just the sight of him still made her bones turn to water.

Without realizing she meant to, she reached up and touched a small scar beneath his eye. "What happened?" she asked huskily.

He caught her hand. "Nothing." His own voice was hoarse. "An argument with a bulkhead."

So close to his beautiful eyes. "You were lucky."

The hot words they'd exchanged seconds before were forgotten. With his eyes locked on hers, Patrick pressed his mouth to her palm. "Kathleen..."

She felt giddy and too warm. Where his mouth lingered, heat and sensation merged and then spread throughout her veins like hot honey. Sweet and rich with pleasure. Bittersweet pleasure. It was wrong to touch him, to allow him to touch her. But her lower body ached with longing. If only she didn't know how it was with Patrick. If only she hadn't once . . .

A knock at the door startled them both, and they sprang apart, scrambling to their feet.

"Hey, boss! We got a helluva problem with—" With one foot inside the door, the man stopped abruptly. "Oh, 'scuse me, boss . . . ma'am. I didn't know there was anybody—"

"It's all right, Mulvaney." Patrick handed Kathleen the coin purse. She took it and dropped it into her bag. Then, without looking at Patrick, she headed for the door.

"Wait, Kathleen—"

"I can come back, boss," Mulvaney said, sensing the tension.

"Yeah, give me two minutes here."

Mulvaney left, but before Kathleen could dart out behind him, Patrick put a hand on the doorknob. "One more thing, Kathleen . . ."

Her gaze went from his to the large hand blocking her escape. "Yes?"

"There is a special luncheon after the launch ceremony tomorrow," he said. "Would you like to attend?"

He sounded cool, almost formal. Nothing in his tone hinted that a few seconds before, they had almost rediscovered each other in a prelude to passion. Her pulse still racing, Kathleen said, "Thank you, no."

"The invitation includes Rutledge too, naturally," Patrick said, although the idea was anathema to him. He cleared his throat. "I'm sorry if what I said about him offended you. You're a free woman. You can do what you please."

"Please let me out, Patrick."

"There will be several navy bigwigs as well as a congressman or two."

"No, I don't think so, Patrick."

"Wade will wring my neck if you don't show up. He often claims that I don't understand the value of publicity."

"He's probably correct."

"I understand it," Patrick said quietly. "I just prefer that someone else do it. I'm a shipbuilder, not a cheerleader. I'll leave that to folks like Wade who seem to get a kick out of tooting their own horns."

"I'll ask Max to send another reporter. That should keep you out of hot water with your father-in-law."

He removed his hand from the doorknob. "Kathleen—"

She wrenched it open. "Goodbye, Patrick." She slipped past him and out into the bright glare of October sunshine.

Brooding and still, Patrick watched her until she turned the corner and disappeared from sight.

CHAPTER EIGHT

PATRICK FOUND HER sterling silver compact beneath his worktable the next afternoon. Picking it up, he turned it over slowly, feeling the silver warm instantly in his hand. It was a beautiful feminine trinket. Expensive. A gift from Rutledge, he guessed. Pressing the catch, he realized that it held wax perfume, not powder. He raised it, inhaling, and the scent of roses filled his head.

He never smelled roses without thinking of Kathleen.

Forbidden thoughts.

She had not attended the launch. Even caught up in the details of the event, he'd found himself watching for her auburn hair and tall, willowy figure. Later, at the luncheon at the country club, he had spotted Maxwell Rutledge sitting at a table with Oscar Ellis, Georgia's senator. But another reporter had covered the festivities for the *Sentinel*. Usually he felt satisfaction and a sense of accomplishment at the launch of a ship, but today something had been missing. No, some*one* had been missing.

It was dangerous, it was foolhardy, it was crazy. It was begging for trouble, but he'd wanted Kathleen.

On top of everything else, he'd quarreled with his wife. God knows, there was nothing traditional about their marriage, but was it unreasonable to expect her to act like a lady for the few hours it took to celebrate a company success?

Because it was a government contract, Patrick had warned her that there would be absolutely no alcohol served at the luncheon. But for Caroline, the occasion had been just too boring to sit through sober. As a member of the country club, she had sources for times like these. From the moment they'd arrived, she had steadily consumed one drink after another on the sly. It hadn't mattered to Caroline that she was an embarrassment to her husband and her father; she disdained playing the role of supportive wife and loving daughter. Instead, she'd flirted shamelessly with Duncan Wheeler. Patrick had no interest in what Caroline did privately, but when she'd taken his name, she'd taken a vow to honor it. At least in public.

It was an argument they'd had many times before. He should know by now that there was no reasoning with her when she was feeling the effects of too much bourbon. She'd stormed off in a huff with a drunken Wheeler trailing behind and every eye in the club on her. Patrick had escaped himself as soon as he decently could and had gone directly to his office to lose himself in his job as he usually did to avoid thinking of the bleakness of his marriage.

For the first time, that trick had not worked.

Leaving his office later that evening, he wandered aimlessly, his emotions still in turmoil. He was feeling angry and resentful and trapped. With a smothered oath, he kicked at a loose stone on the sidewalk and admitted he was also feeling a little sorry for himself. Was this the way he was to spend the rest of his life? Since the moment he'd turned around in Wade Ferguson's living room and found himself looking into Kathleen's eyes, he had been dreaming hopeless dreams, wishing wishes that could never come true.

His hands deep in his pockets, his fingers closed around the compact. He thought of all the reasons he should not return it to Kathleen personally. She belonged to someone else now. He belonged to someone else. Savannah was a temporary stop for her. Rutledge wasn't about to forsake the sophistication of New York City for a sleepy Georgia town. And Kathleen's destiny was apparently linked to Maxwell Rutledge, just as his own destiny was inexorably linked to the Leland Company.

Taking the compact out, he turned it over and over. He traced the engraving with his finger—a single initial *K* and a scroll of flowers and leaves. He could return it by messenger. He should. Or in the mail. Or he could leave it with the receptionist at the *Sentinel*. Seeing Kathleen again, no matter what excuse he trumped up, was undoubtedly a mistake.

Glancing up at a street sign, he realized he had reached the house where Kathleen lived. The walk had done little to banish his demons; he was still tense and edgy. Although it was late—well past ten in the evening—lights were still on throughout the house. He pushed the ornate iron gate open, smothering an oath as it clanged shut behind him. Within seconds, a light went on in the foyer.

Too late to back out now.

He knocked once, softly, and the door was opened instantly.

"Yes?"

"Hello. I'm...ah... Is this where Kathleen Collins lives?"

A tiny woman with bright, inquisitive eyes looked him up and down. "And who wants to know, if I may ask?"

"Patrick O'Connor."

Her eyes narrowed. "Patrick O'Connor. Well, well, well."

Patrick smiled, hearing her Irish accent.

"I'm...an old friend," he said.

The door didn't budge. "Is that a fact, now?"

"Yes, it's a fact." He hadn't counted on having to get beyond a guard, even a diminutive one.

"And what brings you to Kathleen's door after all these years, Patrick O'Connor?"

At something in her tone, he looked at her a little closer. "Have we met?"

"No, sir, we have never met."

He drew in a slow breath. "If Kathleen's at home, I'd like to see her. Is that possible, do you think?"

"Maybe, Patrick O'Connor. And maybe not."

With the light behind her, it was impossible to read her expression, but she didn't sound particularly hostile. Whatever her mood, Patrick realized he probably wouldn't get to see Kathleen if this woman didn't want him to. Deciding to play along, he crossed his arms over his chest. "Would you be the housekeeper, Miss... Mrs...." His eyebrows lifted.

"Lizzie."

He grinned. "Pleased to meet you, Lizzie."

Her mouth quirked up at the corners and she dipped a quick curtsy. "Likewise, Patrick O'Connor."

"You're sure we haven't met?" She shook her head. "Yet you say my name as though you're familiar with it."

"I guess you could say we've almost met," she told him, clearly enjoying herself.

"Oh? And where was that?"

"New York, of course."

"You were Kathleen's housekeeper when she lived in New York?"

She opened the door a little wider. "That's what I called myself and that's what other folks called me, but Kathleen, now..." She shook her head, still smiling. "She wouldn't have it. She—"

"I wouldn't have it because it was ridiculous," Kathleen said, appearing suddenly at Lizzie's shoulder. "Hello, Patrick. I didn't expect to see you tonight, especially at this hour. Lizzie, why are you interrogating a guest? What would Leo say?''

"Leo?'' Patrick repeated, torn between feasting on the sight of Kathleen and trying to follow the conversation.

"Leo Stern, Lizzie's husband,'' Kathleen explained. "Neither of them is a domestic, no matter how insistently Lizzie claims otherwise.''

"Fine,'' Lizzie retorted, relinquishing her hold on the doorknob. "Next time, I'll let you or Mr. Max answer the door.''

"Let Bertha do it,'' Kathleen said.

"Who's Bertha?'' Patrick asked faintly.

"A person Kathleen forced me to hire to do the cooking and cleaning.''

"A housekeeper,'' Kathleen said firmly.

"I can keep house without the likes of Bertha Mc-Farland to help me,'' Lizzie returned, warming to a familiar argument.

"Bertha is an excellent cook and housekeeper,'' Kathleen said.

"Her mulligan stew has no flavor.''

"She says yours is too hot to swallow.''

Lizzie sniffed. "Max and Leo prefer a little spice.''

"Oh, for heaven's sake, Lizzie.'' Kathleen laughed, shaking her head, and motioned Patrick inside. "I should know better. We'll be in the front parlor if Max asks when he comes home.'' She touched Patrick lightly on the arm. "We can talk in here.''

Patrick's good humor faded at the mention of Rutledge. He followed Kathleen through French doors to a sitting room furnished with a rose-colored settee and two brocade chairs. A Tiffany lamp glowed softly on a long, narrow table beneath the window. On the floor was a pretty floral carpet. Patrick knew little about decorating, but there was something cozy and welcoming about the room. Instinctively, he knew it was Kathleen's place.

Rutledge is good to her. Clenching his jaw, he fumbled in his pocket for one of his smokes. He lit it and frowned through the haze, thinking how much pleasure he would take in indulging Kathleen. If she were his.

With his attention elsewhere, Kathleen stole a moment to study Patrick. Was it because the room was small that he seemed so tall? So...so male? Even slightly rumpled in a suit that looked as though he'd walked miles in it, there was something about him that set her heart thumping. His dark good looks were heightened by a stark white shirt, loosened at the collar. He looked tired, she thought. She wanted to... But that thought had to be stopped.

"I like this room," Patrick said, looking around with somber interest. "I can tell it belongs to you."

"This house belongs to Max."

He looked at her then. "But what is Rutledge's is yours, too. Isn't that so?"

"Not in the way you think."

"Then explain it to me, Kathleen."

They stared at each other a long time. "You should not be here, Patrick."

"Maybe not." He shrugged. "Surely not." After a second, he laughed softly. "For what it's worth, I almost didn't get in. Lizzie runs fierce interference."

"Sometimes I get visits from people who disagree with what I write. We've found it's better for Lizzie or Leo to answer the door."

"Good friends to have."

Kathleen nodded. "Yes."

"She seemed to know me. How is that?"

"She was the first friend I made in New York. She worked at the Drummond mansion with me. We shared a room."

"The Drummond mansion?"

"Yes, I told you before that I was mistakenly identified as a woman who had signed a work contract for the Drummonds. Lizzie took care of me until I was on my feet." Kathleen smiled. "She made the eight months I worked there tolerable."

Patrick frowned. "You left after eight months? How? A work contract is legally binding. Where did you go?"

"As for how, Max paid off our indebtedness," Kathleen said quietly, looking him straight in the eye.

She watched him struggle with that, knowing his mind churned with questions. She owed him nothing. Certainly no explanations of her relationship with Max. But something—maybe her memory of their sweet, youthful love—made it hard to hold on to old grudges.

"There was a New Year's Eve party," she said, turning away and fiddling with a small glass bluebird on a table. "I had some...trouble with the chauffeur. He—"

"Trouble?" Patrick said sharply.

"Oh, it's embarrassing to talk about, even now. It was nothing, really. Just one of those situations...you know..."

"He had eyes for you."

Kathleen laughed shortly. "I suppose you could say that."

"Did he touch you?" With a fierce expression, Patrick took a step toward her before catching himself. He looked searchingly into her eyes for a long moment, then drew in a deep breath. "I know it's past, but did he hurt you?"

"You mean, did he actually force me?" Kathleen said, setting the bluebird down. "No, he tried, but as I was telling you, Max happened to be there. He saw it all and...I suppose you could say he rescued me."

Patrick said nothing, just stood straight, his body tense. Smoke curled slowly upward from the cigarillo in his hand, obscuring the grim look of his mouth.

"Well, I knew it was going to be difficult to stay after that. Maybe impossible. But then Max offered me a job and I took it."

With a savage twist, Patrick ground out his cigarillo. She looked at him defiantly. "Women don't have a lot of options sometimes, Patrick. I accepted his offer and it was the best decision of my life."

"Kathleen…" He swung away, biting off an oath. "You don't know what it does to me to hear this. Why? God, why did it have to happen this way? We had such plans, such dreams. To think that you virtually sold yourself!"

"I didn't sell myself, Patrick," she said coldly. "Max hired me to be a companion to his wife, Lily. She was wonderful and wise and intelligent. She became a mother to me. And when she discovered my friendship with Lizzie, she persuaded Max that they needed another maid. So Lizzie's debt was paid, too. By the time Lily died, Lizzie had become a mainstay in the household, as she is to this day." She moved to the window and stood looking out, her back to Patrick. "I don't know why she insists on calling herself our housekeeper. She's not a housekeeper. She's my friend, my dearest friend in the world."

"And is Maxwell Rutledge also a dear friend?"

She turned, expecting sarcasm, but he was only waiting for her answer. Her sigh came out wearily. "Yes. Friend and mentor. Lily had encouraged me as a writer, but Max took such delight in my success. He's almost like a…a father to me," she said huskily. She looked at him. "Can you believe that?"

Patrick stared at his hands, then up at her. "So Lizzie was with you those first few months?" She nodded. "She knew about your pregnancy?"

"Before anyone else," Kathleen said. "As I said, we shared a room. It…it was impossible to keep it a secret."

His eyes seemed unable to meet hers. "Kathleen, Kathleen... I should have been there for you." He swallowed hard. "Did... Was your labor... difficult?"

"Patrick, I don't think we should talk about this."

"Yes!" At her start, he lowered his voice. "I mean... please, tell me about it. Everything, Kathleen. I *need* to know."

"I don't know much myself. I... it was long and... and I've told you how it ended. He was early. He was too... too little...."

"God, Kathleen..." He took a step and reached for her. Closing his arms around her, he crushed her body to his, as they finally allowed themselves to feel the grief and longing and pain. For this one moment, they did not think of the proprieties, guilt or conventions. Standing close, bodies entwined, they were simply two people sharing the ultimate loss.

With his mouth against her temple, Patrick asked, "Did you see him?"

"No, but they told me." Kathleen swallowed hard, eyes closed. "Or at least Lizzie did."

"What did he look like?"

"You. He looked like you."

She felt the catch of his breath and the shudder that went through him. His embrace tightened as he buried his face in her hair. The tears that shimmered on her lashes overflowed suddenly. She had spent many years embroiled in bitterness and grief, much of it directed at this man. Now, as she was held fast in his desperate embrace, as she felt his big body tremble against hers, and heard the rasp of his breath as he fought his own grief and loss, somewhere deep inside her, healing at last began.

For long moments, they rocked slowly, both content to hold and be held. Time was measured by the soft ticking of the clock and the occasional honk of a car horn outside. Since losing her child, Kathleen had been comforted many times by friends—Lizzie, Lily, Max. She realized, with wonder, that it was Patrick with whom she had needed to share her pain.

"I shouldn't be here," he said, drawing in the scent of her with the desperation of a drowning man.

"No."

With his hand buried in her hair, he pressed her head against his chest. "I walked the streets tonight, going over and over all the reasons why I should stay away from you."

"Yes."

"But I couldn't help myself, Kathleen. Even after all these years, it only took one look at you to destroy me. I can't fight this, I swear I can't."

He closed his mouth over hers and instantly they were lost in a deep, hungry kiss, freeing feelings that had been locked up and buried for years. To Kathleen, their love came rushing back like the music of a favorite song.

He tore his mouth from hers with a groan. "Kathleen, Kathleen . . ." Nuzzling her temple, her ear, her cheeks, he caught her face, cradling it. He looked into her eyes, smoky green with passion. "I used to dream about this. I'd lie awake counting off the days it would take for that damn ship to reach New York harbor and I'd imagine all the ways I'd love you."

He lowered his mouth to hers again, kissing her fiercely. His tongue was at first wild and plunging, then teasing and tantalizing. Kathleen gloried in the rediscovery of his taste, his smell, his touch, the strength of his body curved to hers, the hard clasp of his arms, the restless, questing movements of his hands. Dear God, how had she survived without this?

Like a flower blossoming in sunshine, she yielded to his urgency. She sighed when he stroked her shoulders and back. She whimpered when he ran his palms over her breasts and down to her stomach. And she shuddered with longing when he cupped her buttocks and with a groan pulled her flush against him. Deep within her womb was a craving need, a yearning to have her emptiness filled.

Pleasure, poignant and bittersweet.

Breathless hunger.

Need.

The front door closed, and for a moment in her mindlessness, it meant nothing. Then she froze and horror washed over her like the waters of an arctic sea. She heard Lizzie's and then Max's voices, familiar and deep, answering. Tearing herself out of Patrick's embrace, she covered her mouth with her fingers, shocked and shamed. What was she doing? What in heaven's name had come over her? This was wrong, so wrong. Patrick was married. *He had a child!*

Seeing her expression, Patrick reached for her instinctively. "Don't look like that, Kathleen. Please."

Before he touched her, she whirled away. "No, don't! Just leave now, Patrick. Oh, go. Please go."

"Yes, all right. I'm going. But, Kathleen—"

"Don't say any more, Patrick! This was wrong." Wrapping her arms around her waist, she looked at him through a haze of tears. "We had our chance and somehow we lost it. It's too late for us now. Go back to your h-home, to your wife and little girl. I don't want to see you again."

"You can't mean that, Kathleen." There was agony in his eyes. "I won't do anything like this again. I'm sorry things got out of hand. I just..." He raked both hands through his hair, but when he spoke, his voice seemed more controlled. "I forgot myself. I swear, it won't happen again. We can—"

He broke off at a sharp rap on the parlor door.

"It's Max," Kathleen said, hastily wiping her cheeks with both hands. "Let me handle this, Patrick."

"Kathleen?" Max sounded concerned.

Kathleen opened the door, and Max sent a quick, accusing glance beyond her to where Patrick stood. Kathleen knew Max guessed exactly what he had interrupted. She must look scandalously mussed and guilty as sin. Patrick, as well. But it wouldn't be her Max would demand an explanation from. It would be Patrick. And truly this was no more his fault than her own.

"It isn't what you think, Max," she said, putting a hand on his arm as he started toward Patrick.

But it was exactly what he thought, although he cared too much about Kathleen's feelings to contradict her. After a measuring look at them both, Max nodded curtly in Patrick's direction. "O'Connor. I didn't expect to see you here tonight."

"I brought something of Kathleen's," he said, delving into his pocket for the silver compact. Both Kathleen and Max looked at it lying on his palm. "You dropped this yesterday, Kathleen. I found it under my desk when I went back to my office today after the ceremony."

"Oh." She took the compact without touching him. "I hadn't realized it was missing. Thank you."

If Max thought Patrick had taken his time getting around to the reason for his visit, he didn't say so, but there was nothing friendly in his manner as he moved to stand beside Kathleen. "We won't keep you then," he said coolly.

Patrick walked past them to the door of the room, then with his hand on the doorjamb, he hesitated. He might never get another chance to say what he felt. He turned and, ignoring Rutledge, spoke to Kathleen. "I'm not going to apologize, Kathleen. Nothing happened between us tonight that I feel sorry about.''

Kathleen stared at him wide-eyed. The taste of him was still on her lips, and her fingers still tingled from touching him. Most of all, her body still throbbed from that forbidden embrace. How could she bear to lose him twice in a lifetime? But she must.

''I'll show you out, O'Connor.'' Without actually touching Patrick, Max urged him out of the parlor into the hall, where Lizzie stood at the front door. At a signal from Max, she opened it.

''Goodbye, Patrick O'Connor,'' she said softly.

Patrick gave her a startled glance. Was that regret he heard in her voice? Shoving his hands deep in his pockets, he went out into the night.

BREAKFAST ON SUNDAY morning was usually a solitary affair for Kathleen. Max played golf and Lizzie and Leo went to early mass at St. John's. Kathleen attended a different church, but she wasn't sure that she wanted to go this morning. She was still feeling guilty and ashamed for her behavior the night before. Patrick might feel no regret for anything that had happened, but her principles did not stretch to kissing a married man. There were no extenuating circumstances. Period.

She winced as her coffee cup clattered against the saucer. Bending her head, she rubbed her temples. A sleepless night had given her a sick headache, yet she was no closer to working her way out of the dilemma than ever.

''Bad night, hmm?''

''Max!'' She blinked to clear away the pain. ''I thought you would be on the golf course.''

"I decided to pass this morning." He sat down and poured himself a cup of coffee, looking her over shrewdly as he sipped at it. With a sigh, she met his eyes, not even attempting to pretend everything was fine. In her mirror that morning, she'd seen the bruised look around her eyes and the strain around her mouth. She was too pale and her hands were not quite steady. Max knew her too well to be taken in by a false smile and a lie.

With a sympathetic smile, he patted her hand. "Did you take something for that migraine?"

"It's not a migraine yet, but I did take a powder, which usually seems to work very well. I'll be fine in a little while."

His touch was warm and reassuring. What would she do without Max? He surprised her when he suddenly picked up her hand and squeezed it. "Your headache will ease off, yes, and you'll be fine. But I don't think you'll be fine long. I think you've landed in some rather deep trouble here in Savannah, Kathleen."

"Please, Max." Withdrawing, she wrapped both hands around her coffee cup. "I know you mean well, but I just don't think I can bear talking about...him."

"Well, we won't talk about him...but we should and must talk about *you,* love. Do you want to stay here?" She gave him a startled look. "Or do you want to leave?"

"What about this house?" She looked around the spacious dining room. Its cherry furnishings were beautiful and gracious. The view through a wall of French doors was her favorite. There was peace and serenity in gazing at the rustic fish pond shaded with magnolia trees and oaks dripping Spanish moss.

"We have a house in New York," Max reminded her gently. "We also have one on the Cape and another in St. Louis. The question is, do you think putting O'Connor out of your mind is as simple as boarding a train and leaving Savannah?''

Kathleen traced the rim of her cup with one finger. ''I don't think so, Max,'' she said quietly.

''You feel like you should stay and deal with this?''

She looked at him. ''I'm afraid so.''

He frowned. ''I wish you wouldn't use that word.''

''Afraid? I wish I didn't feel it.'' She looked beyond him to the tranquil backyard. ''I don't think running away to St. Louis or Cape Cod or even plunging back into the hectic pace of my life in New York is going to give me back the peace of mind I had before I saw Patrick again, Max. I've just discovered that things in my past that I thought were dead and buried were simply buried, not dead at all. I don't quite know what to do about it.''

''He's a married man, darling.''

With a whimper, she bent her head, kneading the throb between her eyes. ''I know it, Max. I'm not going to have an affair with a married man, please believe that.''

She missed the compassionate look he gave her. ''I know you think it could never come to that.''

She looked up. ''But what? What are you telling me?''

''Sometimes we don't have much control over ourselves, Kathleen, when other...forces are so compelling. I'm older than you. I've been madly in love. I know how utterly enthralled someone can be with that one special person.'' He turned his cup round and round pensively. ''It's almost a form of insanity.''

''Max, I don't think—''

He looked up, unfocused for a second. Then he gave a short, soft laugh. ''Forgive me, dear. My thoughts run away with me sometimes.''

Kathleen studied him thoughtfully, wondering. Had Max ever loved hopelessly? There was no doubt that he and Lily had been devoted to each other, but Lily had been an invalid for many years. Had there been another woman?

"So, we stay in Savannah, I take it?"

She nodded. "I think so. I can't run away from this, Max. If I do, I might never find peace again. Besides, I have things to do. Unlike many women, I'm not dependent on a man to feed and clothe me and provide a roof over my head."

She laughed ruefully. "Although, if something were to happen to *you,* I might not be talking so confidently."

"If something were to happen to me, you would do quite well. Not that I'm thinking of going anywhere, mind you." He reached for a cinnamon bun from a basket in front of them. "Surprisingly, I find I like Savannah."

Kathleen nodded, twirling her coffee cup. "It's very beautiful . . . on the surface."

With his butter knife poised, Max looked up. "Uh-oh. You have that look in your eye."

"I've been thinking of a series of articles."

"Don't tell me." He held up the knife. "An exposé of the atrocious working conditions in the industries along the waterfront."

She leaned back. "How did you know?"

"How could I miss it?" he asked, rolling his eyes. "You've been nosing around the area, interviewing ragtag laborers, trying to ferret out the names of silent investors. I know your style, love."

"It is simply criminal the way some of those businesses are run, Max." She leaned forward, pointing a finger, her headache forgotten. "Why, some of those women are so overworked and mistreated that they may as well be slaves.

Maybe a little adverse publicity will shame the owners into making a few improvements."

Max lounged back in his chair. "My God, you sound just like Lily."

Kathleen's outrage faded into a wry smile. "Thank you."

"She would be very proud of you."

"I hope so."

They both smiled softly, sharing memories. Then Max crossed his legs. "Well, since you won't leave Savannah and your interest seems to be centered on labor reform, you might be interested in something I learned at the club yesterday after the launch."

"What?"

"Several of the businesses you've been investigating are owned by the same group of investors. I don't know who they are, but if we can dig up their names, the articles will carry more weight."

"I'll get right on it," Kathleen said, her mind already leaping ahead to possible angles to explore.

"Surely Monday will be time enough," Max said. "And one more thing..."

"Yes?"

"Wade Ferguson's company is now a full-fledged partner with Leland Shipping. Ferguson already had a seat on the board, you know. Yesterday they announced a name change—the company is now LelandFerguson, Incorporated."

After a second, Kathleen leaned back, shaking her head. "They have cut corners and swindled and cheated to a criminal extent and yet they've prospered hugely. It doesn't seem fair, does it, Max? Why would Ferguson want to get into bed with those sharks? He seems like a decent man."

"Who knows? They also named a new corporate vice president and member of the board," Max said, watching her quietly.

"Who? Who is it?"

"Patrick O'Connor."

CHAPTER NINE

"THIS WOMAN IS A . . . a crazed lunatic!" Tossing the newspaper aside in disgust, Caroline lit a cigarette and inhaled deeply. "I can't imagine why Maxwell Rutledge consorts with a person of such questionable breedin'. I swear, I can't."

"Momma, may I have a jelly biscuit?"

Caroline tapped ashes into her saucer. "He seems like such a nice man."

"Max Rutledge consorting with what woman?" Looking up from his breakfast plate, Wade Ferguson's brows beetled. "What are you talking about, girl?"

Caroline flicked her fingers at the newspaper. "Oh, this . . . this reporter person who calls herself William Collins."

"Momma—"

"Hush, Jessica. Don't you hear me talkin'?" She set her china cup down with a clatter. "I think that's just too silly. Givin' herself a man's name, shamelessly doin' a man's job. Even her red hair is just too vulgar. You know who I mean, Daddy—that woman who lives with Mr. Rutledge."

Patrick grimly studied the bottom of his coffee cup.

"What's this about questionable breeding?" Cutting into a slice of sweet Georgia ham, Wade looked mildly reproachful. "I don't think Miss Collins's bloodlines can be questioned, Caro. She's very gracious and ladylike, or at least, I have certainly found her to be so."

"Everybody's talkin' about her, Daddy."

"Well, now..." Wade lavishly buttered a biscuit. "I don't know about that, honey. If they are, we'll just have to be careful not to fall into the same trap. Gossip can be very damaging, especially to a woman without a man to protect her."

"She's got a man to protect her," Caroline said viciously. "I hope you don't think Max Rutledge is her long-lost uncle."

"Now watch yourself, girl."

"Yes, Caro, watch yourself," Patrick said quietly. "As your father says, Miss Collins is a lady."

For a second, fury burned in Caroline's eyes. "I can't believe—"

"Ple-e-ease, I want a jelly biscuit."

"Shut up, Jessica! I can't believe what I'm hearin' from you two," Caroline said scathingly. "Have you read this latest article, Daddy?"

"Here, baby." Patrick handed a biscuit to Jessy, gently squeezing her small shoulder.

Wade washed a bite of ham down with coffee. "Matter of fact, I *have* read her latest article...that is, if you mean the one lambasting Graham Sherwood's sweatshop factory on Mill Street."

"Graham Sherwood is one of your oldest friends!"

"Acquaintances, my dear. There's a difference."

"The article said something we've all known for years," Patrick said levelly. "Sherwood's facility is a firetrap, and one of these days, a lot of people could be hurt if it burned."

"Maybe he'll make a few changes," Wade said. "It's about time."

"The woman's on a crusade of some kind," Caroline grumbled. "This is the fourth article in as many weeks. Duncan's just furious."

"One of Sherwood's investors, is he?" Patrick said, meeting her look blandly.

Wade folded his napkin beside his plate and got to his feet. "Speaking of Max Rutledge, we've got a golf game scheduled this morning. I'd better get on off to the club if I want to make the tee time."

He paused, looking back at Patrick. "You want to join us, son? We'd enjoy having you."

"No, thanks, Wade. I promised Jessy I'd take her to the fair. Today's the last day and she reminded me last night that she hasn't been yet."

"I'm going to ride the Ferris wheel!" Jessy said. "And eat cotton candy. Daddy promised."

Wade Ferguson gave his daughter a sharp look. "You'll be going with them, won't you, girl?"

"I most certainly will not!" Caroline ground out her cigarette on the bone china. "And I don't want a lecture about it, either. You know I hate that kind of thing, trudging around in the dust—or mud, if it rains, which it probably will. And the crowd. Ugh, poor white trash and hobos, lookin' all ragged and dirty. They ought to keep them out of sight from decent people."

"You can't assume they're indecent because of the way they look, Caroline," Patrick said in a hard tone. "Jobs are scarce all over. The country is in a depression, or haven't you heard?"

"Then they ought to stay in their shacks where they belong," she snapped.

"Some of them don't belong anyplace," he said. "They travel with the carnival because it's work."

With a disgusted sound, Caroline tossed her napkin onto her plate and pushed back her chair. Patrick got politely to his feet, mocking himself for going through the motions. He had no gentlemanly feelings toward his wife.

"Jessica, go wash your hands," Caroline ordered. As the little girl ran off obediently, she turned to Patrick and their eyes locked in cold hostility. They never spoke with anything except hostility anymore, Patrick reminded himself. Why couldn't he remember that? Besides, what was the use in arguing with Caroline? It never solved anything and only added to the misery of Jessy's life.

Jessy. Sweet heaven, sometimes he thought that if it weren't for Jessy, he would just walk out. Forget everything, his mission, his job, his future—everything—and just leave. He was no longer a penniless Irish immigrant. He could build a new life elsewhere.

And he would be free.

But Caroline would eat Jessy alive. The woman was like a bloodthirsty vampire, sucking the life and joy, the very childhood, out of her own daughter. No court in the land would give him full custody, and he couldn't leave her with only Wade to look out for her. Wade was too old to challenge Caroline in those rare moments when he allowed himself to see her as she really was.

No, he had made his bed and he would have to lie in it. Shrugging into his jacket, he heard Jessy telling the maid excitedly about going to the fair. His mouth grim, he reached for one last sip of coffee.

But it was cold and bitter.

"Oh, I LOVE A CARNIVAL!" Turning around and around with her arms wide open, Lizzie lifted her face to the sky and smiled widely. "Smell that? Popcorn and cotton candy and cow poop. It reminds me of my first kiss."

With a startled laugh, Kathleen stared at her friend. "Lizzie!"

"Behave yourself, Lizzie," Leo said softly, but there was a smile in his gray eyes.

Leo Stern, whose demeanor suited his name most of the time, had been with Lily and Max Rutledge for years. His duties ranged from male nurse, chauffeur and handyman to butler. His age was a mystery, at least to Kathleen. Lizzie and Leo had met in New York the summer after Kathleen and Lizzie had gone to work for the Rutledges. Incredibly, it had been love at first sight for both. By Christmas of that year, they were married.

"Oh, get on with you, Leo Stern," Lizzie teased him. "Doesn't the aroma of that big barn over there remind you of anything?"

"Nothing I can discuss here in front of Miss Kathleen," the big man said repressively.

"Do I want to hear this?" Kathleen asked of no one in particular.

"It's where this big lug gave me my first kiss," Lizzie said, leaning her head against Leo's arm. She was so tiny that she barely reached his elbow.

"In a barn?" Kathleen couldn't help it, her nose wrinkled.

"Yes," Lizzie returned, chuckling at Leo's expense. "He was too shy to do it on the Ferris wheel, even at the top where no one but God and his angels could see. So with a line of blarney that wouldn't disgrace an Irishman, he finagled me into the barn among the sheep and cows and horses and chickens."

In spite of herself, Kathleen bit. "And then what?"

"And then that's where he did the deed," Lizzie claimed, ignoring Leo's stone face. "Plus a lot more. Right in front of a big-eyed cow."

Kathleen's eyes danced. Lizzie and Leo were such an unlikely couple, but no two people ever seemed more devoted. It was a joy just to be with them.

"I've been wondering about the livestock in this fair," Lizzie said, looking around innocently.

"Lizzie—" Leo's deep voice was soft. Suspiciously soft.

"And I have a hankering for cotton candy all of a sudden," Kathleen said hastily. "I'll meet you two at the car in two hours, okay?"

Leo checked her with one big hand on her arm. "Will you be all right on your own, Miss Kathleen?" He didn't quite look her in the eye. Even after five years of marriage, Lizzie's teasing still made him blush like a boy.

"I'll be fine."

She was still smiling as she approached the cotton candy stand. The treat, looking like a puff of pink cloud, was made in a shallow tub. Cooked sugar was spun out of a revolving center, then captured by the candy man on a paper cone. With nearly as much fascination as the two boys just ahead of her, Kathleen watched the process, smiling as the boys were handed a cone apiece.

"How many, ma'am?" the candy man asked, turning to her.

"Two, please," said a familiar deep voice from close behind her.

"Patrick..." Her heart, which had stayed quiet and even through a ride on a roller coaster and a trip through the horror house with Leo and Lizzie, tripped into double time. Were the fates conspiring against her? She hadn't seen or heard from Patrick since the night he'd come to her. It was better that way. After countless nights spent tossing and turning, her body aching in shameless need, she knew Patrick could never be just a friend.

"And Jessy." With his eyes clinging to hers, Patrick nudged Jessy slightly forward from her place at his side. "You remember Jessy, don't you, Kathleen?"

"Yes," she said faintly. Then, managing a smile, she said, "Hello, Jessy."

"Are you having cotton candy?" Jessy asked, eyeing the large pink bundle of fluff the candy man handed her.

"Yes, I am."

"I thought it was only for children, like me."

Bending slightly, Kathleen handed hers to Jessy. "No, it can be for anybody, even grown-ups. Here, you can have mine and I'll wait for another one."

"Did you hear that, Daddy? Do you want one, too?" Sticking out her tongue, Jessy took a tiny taste.

"I think I'd rather have popcorn, Cricket," he said, wiping off a blob on the end of her small nose with his handkerchief. "Uh-oh, this might be a big mess if we aren't careful."

"You don't mean we! You mean me!"

"Right, little lady, so you just remember that," he teased, poking her gently in the tummy. "Otherwise, I might have to take you over to the elephants and let them wash you off."

Jessy giggled, fending him off playfully. "Oh, Daddy."

As the candy man passed the second cone to Kathleen, Patrick quickly paid for both and then looked around at the people near them. With a frown, he asked, "You're not here alone, are you?"

"No, Leo and Lizzie are in the livestock barn."

"The livestock barn is on the other side of the fairgrounds."

She smiled, then took a tiny bite of pink fluff. "I'm not lost, Patrick. I'm old enough to go to the fair by myself."

With brooding eyes, he watched her trying to capture a piece of spun sugar that stuck to her cheek. Not thinking, he did exactly what he'd done with Jessy. He cleaned it away with his handkerchief.

It was a mistake to touch her. Drawing in a deep breath, he stepped back. Only moments before, the smell of the carnival had been overwhelming—popcorn, smoke from the food grills, people and more people, the livestock barn. Now, none of that registered. He smelled only the heady scent of roses, and that was what filled his head and undermined his good intentions.

He did have good intentions. If he didn't, weeks ago he would have yielded to the temptation to see her. But seeing her would just lead to other things, a touch, then a kiss, and then...

"Daddy, Daddy..."

He glanced down at Jessy, tugging at his pants leg. "What is it, Cricket?"

"Look, there are some ragged, dirty people, just like Momma said." She pointed at a family with several unkempt children. "Are they poor white trash?"

"Hush, Jessy!" Squatting down in front of her, Patrick caught her chin, forcing her to look directly at him. "That is an ugly way to describe people. Look again...that is a family, a mother and daddy and their children. Their clothes are mended and neat. They aren't dirty. Maybe their daddy doesn't have a good job."

"But Momma said it," she murmured, her small bottom lip trembling.

"Your mother was wrong to say it," Patrick said firmly.

"You want me to apologize?" she asked with obvious trepidation.

"I don't think they heard you, and wasn't that lucky?" He cupped her small neck in one hand affectionately. "But Kathleen and I heard you."

Jessy looked up at Kathleen. "Are you mad at me?"

"No." Kathleen smiled and touched her hair.

"I'm glad, 'cause when Momma gets mad at me, she slaps me and yells at me. It's awful. I get scared."

"Jessy..." Glancing up, Patrick wasn't surprised to see Kathleen's shocked expression. He looked around for a distraction before recollections of his wife ruined the whole day. "Look, there's the cage with monkeys in it. I bought some peanuts for them a few minutes ago. Want to feed them, Jessy?"

"Yes, can I?"

"Careful with your cotton candy," Kathleen reminded her, then realized that Patrick was the parent here. Where was Jessy's mother? she wondered. And was Jessy's remark simply a child's exaggeration? Surely the woman wasn't as harsh as she sounded.

"I know what you're thinking," Patrick said quietly, "but—"

"I'm thinking your personal life is none of my business," Kathleen said quickly. She could almost feel his frustration. Did he want to defend Caroline? Hearing Patrick make excuses for his wife would be too much. She didn't think she could bear that.

"No matter what I think about your wife as a mother, you make a good father, Patrick. I admired the way you handled the incident with the poor family," she said. "Jessy probably will never use that term to describe people again, even when they might deserve it."

"No thanks to her mother," he said bitterly. "You would think she'd want to show Jessy the county fair."

"It's good family fun," Kathleen murmured noncommitally.

"Caroline isn't interested in family entertainment."

Is she interested in her family? But naturally she couldn't say that, Kathleen thought. He had made no effort to hide his bitterness when he mentioned Caroline. What kind of woman was she? What kind of marriage did he have?

"Daddy, there's where you get popcorn!" The peanuts gone, Jessy pointed to a vendor who was approaching them hawking popcorn. "And a soda! I want a soda, too."

Kathleen looked at him. "Were you going to get popcorn?"

"It's neater than cotton candy."

She made a rueful face, holding the sticky fluff well away from her clothes. "Too true."

Jessy scooted around until she was in front of them. "Can I have a hot dog, too?" she begged, dancing from one foot to the other.

Patrick looked helplessly at Kathleen. She laughed, tossing her half-eaten cotton candy into a nearby trash barrel, and reached down to take Jessy's hand. With a purposeful air, she went down on her haunches in front of the little girl. "Jessy, do you want to know the nicest thing about being at the fair?"

Held still, at least for a moment or two, Jessy thought hard. "No, what?"

"It's popcorn and hot dogs and cotton candy and candied apples, all the wonderful treats that you never get to eat when you're at home." Glancing up, she saw that Patrick did not look relieved. "The second best thing at the fair are all the wonderful sights to see, the wild animals, tigers and lions and elephants, the sword swallower, the tattooed lady, the man who eats fire, the—"

"Eats fire! Really?" Jessy's eyes were round with wonder.

"Yes, really. And riding the Ferris wheel and the roller coaster."

"I'm gonna do all of that!"

"But you know what the worst thing is?"

"Uh-uh, what?"

"It's when you eat too much of that good stuff and you get a tummy ache and you have to go home before you get to see the other things." Sneaking a look at Patrick, she saw a smile hovering near his mouth.

"I don't want to get sick."

"I know you don't, Cricket." Kathleen plucked the cotton candy out of Jessy's hand and the two of them studied it seriously for a few seconds. "I think this particular treat is ready for the trash. What do you think?"

"Me, too. Later I may want a hot dog. Do you think that would be okay?"

Smiling, Kathleen stood up and looked at Patrick. "What do you think, Daddy?"

For Jessy's benefit, he stroked his chin as he considered the question. "Hmm, hot dogs and lemonade for all of us," he decided, winking at Kathleen. "But only after we've seen the fire-eating man."

"Yaay!"

Kathleen dumped the cotton candy into the barrel and dusted off her hands. Then, falling into step beside Jessy, she took one small, slightly sticky hand while Patrick took the other.

"You did that very well," he told her, smiling into her eyes. "Thanks."

"Basic psychology. Jessy's bright enough to understand and sweet enough to be persuaded."

"Put that way, it sounds simple."

She laughed. "Probably because I'm not a mother."

His smile disappeared and Kathleen was suddenly breathless. He was thinking of their child, she knew. They were both thinking of their child. "You would make a wonderful mother," he said softly.

"It was not meant to be, Patrick."

"You're still young."

"I have a career. It is not the destiny of every woman to be a wife and mother."

"Daddy..." Jessy tugged on his hand. "Is Kathleen going to see the fair with us?"

And so, without actually knowing how it happened, Kathleen found that she would not be spending the next two hours at the fair by herself, after all.

Kathleen and Patrick got off the Ferris wheel, muffling their laughter to keep from waking Jessy as Kathleen juggled teddy bears, two Kewpie dolls and a glass kitty cat filled with sugar candy. It was their fourth turn on the Ferris wheel and absolutely the final one, Patrick had declared. But his eyes had been laughing. Sure enough, halfway through, Jessy had finally fallen asleep.

"This is one grimy, exhausted but very happy little girl," Patrick said, lifting her gently to his shoulder. "I don't think she would have enjoyed the day nearly so much without you. A few times there, I felt like the only one over twelve years old."

"You don't laugh enough."

Patrick looked at her quickly, catching his breath at the sight of her. Most of the time, he'd carefully avoided thinking of her as anyone but a friend to enjoy the fair with him and his daughter. A good part of the time, he'd even managed it.

But now...

"I shouldn't say that." She shifted some of the souvenirs in her arms, avoiding his eyes. "Besides, I should be thanking *you*. I wouldn't have had half as much fun alone either. A carnival should be enjoyed through the eyes of a child."

She grabbed for a teddy bear that almost toppled to the ground. "Heavens! How are you going to get all this back to your car?"

"You're going to help me?" When she threw him a startled look, he shrugged—as much as he was able with Jessy's deadweight draped over his shoulder. "Please?"

"Well..." She glanced at her watch. "Oh, Lord, it's time for me to meet Leo and Lizzie!"

"Where?"

"At the car." She looked distractedly toward the area where cars were parked. "The problem is, I'm not sure—"

"I'll help you find them after we put Jessy in my car," he said, obviously expecting her to fall into step beside him. "Let's head out that way. Can you manage?"

She rearranged the teddy bears and nodded. "I've got it all, I think."

"I've been reading your articles," he said, striding ahead, his tall, solid breadth parting the crowd with ease. "It's pretty provocative stuff, Kathleen. Savannah's as hard hit by the Depression as other cities. Sometimes businesses have to make decisions that seem harsh on workers just to stay competitive."

"I don't think we should talk about this, Patrick."

"I'm only mentioning it because I've heard a few grumblings among some of the businessmen. Just keep in mind that times are hard. People sometimes do desperate things when they feel desperate."

"I assume you speak from an owner's point of view. I was writing from the workers' point of view. There's a big difference. But since you use the word desperate, I think the workers in some of those warehouses in the Mill Street district truly understand the word far better than the fat-cat owners."

He sighed heavily. "Kathleen, I'm telling you this for your own good. You're stirring up some people who might not respect the fact that you're a woman. They could get rough."

"Thank you for warning me, but there really is no need for you to worry. I can manage." She shrugged. "How could anything in Savannah be half as bad as the controversy I survived in New York?"

"I'm not talking about controversy, for God's sake! I'm talking about somebody doing physical harm to you."

"Are you sure you're not trying to call me off before I get around to your business?"

He looked at her. "What am I supposed to make of that statement? I will put working conditions at my shipyard alongside those of my competitors in the south, lady. And we pay our workers a fair wage, too. I don't have anything to feel guilty about."

Her silence said more than an out-and-out argument.

"Is there something I should know?"

"My next column isn't about the shipyard, it's about LelandFerguson."

The name seemed to throw him for a second, but he recovered. "What about LelandFerguson?"

"I heard about your promotion. Congratulations."

"You don't sound congratulatory. You sound contemptuous. I worked very hard to get that vice presidency, Kathleen."

"I hope you didn't sell your soul."

They were at the car. Without another word, she pulled the door open and waited while he laid Jessy gently on the seat and pulled a blanket from the back. Covering the little girl, he closed the door as softly as he could.

"Now, let's talk about this some more," he said. Leaning against the car, he looked as though he planned to be there all night.

She glanced beyond him to where the Hudson was parked. She could see Leo and Lizzie watching them, obviously recognizing Patrick. She would have to suffer a cross-examination from both of them on the trip home.

"I really must go, Patrick."

"Then tomorrow. I'll come to your office."

"I have an appointment."

"Then later."

"My appointment will take most of the day. I can't say when I'll be back."

"You're going out of town?"

"No, I'm following up on some information that came across my desk. I'll need to check it out personally. I can't tell you any more than that, Patrick," she said, seeing by his expression that he wanted to argue.

"Does it have anything to do with your investigations of the Mill Street businesses?"

"Why do you ask that?"

"I've told you. That's dangerous territory for you to be fooling around in, Kathleen." He rubbed impatiently at his neck. "Since you've as good as promised me you won't pull any punches in your editorials, I'll just tell you that some bad people are involved in those warehouses along the waterfront. You want to stay away from there."

"I'm an investigative journalist, Patrick. I don't stay away from sensitive issues."

"Not even if it jeopardizes your life?"

"I'll have to be the judge of that."

"No. Hell no! I'm not going to just stand around and let you risk your silly little neck. Dammit! You don't realize what—"

"My work is not silly," she said, interrupting him icily. "*You* may have lost the ability to care about injustices to working people since you came to America and found such stunning success, but I still burn for the outrages perpetrated against workers, women and children especially. It's shameful the things they have to suffer just to get a paltry wage, Patrick. I think that's something people should think about. You used to think about it. You used to deplore it. I can't imagine what happened to make you change this way, but so be it. You've made your choices. You live your way and I'll live mine. And please remember that you aren't in any position to dictate what I can or can't do. You gave up that right a long time ago.''

He pushed away from the car and looked her squarely in the face. ''I may have given up the rights a husband could exercise, Kathleen, but I didn't give up the right to care about you. And if you don't heed me in this, then I'll find a way to make you listen.''

''Empty threats, Patrick,'' she said with asperity. ''What could you do?''

''What can I do?''

''Yes, what? Or is it that you're pretending concern for my welfare when it's actually concern for the effect of my column? Are you afraid I'll print something that will cost LelandFerguson?''

''I don't need to repeat what I said about my shipyard,'' he said abruptly. ''And I don't pretend where you're concerned, Kathleen.''

He reached out and touched her collar, a whisper-soft, delicate touch. But there was an implied sense of possession in it, and Kathleen almost let him see that she felt it.

''As for what I can do,'' he said, his tone as soft as his touch. ''I suppose I could go directly to your esteemed mentor.''

She frowned. ''Max? You would tell Max?''

''You bet your life. And if I know the man, he will see eye to eye with me on this one.'' He shrugged, taking his hand away. ''It's up to you.''

For a long moment, the air literally hummed with the force of their emotions. Her frustration, his obstinacy. Their mutual anger. She wasn't used to anybody interfering when she made up her mind. Patrick was accustomed to issuing orders and having them carried out without question. In their separate lives, few people challenged either of them. What was it that made them challenge each other?

With a furious movement, Kathleen tossed everything in her arms—teddy bears, Kewpie dolls, glass kitty, everything—into his face and stalked off.

CHAPTER TEN

TWO STIFF DRINKS and Patrick was still wound as tight as an eight-day clock. And still stinging over Kathleen's fierce attack. She was a woman who was prepared to stand up for her principles, no matter what the cost. At one time, she had believed him to be the same kind of man.

It nearly destroyed him to know she no longer believed that.

It hurt even more that she rejected his help when she so obviously needed a protector. She had made it plain that she was not a woman who was used to having a man interfering in her life. She wouldn't call what he was suggesting protection. She would call it interference.

She didn't even believe there was serious reason to fear reprisal from those she targeted in her articles. Patrick knew better. He hadn't been overreacting when he cautioned her. He made it his business to keep his finger on the pulse of business in Savannah, and word was that Kathleen Collins needed to be taught a thing or two. He was afraid that the appointment she'd mentioned for sometime tomorrow might be a setup. If these people were forced to alter the way they ran their factories, it would cost them a lot of money. Using a man's pseudonym wasn't going to save her if she didn't ease up.

But it wasn't her nature to ease up.

Moving to the liquor cabinet, he took out the bottle of whiskey. He supposed the logical thing, the honorable thing, would be to go to Maxwell Rutledge and lay out everything he knew. Rutledge was, after all, her employer. It was because of her job and how damned good she was at it that she was in this mess in the first place. It was Rutledge's responsibility.

Biting off an oath, he swallowed the whiskey, almost relishing the way it burned going down. She might belong to Max Rutledge, but God in heaven, it didn't feel that way. With every fiber of his being, he still felt like she was his.

At the breakfast table that morning when Caroline had been maligning Kathleen, it had taken every ounce of control at his command to keep from ordering his wife to shut up. Her criticisms stemmed from spite and petty jealousy. She didn't really care about the content of Kathleen's columns. Patrick doubted she had even read them. She had simply been parroting what Duncan Wheeler said. If she should ever get even a hint of the past that he and Kathleen shared, her pettiness would turn vicious in the twinkling of an eye. And then Kathleen would be faced with another threat. Knowing his wife, Patrick did not discount the harm Caroline could do if she set out to hurt Kathleen. With a groan, Patrick tossed off the rest of his drink. Deep inside he knew that it was going to take more than whiskey to soothe what ailed him tonight. And whether Kathleen approved or not, he was going to see Rutledge the first chance he got and tell him to keep an eye on her.

He lifted the bottle to pour another hefty shot when he heard a sound. He closed the liquor cabinet just as the door of his bedroom flew open, slamming with a crash against the wall.

"You son of a bitch! You miserable, two-timin' son of a bitch!" Caroline confronted him, literally shaking with rage. Eyes wild, chest heaving, she looked ready to launch herself at him. "I just left the club and I know every-thing!"

Walking swiftly, Patrick closed the door before turning to face her. He kept a wary distance, knowing from experi-ence what damage she could do with those long scarlet nails. "Caroline, what the hell are—"

"Don't you dare take that mealymouthed tone with me, you bastard! I know where you've been all the damned day, and with my child, too. You miserable *snake!* You took my baby with you to... to fornicate with that bitch."

With an oath, he caught her by the wrist and pulled her to the other side of his bedroom, as far away from the door as possible. The last thing Jessy needed tonight was to wake up and hear her mother ranting and raving like a crazy woman.

"Get hold of yourself! If you want to discuss this, then keep your voice down."

"I won't keep my voice down!" she screamed. "I'll shout it from the rooftops if I please, you... you weasel!"

"You'll shout it to an empty room then," he muttered, grabbing up his jacket. He was halfway to the door when she caught him by the arm.

"Don't you dare walk out on me." She was still nearly wild with rage, but her tone was tempered. Watching her, Patrick knew the effort it took and was undecided whether to have it out with her now or wait until morning. Better to do it now. He wouldn't put it past her to storm over and at-tack Kathleen.

He shook her hand from his arm and tossed his jacket on his bed. Knowing she was too agitated to sit, he reached for a cigarette box on the table in front of the sofa and offered her one. "Here. Now calm down so I can make some sense out of all this."

Caroline ignored the proffered cigarette. She still trembled with the force of her wrath. "You think you're so clever, so superior, don't you?" she snarled, watching as he calmly lit a cigarette for himself. "Well, this time you aren't so lily white. I guess you thought you could flaunt that...that tart in front of my own child and nobody would notice." Her lip curled. "You've been found out, Mr. Holier Than Thou!"

Patrick inhaled, then blew the smoke away from them. "Found out doing what, Caro? Walking around at the fair with my own daughter and a friend in front of hundreds of people?"

"A friend? Do you take me for a fool, Patrick?"

"You're many things, Caro, but not a fool." Again he offered her a cigarette, and this time Caroline took it, so agitated that she could barely light it.

"I'm going to see that Daddy hears about this," she said, inhaling jerkily. "Your bubble will be burst then, wait and see."

"What bubble? I don't exactly live a charmed life to begin with."

She flung out an arm, encompassing his large bedroom. "This looks pretty charmin' to me. And I don't notice you turnin' down fat bonuses or promotions or special favors or—"

"What special favors?"

"A partnership in my father's company! If you don't consider that a special favor, then you're a fool."

"I've had no special favors. I worked hard for every promotion I ever got, as Wade himself would testify. On top of that, I plowed most of my salary and bonuses back into the shipyard. As for this house, actually I own it, not your father." Ignoring her astonishment, he ground the cigarette out. "But I don't have to defend myself to you, Caroline.

Your father and I understand exactly what my role is, and he's satisfied. I don't have to try to make you happy, too.''

"You've never tried to make me happy!" she charged, whirling around to pace across the room and back. "From the day you married me, you haven't given two thoughts to my happiness."

He stared at her pointedly. "That's not the way I remember it, Caro. I seem to recall that one month after our wedding, you reminded me that Wade had bought and paid for me and that you would decide when and if we ever had sex again. Furthermore, you told me that our marriage was a farce. I admit frankly that I didn't concern myself overly much with making you happy from that day."

"I would have had a divorce, too, if Daddy had been reasonable," she said furiously. "But, no, he's never been able to see your faults." Her eyes narrowed. "But this time he will. This time you've cut your own throat. Two-timin' me with that redheaded slut was a big mistake on your part, Patrick." She laughed softly, viciously. "Daddy won't forgive that, no matter how you try to wriggle out of it."

"I haven't two-timed you, Caroline. Don't be ridiculous."

"Everyone saw you," she said, caught up in her own sense of betrayal. "All my friends, simply *all* of them. It's even more humiliatin' that she's tall and skinny as a beanpole. I'll never be able to hold up my head in public again."

For a moment, Patrick simply stared. "I don't believe what I'm hearing, Caroline. For years you've flaunted your affairs in my face, ignoring the scandal. Right now you're sleeping with Duncan Wheeler, and every one of your so-called friends at the club knows it. The time Jessy and I spent with Kathleen Collins was innocent. What could happen with a five-year-old watching in the middle of the crowd at the fair? But even so, it's odd that you say you care.''

As he reached for his drink, there was a firm rap on the bedroom door. With a sigh, Patrick walked over and opened it.

"Wade. You must have heard the ruckus." Stepping back, he motioned his father-in-law in, adding mockingly, "Join the party."

Wade looked tired, Patrick thought. There was a hint of strain on his face, and the starch in his usually squared-off shoulders was missing. He must have come from his bed, because he was in pajamas and a robe.

"I don't like to intrude on this, Patrick, but Jessy came to my bedroom crying pitifully. She said her mama was screaming at you. I took her back to her bed and tucked her in." He looked beyond Patrick to his daughter with disapproval. "I hope you have a good excuse for upsetting the household this way, young lady."

Wade seldom lost his temper with Caroline. From the look on her face, she was surprised to hear him scolding her.

"It's not my fault, Daddy," she said, lighting another cigarette. "This time it's your precious Patrick who has fallen from grace."

"Your little girl is crying in her bed, Caroline," Wade said in a grave tone. "I know her daddy here gave her a good time at the fair today while you went off gallivanting with that milksop Duncan Wheeler. I know, too, that they met up with Kathleen Collins and enjoyed a few of the sights. As old friends, it was a perfectly understandable thing to do, and with Jessy along, not at all questionable."

"Hah!" With a malicious look, Caroline turned to Patrick. "'Old friends' doesn't quite describe that relationship, does it, Patrick, darlin'?"

Before Patrick could reply, Wade spoke. "I think it does, Caro. They have their Irish background in common," he said in a patient voice, rubbing the side of his head slowly. "And they lived in the same neighborhood in New York. Max mentioned it on the golf course," he explained to Patrick with the ghost of a smile.

Patrick pushed his hands deep in his pockets, not sure how to respond. What good would it do if he revealed the whole truth? That it might harm Kathleen, he had no doubt. With Caroline's anger at a fever pitch, she was capable of anything.

Caroline smiled like a cat with a secret. "Is that the story y'all have decided on, Patrick?"

"We're all tired, Caroline," he said. "Just say straight out whatever it is you think you know."

"I don't think I know anything, dear husband. I know I know." She studied the end of her cigarette a moment, then sneered at him. "You never knew Kathleen in New York. The two of you go 'way back, all the way to Ireland, where you were *very* close. Isn't that so? She was pregnant with your brat when she got to this country!"

"Caroline!" Wade thundered.

Patrick wasted no more than a second or two wondering how she'd found out. His overriding instinct was to protect Kathleen. "Be very careful, Caroline," he said softly. "Miss Collins is no longer a destitute, friendless immigrant. She's a successful journalist. A respected professional in Savannah. You are not above the law. Unless you can prove what you say, you're asking for a slander suit."

She whirled to face her father. "You heard what I said, didn't you, Daddy? I'm not makin' this up. Patrick's a hypocrite! Pretendin' he doesn't know that slut. Well, he doesn't fool me. Now what do you think?"

Wearily, Wade rubbed his temple again. "I think you're dabbling in something you should stay out of."

She stared. "Is that it? Is that all you have to say?"

Patrick spoke. "Where did you dig this up, Caroline?"

She looked at him coldly. "I have my sources."

"Where," he repeated implacably. "And how long ago?"

"I hired a detective right after I agreed to marry you," she said defiantly. "I knew all along that you were moonin' over some other woman. I wanted to know about her. It was almost too easy. My man traced her through your first job, if you must know. She's nothin' but a tramp and I put her out of my mind."

Patrick thought he had become accustomed to Caroline's cruelty, but he found that he hadn't. A wave of fury started from deep inside him, filling his chest and head so that he could hardly speak. To think that his wife had known of his heartache all along and had secretly enjoyed it. He looked at her now as though she were a specimen of some alien species. What made a woman so...evil? He swallowed hard. It was too late now, and he'd be damned if he'd give Caroline the satisfaction of admitting everything. He could do that much to protect Kathleen, at least. "Just remember that I warned you, Caroline. Slander is a punishable offense."

She laughed harshly. "I'll say what I please when I please, and you can't do a damn thing about it."

"*I* can and will," Wade said suddenly. "Don't let me hear you talking this rubbish, my girl. If so, you'll answer to me."

"Oohh, both of you just disgust me!" She swore furiously at Patrick. "If only I'd known then what I know now, I would never have tied myself to you, Patrick O'Connor!"

Patrick took a deep breath, forgetting for a minute that his father-in-law was watching. "Then that makes two of us," he said quietly. "Because, from the outset, I have regretted marrying you."

The look they exchanged was hostile. Then she turned to Wade. "I want a divorce, Daddy."

He raked a hand over his face tiredly. "Not tonight, baby."

Caroline stamped her foot. "Stop treatin' me like . . . like I'm no older than Jessy! You talked me into shacklin' myself to this . . . ill-mannered, common, insensitive . . . Irishman. And I've been unhappy from the beginnin'. I want to be free, Daddy."

Her father looked at her sadly. "Maybe I treat you like Jessy because most of the time you don't seem much older than Jessy, Caroline. I declare, girl, I don't know where I went wrong."

"Oh, hush, Daddy! What does that kind of drivel have to do with my divorce?"

"You don't need a divorce, honey. You need to go to your room and sleep off such an insane notion." He gave her a narrow-eyed look. "How much drinking have you done tonight?"

"Not that again!" She flounced away, turning her back on them. "I haven't had too much to drink. What woman wouldn't lose her temper when she finds out her husband has been foolin' around with another woman?"

Patrick released an impatient breath. "I haven't been unfaithful to you, Caroline."

She faced him angrily. "And I'm supposed to believe that?"

"Yes," he said quietly.

She turned to her father and spoke feverishly. "Daddy, get rid of him. We don't need him. You ran the company just fine before he got here. He doesn't even have a decent education. We can find someone to replace him. We can find a dozen men to replace him."

"Now, Caroline—"

"Aren't you hearin' me, Daddy!" she screeched. "Are you just goin' to let me suffer forever?" Large watery tears welled up in her dark eyes and slowly overflowed.

"The subject is closed, Caro." Wade tightened the belt on his robe with unsteady hands. Looking at him closely, Patrick saw his pallor and felt alarmed.

"Sir, are you all right?"

The old man rubbed his temple. "It's nothing, son. Just a headache. It's been nagging me for a couple of days now." He conjured up a weak smile. "A good night's sleep and I'll be fine."

Unconvinced, Patrick went with him to the door. "I need a breath of fresh air. I'll just walk with you to your room, then take a turn outside."

"And keep right on goin' to that hussy's house?" Caroline said, her voice hard and condemning. With her arms crossed over her chest, her expression challenged them both. With the last of his flagging energy, Wade Ferguson drew in a deep breath.

"Caroline, honey, looks like there's no getting around this tonight. I'm more tired than I can remember being in a long time. But there are a few things I think I must tell you. I've waited too long, I guess, but . . ." He shrugged, staring momentarily at his feet.

"Wade, don't you think—"

"No, son. I think I need to get this over with."

Caroline stared at them both. "What? What is it?"

"You speak of a divorce, girl, as though a piece of paper is going to be your ticket to happiness. More likely it would be your ticket to ruin. You say I should sack this man you've

married, a man who's been good to you under trying circumstances, who has revitalized my business and single-
handedly taken over the merger with the Leland folks."
Shaking his head, he studied her with a baffled frown. "You
amaze me, Caroline. I'd like to think a daughter of mine
would have better sense. Don't you know when you have it
good, girl?"

Alarmed by the grayness of Wade's skin, Patrick touched
his arm. "Wade, maybe we should head toward your
room."

"In a minute, son."

"Son," Caroline said spitefully. "That's really what this
is all about, isn't it? You don't care about my happiness, do
you, Daddy? No more than Patrick. He's male and there-
fore your soulmate. He can step into your shoes, carry on
your business in a way that's impossible for me. He's the son
you never had."

She turned to Patrick. "Is that how you did it? By playin'
on my father's need to have a son? So that now, even when
you've betrayed me, he takes your side?"

"Patrick has not betrayed you, girl," Wade repeated
wearily. "And he hasn't stepped into my shoes. He didn't
need to. By his own hard work and shrewd management, he
owns half of the company and this house. And if he had
wanted to, he could own all of it. It's because he's a man of
integrity that he hasn't acted on that option. I should have
told you how things were before this, but I suppose I wanted
to spare you. I'm ashamed of you for poking into his private life and then throwing it up to him like you did. I honestly don't know what to make of you sometimes, girl.
You—"

"I don't have to listen to this!" she snapped, shouldering past her father and Patrick. "And I don't have to stay
around here and be treated like a stepchild."

"Caroline!" Wade's tone, intended to reprimand, sounded weak. "Where are you going, girl?"

"What do you care!" She flung the words over her shoulder as she burst into tears and ran down the stairs.

That night, Wade Ferguson suffered a severe stroke. For three days, he hovered between life and death. Keeping vigil by his bedside with Caroline, Patrick had too much time for thinking. A man's hold on life was at best a tenuous and fragile thread. One quick, shattering moment and it was severed.

As he watched Wade balanced on the brink, he kept thinking there was a lesson to be learned. His own marriage was a travesty. He had no close friends. He took little pleasure in his work. His spare time and every decision he made professionally was focused on one goal: to bring down the Leland company. Was he wasting his life?

SOMEONE WAS IN the warehouse. Listening in the twilit gloom, Kathleen heard a brief, furtive sound. But there was nothing but silence when she peered into the building's deep shadows. It was enough to tell her that she was no longer alone in the huge, abandoned building. Hastily, she shoved her notebook into her big tapestry bag and glanced uneasily at the stacks of wooden crates. Far too many hiding places stood between her and the big closed door leading outside.

Had she closed the door? She was almost certain she had not.

Why hadn't she wrapped up the interviews while it was still full daylight? Because the women were so eager to talk. Because the material she had scribbled down had exceeded her wildest expectations. Half a dozen women with the courage to speak out. Who could guess that the results of an anonymous call would be so spectacular? Kathleen had simply been unable to close her notebook until she'd recorded every last injustice perpetrated against the women in their jobs at the woolen mill.

But it was nearly dark now, an hour past the time when she should have started back to the offices of the *Sentinel*. And long past the time when the building should be empty, someone was in the warehouse.

Oh, God, was this what Patrick had warned her about?

She slipped a hand inside her bag, searching for something, anything, that would serve as a weapon. Sifting through the contents, she found nothing except her hairbrush. Drawing a shaky breath, she closed her fingers around the sterling silver handle.

The distance to the exit looked like forever, but she couldn't stay here all night. Hefting the bag onto her shoulder, and taking a deep breath, she ran for the door.

She was broadsided as she shot past a crate. The hairbrush went flying along with her bag. The scream that began in her throat was smothered by a heavy hand closing over her mouth and nose, shutting off oxygen. She made only a grunt as she was jerked back against a hard, broad chest. Kicking frantically and flailing her arms wildly, she fought to free herself. Her captor cursed in her ear, crude, blasphemous demands. Kathleen fought harder. Her only hope lay in resisting whatever he planned.

Suddenly he landed a hard, vicious blow to her head and clenched her chest, forcing the air out of her lungs with the savage strength in his thick arms. As dark mist clouded her brain, Kathleen slumped into semiconsciousness. She would have sunk to the floor, but he wouldn't allow it. Yanking her by her hair, he slammed her up against one of the crates and pinned her there.

Then she was gulping in long, gasping breaths, blinking and frowning to clear the haze of pain. With a hand clamped to her jaw, her captor forced her head sideways. Even in her fear, she realized he did not intend for her to get a look at him.

Maybe he wasn't going to kill her.

Maybe it would be worse than death.

"Not so cocky now, are you, Miss Busybody Loud-mouth Bitch Reporter?" he spat when he could catch a breath. From somewhere inside her, somewhere that hadn't yet been frightened beyond coherence, Kathleen felt savagely glad that she'd given him enough resistance to at least wind him.

"What do you want?"

She cried out as he yanked a handful of her hair. "To teach you a lesson, that's what. Keep your busybody nose out of things in this town that don't concern you, you hear me? Or you might find yourself shipped back to New York City in a box."

She held herself as still as marble and said nothing.

"You better hear me, bitch!" he shouted, shaking her savagely. Like a rag doll, she bounced against the crate, and another shower of stars exploded in her head.

"I hear you," she whispered weakly.

"Good. Now, where are the goddamn notes?"

"Notes?"

He spewed out a string of profanity and slapped her across her face. When her senses returned, she could not think for a few seconds. He seemed to know that, because she felt him waiting, his evil barely restrained.

"Now," he said, his tone ugly as he repeated slowly, "where . . . is . . . the goddamn notebook?"

"In my bag."

"Now we're cookin'."

He stepped back to pick up her bag, leaving her to crumple to the floor like a puppet with broken strings. Her head was spinning and her ears rang. She heard the sounds as he found the notebook, but she was unable to look up, to focus on his face, even though she knew it was important to see him. She would make him pay for this. Somehow.

Suddenly he loomed above her. "Go home, Yankee woman," he said, emptying the contents of her bag over her. Things rained down on her, striking her face and head and chest like sluggish bullets. "We don't need your kind in Savannah."

With another lewd epithet, he turned and swaggered toward the door. With every ounce of energy at her command, Kathleen struggled to look. Blinking to clear her vision, she finally focused. He was short, broad, thick necked. As he pulled the big door open, he was caught momentarily in the gleam of a passing car's headlights. He was bald. Completely bald.

The silence after he left was oppressive, as dark and ominous as the swiftly falling shades of night. Kathleen gingerly touched her mouth and winced. Her lip was puffy. Inside, the skin was broken and she tasted blood.

With a groan, she drew her legs up and, using the crate for leverage, managed to get to her feet. She was swamped by darkly swirling mists and a roaring in her ears that threatened to buckle her knees again. She stood swaying, bracing herself while the dizziness passed.

Stumbling over her tapestry bag, she bent down slowly, carefully, and raked her things back into it. He had taken only her notebook. She had a good memory: as soon as she got home, she could reconstruct the interviews in her mind and write the article exactly as she had originally planned.

They would have to do more than beat her to shut her up.

MAXWELL RUTLEDGE WAS collecting his thoughts for a Thursday morning meeting with the managing editor of the

Sentinel when Patrick O'Connor showed up instead. Max got to his feet, his eyes shrewdly assessing the man who had stolen Kathleen's heart when she was a seventeen-year-old girl and, whether Patrick knew it or not, still held it as securely as though she was married to him in the eyes of God and man.

"O'Connor," he said levelly. "What can I do for you?"

He hadn't seen or heard from O'Connor since the night he had slipped into the house and spent a few stolen minutes with Kathleen. He wasn't sure what had happened between them that night, but Kathleen's reaction had alarmed Max. He hadn't seen her smile genuinely since. He studied the big Irishman now and decided O'Connor wasn't paying a social call. What had brought him to town?

"Mind if I smoke?" Patrick asked, his cigarillo suspended unlit in his hand until Max nodded.

"The last thing I'd ever do is try to tell a man how to run his business," Patrick began after lighting up. "It would sure get my back up if you were to come into the shipyard and start offering me advice on shipbuilding."

"I see," Max said, although he didn't. "I assume then that you're here to say something about how the *Sentinel* is run."

"Not exactly."

"Why don't you have a seat, O'Connor."

"Thanks." Patrick sat but didn't lean back. He seemed edgy, looking around Max's office without taking in much. "Did you hear about Wade's stroke?"

"Yes, I did. A pity. I also hear he's holding his own."

"He's been pretty sick. I spent most of the past three days at the hospital, which is why I haven't been here before now. The doctors tell us he's likely to recover, at least somewhat. He'll never be the same, naturally, but..."

"Yes. But I imagine he'd be much more worried and less likely to recover his spirits if he didn't have you to run things at the shipyard. On the golf course, he can't say enough about you."

"I owe him a lot."

"Did you come here to talk about Wade?"

"No." He got up and paced a round or two as Max watched him with a thoughtful expression. "I came to talk about Kathleen."

"Ah."

Patrick glanced up quickly. "Not in a personal sense."

"No? Then what?"

"I read her article in this morning's paper about conditions at the woolen mill."

Max's scrutiny was more intense than ever. "And what did you think?"

"I think she's taking some damn fool chances of getting hurt, that's what I think." Patrick resumed pacing. "I warned her, but she obviously won't pay any attention to me. That's—"

"You warned her?"

"Yes, the night we met at the fair." He stopped, looking at Max. "Did she mention that?"

"No. What do you mean, you warned her?"

He moved restlessly to the window. "I guess I should have come to you in the first place. Seems you're the only one she pays any attention to. I told her that her articles were inflaming a lot of influential people, people who wouldn't let a little thing like the fact she's a woman stop them if they decided she's gone too far." He made a humorless sound. "Then I opened the paper this morning and found that article about the woolen mill. It just goes to show you how much she values my judgment."

Max was on his feet by the time Patrick finished. "You say you suspected she would be hurt? And you didn't come to me? Do you realize what you've done?"

"I couldn't come to you. I told you, I've been at the hospital with Wade, and I have other—" As Max's words registered, Patrick hesitated. "Why? What are you talking about? Did something happen?"

"Who did it? Can you name names?"

"Did what?" Patrick looked around as though searching for Kathleen. "Where is she?"

"She's safe at home."

Patrick swallowed. "Did they try to hurt her?"

"They did hurt her," Max said through his teeth. "And if you know something about it, you tell me now or we're going to the authorities and you can tell them."

"God in heaven." Patrick raked an unsteady hand over his face, then looked at Max. "How bad is it?"

"Bad enough. She—"

But he was talking to an empty room. Patrick was already through the door and running.

CHAPTER ELEVEN

November 7, 1932

The ambience of this town is deceiving. Savannah, beneath its sleepy southern languor, its sultry beauty and the friendliness of its people, harbors greed and injustice and violence. I was given a taste of it three days ago. It was a frightening experience. Max was nearly wild when he saw my bumps and bruises. He wants me to cease and desist from "inciting the natives." His words, not mine. But if he could have seen those women, heard their stories. They work in dismal conditions for long hours at scandalously low wages. The mill is unsafe, a fire hazard and riddled with incidents of injury to women. Perhaps what shocked me most was the fact that there are so many young girls there, some only thirteen or fourteen, in blatant disregard of labor laws. What a miserable existence for them. The assault on my person was terrifying. But more terrifying is the thought that if I stop now, nothing will be done to liberate these women. It will be business as usual.

I cannot quit. I won't quit.

WITH HER THOUGHTS WRITTEN, Kathleen laid her pen down and leaned back in her chair. The afternoon was warm and restful, lulling her into dreamy relaxation. Bird calls echoed and sounds of street traffic drifted through the thick ligustrum hedge surrounding the patio. But all was hazy, as though coming to her through a tunnel. As though pulled by a thread, her gaze went up... up...

To the dark green foliage of the magnolia tree shot through with shafts of November sunshine. Soft, mellow sunshine. And then more vivid. Bright. Searing. And then, before her eyes, the sunbeams became hot, licking tongues of fire.

Transfixed, lost to the reality around her, she watched as the magnolia tree altered, reformed into a huge, many-windowed building. And from those windows orange-red flames shot out, leaping and roaring and crackling, unbridled and devouring. Dense black smoke boiled up, becoming ugly, harsh plumes disfiguring the bright blue of the afternoon sky. With a soft moan, Kathleen realized she was experiencing her Dream Sight.

With the terrifying spectacle came the noise, the clang of fire engines, the shouts of panicked people, running footsteps. In her own chest, she felt their fear. Her heart raced and her lungs fought to breathe.

Then came the screams. No, no, the screams...

THE DRIVE TO KATHLEEN'S house seemed endless. Patrick cursed, banging his fist on the steering wheel of his brand-new Packard. It was still almost too much for him to take in. While he'd been sitting in the hospital with Wade, Kathleen had been assaulted and threatened by some thug. He thought of her pale skin, her beautiful face violated by scum who didn't even deserve to know her name and he shuddered with the desire to tear someone from limb to limb.

"Rotten SOB," he muttered through his teeth. Rutledge had said she was hurt "bad enough." What did that mean? If she was bruised and broken, he didn't know what he would do. With a swift, agonizing pang, Patrick thought of other, more lasting violence. Unthinkable violence.

His chest filled suddenly with a surge of possessiveness, and his hands shook as he turned the corner at Bull Street and shot forward toward Oglethorpe Square. He cursed himself for not acting sooner. The very night he'd learned she planned to meet with an anonymous caller, he should have stepped in. Would have if Wade hadn't collapsed. What the hell did he care if she didn't want him interfering? If he'd interfered, she wouldn't be hurt now.

Kathleen, Kathleen...

Lizzie let him in before he even rang the doorbell. "Well, if it isn't Patrick O'Connor," she said, swinging the door wide enough for him to step inside. "We've been expecting you."

"We?"

"Leo and me, we have a little wager going. But I'll save the details for later. You've come to see about Kathleen, have you?"

"Where is she, Lizzie?"

"In the patio garden off her sitting room. It's sunny today. The fresh air will do her good, and so I told her."

"Through here?"

Lizzie nodded, pointing him to the French doors. The night he'd been with her in her special room, he hadn't noticed the doors opening onto a patio. Now he approached quietly, slipping through the doors, which were ajar, and made a valiant effort to calm himself before she knew he was there.

She was sitting in a pool of sunshine, utterly still, her face turned from him toward the beauty of the garden. In the sun, her unbound auburn hair was like a fiery nimbus around her head. On her lap lay a book, forgotten. While his heart slammed in his chest, Patrick took in the scene before him.

She wasn't bandaged or broken. Whatever had happened, she appeared well as far as he could see. Relief was so strong that it weakened his knees. Beneath the edge of the lap robe that was draped over her knees, he could see the tips of her shoes. High-buttoned, oddly old-fashioned shoes when she was anything but. No, his Kathleen was a modern woman, independent and self-reliant. Maybe too much so. Lord, how the sight of her affected him. If she suspected how much she tore him up inside, she would probably bar him from ever looking at her or saying another word to her again.

"Kathleen . . ."

Slowly, as though waking from a dream, she closed the book—he saw now that it was her journal—and laid it aside before looking up into his face.

She had been badly hurt, after all.

With a shattered feeling, he took in the evidence of the violence she'd suffered. A bruised cheek, a purple mark above her eyebrow, a deep cut at the side of her mouth. And pale. She was so pale.

He turned away and with shaking hands lit a cigarillo. "I would have been here before, but I just found out from Max."

"He called you?"

"No, I went by to see him."

"Why?"

"To tell him that you were in danger. A little late, as it turned out," he said bitterly.

"I told you not to interfere, Patrick." Her hand trembled slightly as she rubbed her eyes.

He threw the unsmoked cigarillo down and crushed it beneath his foot. "And I told you this would happen! Why didn't you listen to me, Kathleen? You could have been killed. You could have been—"

But he couldn't even say it. With a broken sound, he went to her, dropping to his haunches. "Kathleen, did he... Were you..." He caught her hand and held it tight. "God, Kathleen, tell me he didn't touch you that way!"

She touched his cheek. "I wasn't raped, Patrick."

He bent his head and kissed her palm. For a few seconds, he just stayed there, his forehead resting on her knees, surrounded by the scent of the flowers and the feel of sunshine on his back.

"I almost died when I heard," he whispered against her fingers.

"It was bad, Patrick," she admitted. "I should have listened to you. Leo would have been glad to stand by while I spoke with those women. I underestimated the malevolence of the people you warned me about."

The admission gave him no satisfaction. "Now you believe me, when it's too late. You posed a serious threat to somebody, and that meant you were treading on dangerous ground."

"I knew that, of course. I just didn't expect them to... to... actually do something violent."

He looked up. "What did you expect, a formal request in the mail that you shut up and go away?"

She shrugged, wincing because it hurt the sprained muscles in her neck and shoulders. "No, of course not. I expected a call to the editor of the paper. Or a hint to Max at the country club, something like that, I suppose."

He shook his head at her naiveté. "And this after living in New York," he muttered, sitting back on his heels. "Did you recognize the man who did it?"

"No, I couldn't see his face, but if I see him again, I'll know him. He was short and thick and mean."

"That probably narrows it down to about a thousand men in the area."

"He also has a bald head."

He looked at her. "A bald head."

She smiled. "A very bald head. Completely bald head. Bald as a billiard ball."

"I get the idea. Now we look for a short, thick, mean man wearing a hat."

They laughed together. He thought how utterly captivating she looked in spite of her bruises. The idea of any man hitting her—hitting her!—was appalling.

He reached out and gently touched the small cut on her lip. "Will this leave a scar?"

She trembled at his touch. "The doctor says no."

With his thumb, he caressed the soft fullness of her lips. "I wish—" What? That he could kiss her? That he was free to kiss her? Hell, he wasn't even free to say it!

He straightened abruptly. "After what happened, I'm surprised Rutledge ran the article," he said, venting his frustration and guilt by criticizing Max. "I thought he cared more for you than that. It was damned reckless. And running your byline as though the series was no more than a fluff piece about blue-ribbon winners at the fair." He stopped, scowling at her. "It was irresponsible, and I plan to call him on it. Next time you could be killed."

"Calm down, Patrick, please. Max isn't to blame. I insisted."

"Hah! Now you're telling me he doesn't control what's printed in his own paper? You'll have to do better than that, Kathleen."

"I told him if he didn't run it, I'd give the article to the *Sun Times*."

He blinked, staring at her. "And he believed you?"

"He believed me because he knew I would definitely do just that." She brushed away a leaf that had landed on her lap. "I'm a journalist, Patrick, and an American citizen. I won't be cheated of my rights under the first amendment to say what I think."

"Fine! Then you can recuperate in the hospital the next time you feel compelled to tweak the tail of a very mean tiger."

She threw off the lap robe and stood up. "I'm glad you said that, Patrick, because I want to ask you a few questions."

"Like what?" He was suddenly wary.

"Who is the tiger? Exactly who owns the woolen mill? And don't slough off my questions with half truths. I know a group of businessmen own it. Who are they?"

"What makes you think I know the answer to that, Kathleen?" he asked quietly. "Do you think I'm one of those businessmen?"

"No, of course not, but—"

"But you think I might have reasons of my own for not wanting to give you their names."

Their eyes locked and then Kathleen sighed. "Honestly, I don't know what to think, Patrick, but I can see I made a mistake thinking we could discuss this particular subject intelligently."

Fine. He needed to get out of here, away from her, anyway. It bothered him far more than he had ever expected that he couldn't tell her everything he knew, but he couldn't take the chance, especially now that she was digging into the town's secrets.

He stepped back, putting a little distance between them. "Are you sure you're all right?"

She nodded, but there was something about her, an air of distraction. Her gaze was fixed beyond him, but he had an odd feeling that she was seeing . . . what?

"What is it, Kathleen?"

She blinked before looking at him. "A strange thing happened just before you came, Patrick. I had a . . . visitation . . . here, in the garden."

He frowned and drew closer to her. "In daylight? Were you sleeping?"

"No, no. I was just sitting here enjoying the sunshine and suddenly I saw a large building with fire and smoke pouring out of the windows. People were screaming. It was terrible."

"Maybe it was brought on by what happened to you in that warehouse. Did you have a concussion?"

"No. Oh, he bumped me up against a wooden crate and I saw a few stars, but I never actually lost consciousness." She glanced at him then and realized that he was struggling to accept what she was telling him without exploding. She touched his hand. "Truly, I was lucky. He could have done far more damage than he did."

Patrick grunted, then said bleakly, "You don't have to tell me that."

"This wasn't a hallucination caused by a bump on my head, Patrick. This was a real visitation."

"What do you think it means?"

She leaned back, relieved to be able to talk about it. Patrick was the only person besides Lizzie who knew her secret.

She studied her hands intently for a few seconds, then looked up. "Did you know that was one of the things I most . . . valued about you when we were together?"

"What? The fact that I believed?" Her smile was contagious. Rocking back on his heels, he basked in the warmth of it. "I will always believe in you, Kathleen."

They were talking about more than her Dream Sight, and both knew it. But that was forbidden ground. Her gaze assumed a hazy aspect as she looked beyond him, and he knew she was seeing it again. "It was real, Patrick, and it's an omen. I just don't know what to do about it. I don't know where the building is or when the fire will be." She wrapped her arms around herself. "I feel a sense of urgency, though."

"Do you think—" He broke off at a sound from the French doors. Both looked up as Lizzie hurried across the patio.

Kathleen's expression instantly turned anxious. "What's wrong, Lizzie?"

"It's Bertha," she said, directing a worried look back at the house. "She's nearly having hysterics. Something terrible has happened."

"Did she hurt herself?" As Kathleen hurried beside Lizzie, Patrick followed.

"There's a fire at that mill," Lizzie explained. "You know, the one that was in your article. Her niece, Meggy, works there."

"Oh, Lord, that's it!" Kathleen reached out blindly and Patrick took her hand.

"It looks bad. Bertha's husband came all the way over here to tell her. They've got fire engines from every station in Savannah."

Jim, Bertha's husband, looked up as they reached the foyer. The housekeeper was white-faced and shaken as he helped her into a coat. Leo hovered in the background.

Kathleen touched the woman's arm. "Bertha, it may not be as bad as you think. Do you want Lizzie and me to go with you? Leo can drive us."

"You know he can't, Kathleen." Lizzie was already shrugging into her coat. "Leo has orders to keep an eye on you. It would be worth his job if he took you to the waterfront after what happened Sunday night. We'll take the car. Jim can drive."

As Jim pulled the front door open, Lizzie wrapped an arm around Bertha's shoulders. "Now, Bertha, let's don't expect the worst. Like Kathleen says, we don't know it's that bad. Meggy's a smart girl, cool in an emergency. You'll see."

"Leo will drive you," Kathleen repeated firmly.

"And when we're out of sight," Lizzie said with exasperation, "you're thinking to persuade Patrick here to drive you, aren't you, my girl?"

Kathleen held her gaze steadily. "Everyone's waiting, Lizzie."

With a muttered Irish oath, Lizzie flounced outside. Leo, at an imperious look from Kathleen, followed. At the street, Lizzie caught Patrick's eye. "I'm counting on you to keep her away from that fire, Patrick O'Connor."

The moment the big Hudson pulled away, Kathleen was snatching her coat out of the closet. She put it on while looking around for her notebook. "I must have left it on the patio," she murmured. Turning to Patrick, she said, "Will you get my notebook, please? I think I left it on the patio."

"You aren't going to the scene of that fire, Kathleen. For once, Maxwell Rutledge and I are in agreement."

"I don't have time to argue with you, Patrick." Leaving him where he stood, she hurried through the house and out to the patio. Snatching up her notebook, she checked to see that she had pencils, stuffed everything in her bag, and then hurried back to the front door where Patrick stood wearing an implacable look. With his arms crossed on his chest, he made a formidable barrier between her and the door.

She faced him. "Will you drive me or must I call a taxi-cab?"

"You'll do neither. You aren't going to risk your life by reporting this fire. Let someone else handle it, Kathleen."

She drew in an impatient breath. "I don't have time to debate this with you now, Patrick. If you refuse to drive me, that's your decision. Now, I'm going to report this fire. Wild horses couldn't keep me away from this fire. You, least of all, won't keep me from this fire."

With a burst of profanity that was truly impressive, Patrick jerked the door open and stalked down the steps. For a second, Kathleen hesitated, glaring at his backside, then followed him.

At the car, she threw him a challenging look before climbing past the door he held open. Grudgingly. "You can argue all you want, Patrick," she muttered, snatching at her skirt to keep it from getting caught. "But I'm covering this fire."

He slammed the door.

"COME, KATHLEEN, I must get you home."

She was distantly aware of the pressure of Patrick's arm around her shoulders urging her away from the carnage. Smoke still hung around the scene, drifting skyward from the blackened hulk that had once been the woolen mill. The smell of charred wood and wool mingled in the dampness of the night. Around them, firemen and a few straggling on-lookers tramped among the litter and puddled water. Some of the frightened, weeping women who had been rescued had been driven away to hospitals, the luckier ones, to their homes.

The dead had been driven to the morgue.

"Bertha and Jim..." Kathleen said, looking around bleakly. "Are they... Did they... Did Leo drive them home?"

"Yes. Lizzie will stay the night with them."

"That's good. Bertha will need someone."

Bertha's niece had died in the fire along with three others. Kathleen's throat tightened with unshed tears. If only the revelation she'd had about the fire had been more than simple knowledge of the event. If only she had known where and how and when. If only...

"There was nothing you could do, Kathleen."

Tears threatened, but she blinked them away. "I know, but it still feels as though I should have been able to do something."

"Come. The car is over here."

She let Patrick guide her over to the Packard and waited while he pulled the door open. Within minutes of arriving at the fire, she had written the article she would hand over to the *Sentinel*. Only the details and names of the dead remained to be added. Meggy, she thought, a postscript in a story that should never have been written.

"Climb in, Kathleen, please. You need to get home to bed."

"I can't go home yet," she said, resting her head wearily against the seat. "I need to get the story to the *Sentinel* before deadline."

After a second or two of silence, Patrick closed the car door hard, his curse muffled. "I don't suppose you would let me take the blasted thing to the *Sentinel* for you, after I've dropped you off at Oglethorpe Square, would you?" he asked when he'd climbed in beside her.

"No. I'll take it myself."

"Be reasonable, Kathleen. You're reeling with exhaustion."

And guilt. And bewilderment. And grief. Why? Why was she allowed to know these things and yet be denied the power to do anything? Closing her eyes, she let her head loll against the back of the seat. "Don't nag, Patrick. Not tonight."

With his jaw clamped, he pulled away from the fire scene and bore down on the accelerator. The damn article. Reason, he could see, came in a distant second. In ten minutes, they pulled up at the *Sentinel*'s offices.

He went with her to the desk of the night editor, listening only vaguely while they discussed technicalities. Kathleen seemed all right, but Patrick was uneasy. He watched her closely, noting the pallor of her skin and the shattered look in her green eyes. She should have been home in bed hours ago.

He wasn't relieved to realize she was trembling as he helped her back into the Packard. Before he started the car, he swept up a blanket from the back seat and tucked it around her. When she didn't resist, his alarm increased. Hell, Lizzie wasn't even home to put her to bed.

He pulled away from the curb and decided to take a roundabout way home. Balanced on the edge as she was, he needed to know that she was all right before he could bear to let her out of his sight.

The lights of Savannah were behind them before Kathleen realized that Patrick was not driving her directly to Oglethorpe Square. Her throat was thick with unshed tears and the stress of holding herself together. If he said anything more about the fire, about Meggy, about her Dream Sight, she would shatter into a thousand pieces.

"I was always awed by your Dream Sight," he said softly in the thick silence. "Did I ever tell you that?"

"No."

"Well, it's true. I always thought—"

At her quick, choked sound, he glanced from the road to Kathleen. She was bent double, her hands covering her face. Heartrending sobs tore through her. "Kathleen, sweetheart!"

Putting on the brakes, he wrenched the car to the side of the road. He slid over, reaching for her at the same time, and hauled her into his arms. "It's all right, love. It was a terrible thing. At least we can be thankful most of the women escaped unharmed." Instead of easing, her crying intensified. "Oh, damn..." He found the soft, silky skin of her nape and rubbed it gently, his cheek resting on top of her head. "Just cry it out, *mavourneen*."

With her nose buried in his throat, Kathleen sobbed out her pain and bewilderment and her anguish over the wasted lives of four women. "Oh, why did they have to d-die, Patrick?"

"I don't know the answer to that, love. No one does."

"One minute Meggy was alive and well, an innocent fifteen-year-old girl, and the next she was..."

"Gone, yes. It's mystifying, sweetheart. I watched Wade struggle to survive his stroke feeling the same things. I kept thinking how on Sunday morning he was fine. God, he was on the golf course with Rutledge just that day. Then only hours later he was a heartbeat away from death."

Sniffing, Kathleen wiped her cheeks with her fingers. "It's torture for me to see these things in my head and then watch helplessly when they come to pass. You don't know how I felt about those people on the *Irish Queen* and the women in the factory on Seventh Avenue. And now B-Bertha's niece." Her tears overflowed again.

"Ahh, don't, sweetheart, you'll make yourself sick." Patrick held her fast, his heart aching.

"Why, why does it have to be this way? I hate it! I hate having this...this...aberration. I can't bear it that I see these things and can't do anything, Patrick. It's cruel. It hurts so much."

Holding her, Patrick felt her pain as though it was his own. Though he had no more understanding of her mysterious gift than she, he revered it. "There must be a purpose for your gift, Kathleen."

"Gift?" She said the word in disgust. "It's no gift, it's a curse."

"Not a curse, *mavourneen*," he said gently, feeling his way. "I don't understand it, but I know it is not a cruel thing, certainly not an evil one."

Now that the storm had passed, she lay against him in silence. Her hands, which had clenched in his shirtfront, relaxed and, unconsciously, he thought, smoothed the soft cotton. "I had a lot of time to think after our baby died," she said suddenly in a husky voice. Patrick's heart stopped. Then, holding her fiercely, he waited to hear what she would tell him about their child.

She lifted her head and looked at him. "Why didn't I have a vision then about my own child? Where was my precious gift then? One day he was alive inside my body, and when my labor began, I had no premonition, nothing. I had no Dream Sight that night. I woke up to find that he was gone." In the dark interior of the car, the glitter of tears shone in her eyes, but she did not cry for their child. Long ago her tears for him had all been shed.

"I'm so sorry, sweetheart." He framed her face with his hands, his thumbs caressing her soft skin. "I should have been there. Can you ever forgive me?" Then, with his hand spread wide on her hair, he tucked her head against his heart, longing to say words that by all rights should stay locked away.

Holding her, touching her, was pain and pleasure. The scent of roses came from her hair. Patrick drew in a deep breath. He brushed tiny kisses on her temple, her cheeks, her eyes. It was delicious, sweet agony.

At the touch of his mouth on her eyes, Kathleen's lashes fluttered and closed. He was as gentle as rain and she was oh, so thirsty. She shuddered when his warm breath invaded her ear and sighed, a deep, trembling, homecoming sigh. Seduced by her own need, she turned her lips to meet his. It was a tender kiss at first, a gentle blending, a sweet exploration of taste and sensation, tentative and tear flavored. With her face held in his hands, Patrick opened his mouth on hers and Kathleen did the same, both savoring and prolonging the pleasure. Their tongues touched, lingered, withdrew.

Both drew back and simply stared at each other. Kathleen's lashes were wet from her tears, her lips parted and vulnerable. Patrick was a man torn. Neither moved a muscle as both fought the attraction that was like a living thing between them.

He was rumpled, he smelled of smoke and he needed a shave, but to her mind he was everything a man should be.

She was disheveled, bruised and trembling, her nose red from weeping, and yet she was, and always would be, his ideal woman.

Moving as one, they came together with hungry passion. As though a floodgate had been thrown wide, they tumbled headlong into a frenzy of loving. Mouths fused, they kissed with the fervor of star-crossed lovers. Whispers, murmurs, moans flowed freely as they kissed. Again and again. Desperation and guilt combined with fierce need.

Patrick ran his mouth down her throat, nosing aside her collar as he sought the soft, fragrant skin at the cleft of her breasts. Moaning, Kathleen clasped his head, pressed him against her eagerly, yearning for more and more and more. Gasping, Patrick shifted and fumbled to unbutton her bodice. Then he spread the folds wide apart and closed his hand around one breast, fanning the nipple with his thumb while he kissed the other.

Kathleen whimpered with the sensation. His mouth was warm. Every stroke of his tongue sent a thrill through her middle to the deep, secret, female core of her.

"Patrick, oh, Patrick..." She whirled on a sea of passion, shifting and arching and throbbing to his touch. What were the rules that governed every phase of her life compared to this delicious pleasure? This forbidden pleasure...

"Ohh!" Shoving at him, twisting and scrambling away, Kathleen drew herself into a tight ball against the door. "I can't... We can't do this, Patrick!"

"No, oh God, I didn't mean—" Squeezing his eyes shut, Patrick turned away, scrubbing his face with a shaking hand. He glanced back over his shoulder and winced when he saw Kathleen's misery. Her face was contorted with grief. Even as he cursed himself for a selfish, lustful bastard, his erection was steel hard and throbbing, an aching, compelling reminder of unfulfilled need. It was all he could do not to drag her back where she belonged, to crush her softness to his body, making them as close as two people could get.

He fumbled at the latch, swore when it didn't immediately release, then flung himself out to stumble along the shoulder of the road. At the rear of the car, he braced his arms against the cold metal, and with his head dropped, gulped air into his lungs.

"We can't go on this way, Patrick."

He hadn't heard her approach. He stared down at her, wondering whether she would ever let him come within a mile of her again. Knowing that if she wouldn't, it was no more than he deserved. "I know. I don't know how it... I never intended for this to happen when I drove you out here, Kathleen. You have to believe that."

"Oh, Patrick..." With a weary sigh, she leaned her head against him and he instantly wrapped his arm around her. "I know that." He made a clumsy attempt to smooth her tumbled hair and then bracketed her face in his hands.

"I can't stand the torture, Kathleen. I want you too much."

"I want you, too."

"It's wrong."

"Yes."

He removed his hands and stood looking beyond her down the stretch of dark, lonely road. "It will be hell, but I won't try to see you again. I thought we could be...friends, that I could still somehow take care of you." His soft laugh mocked the likelihood of that. "I was lying to myself, trying to find a way to have you in my life. There is no way."

With the same weary acceptance, she nodded.

"For myself, I don't care about what the rest of the world thinks, Kathleen, but it isn't fair to you."

"Or to your wife and child," she said softly.

He felt himself color with shame, and before he could say anything more, she turned and walked back to get into the car.

They drove back to Oglethorpe Square in silence. He drew up in front of the house she shared with Maxwell Rutledge, then, looking straight ahead, he asked, "Will you be all right now?"

Yes. She could manage without Patrick in her life. Hadn't she done exactly that for six years now? After a moment, as though she'd reached some kind of decision, she turned to him. "I have another vision sometimes," she said, her tone unemotional and flat. "Or perhaps it's only a dream ... I don't know."

"Tell me."

"It's about a baby."

"A baby?"

"It's night and there's a car on a winding road. A country road, I think, because I'm not aware of any other houses. Then the car comes to an iron fence with ornate, massive gates. There is scrollwork and maybe an initial. I'm never sure. ..."

"Who's in the car?"

"I'm not sure about that, either. Besides the driver, two people, I think. A man and a woman. But the baby is crying. It's horrible, because when I have this dream, I feel as though the baby is crying out to me, calling me in some way."

He watched her intently. "What happens?"

"Nothing much, really. The doors swing open and the car drives inside."

"And that's all?"

"I always wake up then. The sound of the gates closing wakes me."

He leaned back slowly, his eyes fixed on her. "You say you've had this dream more than once?"

"Many times." She rubbed a spot between her eyes. "It comes now and then with no rhyme nor reason. I don't know what it means. I suppose it's linked to my pregnancy. Maybe women whose babies ... don't survive ..." She swallowed hard. "Maybe it's understandable."

Patrick burned to touch her. He cleared his own throat of thickness and regret. "And you say it started ... when?"

She gazed at her fingers laced tight in her lap. "Right about the time I left the Drummonds'."

Right after the birth of their child. With his gaze fixed beyond her, Patrick turned her words over in his mind. A few minutes passed in silence. He was distracted by Kathleen's efforts to open the car door.

"I'll do that." He got out and went around to assist her out of the Packard, but she was already standing on the sidewalk. With her bag held close against her breasts, she looked up at him. In the moonlight, the sheen of her fair skin was like fire opals against black velvet. She was so beautiful to him that she stole his breath away.

"I don't know why I told you about that old dream," she said, shaking herself as though to dispel a chill. "I don't know why I even thought of it tonight."

He simply stood and stared. "You need to get inside," he told her when the moment had stretched too long. Turning her gently with a hand on her shoulder, he urged her through the wrought-iron gate. "It's turning cold and you've had more than enough to cope with for one day."

At the bottom of the steps, before he sent her inside and found himself banished from her life forever, Patrick caught her hand and brought it to his mouth. Closing his eyes, he savored the scent of roses mixed with Kathleen's own flavor.

"Kathleen, promise me that you'll be careful in the future." She stepped back, instantly defensive. "I don't mean that the way you think. You're going ahead with your series, I accept that. But Rutledge's security measures are right and necessary. Please don't take any more foolish chances."

With a sad smile, he touched her cheek. "I have no right to wring promises from you, I know that better than anyone, but I'll say this, anyway. Promise me you'll take care."

With a sigh, Kathleen nodded. "I'll be careful."

He bent a little at the knees so that he could see into her eyes. "Promise?"

"I promise, Patrick."

After a moment, he nodded just once. "Then I'll let you go. Good night, Kathleen."

Kathleen didn't wait to see him leave.

DEEP IN THE NIGHT, she woke up. Almost in a dream state, she pushed the covers aside and walked over to her small desk. In her long, white cotton gown, she was at one with other ghostly presences in the room. Sitting at the desk, she opened her journal. With her hair curling in wild disarray over her shoulders and down her back, she bent and began writing.

November 7, 1932
Tonight I dreamed the Baby Dream again. I know why. Today is his birthday. He would have been six years old.

CHAPTER TWELVE

INSTEAD OF GOING straight home, Patrick went to the hospital to see Wade. It was long past regular visiting hours and the hall was quiet and still as he made his way to the room. A nurse seated behind a glass-enclosed cubicle looked up as he passed, but she made no move to stop him. At the door to Wade's room, he met another nurse, who recognized him, and after a moment's hesitation, motioned him in.

"How is he?" he asked, keeping his voice low.

"Holding his own," the woman replied. "I've just taken his blood pressure and it's stable. All his vitals are fine. He even managed to swallow a bit of soup at suppertime."

"That's good, isn't it?"

"Very good for a man who has suffered a massive stroke."

As she bent to post something on the chart, Patrick moved close enough to look down into Wade's face. His color was better and he seemed to be breathing evenly. It was hard to watch a strong, vital man like Wade brought so low.

"I'd like to stay awhile if there's no objection," he said to the nurse, pulling a chair closer to Wade.

"I think it would be all right, Mr. O'Connor." She bent to straighten a loose corner of the bedsheet as she passed the foot of the bed. "Talk to him if you like. I've seen many of these stroke victims, and to my way of thinking, they recover better and faster when family members talk to them.

Just like the rest of us, they need to know they're still loved."

When she was gone, Patrick eased into the chair and sat for a few minutes. At length he sighed, massaging the bridge of his nose. The light in the room was turned off; the only illumination came from a small bedside lamp. He bent forward in the gloom, resting his elbows on his knees. He had never been so confused in his life. Why was he here?

Because the last place he wanted to be was in his own house. And the last person he wanted to see was his own wife. Not that he could be sure she would be there. But if she was, he didn't want to see her. He had never been unfaithful, but tonight he had come close. Too close. Only by the grace of God and Kathleen's sense of strong morality had he missed falling into the trap. And dishonoring Kathleen.

Oh, God, to be free to love her. To marry her.

"Pa...Pat...glad...see you."

He glanced up quickly and found Wade's faded brown eyes fixed on him. Reaching for the older man's hand, Patrick squeezed it reassuringly. "I'm glad to see you, too, Wade."

Although there was little use in his fingers, Wade blinked twice in an effort to convey a rueful apology. "So...rry, too m...uch trouble."

"Don't talk rubbish, man."

Wade managed a hint of a smile. Speaking seemed a monumental effort, and Patrick wondered if it could be good for him. He glanced around to locate the thing that signaled the nurse, but Wade blinked in agitation. "You don't want me to call the nurse?"

"No...nurse." He swallowed with difficulty. "What... hap...pened?"

"You had a stroke, my friend. You're in the hospital and doing so well that you're amazing them all. And that nurse you don't want me to call says you'll be up and asking for a steak before too long."

"Whop...per."

Patrick smiled. "Would I lie?"

Wade grunted. At length, he said, "Ca...Caroline?"

Patrick's smile did not falter. "She'll probably be here first thing tomorrow," he lied. After waiting around just long enough to know Wade would probably pull through, Caroline had avoided further visits to the hospital. Now that Wade had asked for her, even if Patrick had to rout her out of Duncan Wheeler's bed, he would see that she visited her father. He had tolerated her excuses to stay away from the hospital as long as Wade was unconscious, but now she would have to put in an appearance.

But Wade knew her too well. "Let...her...b...be, son."

"I'll bring Jessy, Wade."

"G...good." Another minute passed. "Com...pany okay?"

"Everything's under control, Wade. You can rest easy on that score."

"W...w..."

Patrick bent forward a little. "What, Wade? I can't make out..."

"W...will...new..."

Will? Someone's name? Patrick sorted quickly through his memory, but drew a blank. He glanced at Wade and found him struggling to form words.

"W...will!" He swallowed with difficulty. "Will... testa...ment."

Will and testament. Patrick scowled. "You don't need to talk about your will, because you're not going to need it, Wade. You're going to be on your feet in no time. The doctor says so."

"No...di...vorce."

God. Patrick dropped his head, his thoughts scattering like billiard balls. Around him, hospital sounds receded until they seemed to come through a tunnel—the faint clink of glass in the room next door, a patient's moan, the soft swish of skirts as a nurse hurried past.

"Wade—"

"Fam ... fam ... ly ... needs ... you. *Business* ... needs ... you."

He looked the old man in the eye. "I know my responsibilities, Wade."

"No ... divorce!"

Patrick stood up, turning away from Wade. "There won't be a divorce."

"Prom ... ise."

Somewhere down the hall a door closed and a bolt was rammed home as the hospital was secured for the night. Locked. He looked back at Wade. The old man was trembling, his eyes begging. "Please, Pat ... rick."

"Yes. I promise."

KATHLEEN VOWED that Meggy and the three other women who'd perished in the factory fire would not be forgotten. As in the tragedy she had seen in New York, death had come from smoke inhalation, not burns. Old, rickety fire escapes had given way when overloaded. When they collapsed, Meggy, who had allowed some of the older, slower women to descend ahead of her, had been stranded. By the time the firemen got to the third floor where she worked, she and the three other women were unconscious.

A stitch in time saves nine.

It would certainly have saved four. A sturdy fire escape was a good investment. Why hadn't the owners seen to it? What kind of people cared so little for the lives of their employees?

"Who are the owners? Did you unearth any names yet?"

Kathleen sighed and leaned back, tossing her pen on the desk. "It's a dead end so far, Max. There is a group of businessmen who own a stretch of real estate along the riverfront. The woolen mill was part of the holdings along with another textile mill, a lumber mill and a paper mill. Incidentally, did you know that the *Sentinel* buys its paper from that company?"

Max swore. "No! I'll look into it right away."

"No, not until I've flushed out the owners. I don't want to alert them. Once I have their names, I want to look into their personal fortunes." Her mouth twisted. "I'm betting they will all be very rich men."

"Rich men." Max gave her a look that stopped her. "And is that very bad?" he demanded in a softly chiding tone.

"To be a rich man? Of course not," she said. "So long as a man is fair-minded and decent at the same time. The men who make up this group have demonstrated that they have very little decency. Their employees, especially if they're women, are victimized."

"They operate legally under the system, Kathleen."

"Then the system must be changed."

Max sat on the edge of her desk. "It is changing, albeit slowly," he said, laying the latest issue of *Time* magazine in front of her. "*Time*'s Man of the Year is the labor activist in Washington, Herbert Johnson. He's been lobbying Congress about a minimum wage, among other labor reforms. He's finally managed it."

Kathleen glanced at the article. "How much is it?"

"A man can demand twelve dollars a week as a laborer. If he's paid any less, it's a violation of federal law."

Kathleen pushed the magazine aside cynically. "How about a woman? I'll bet the law doesn't apply if you're female."

He smiled, crossing his arms. "Then maybe it's up to women journalists to bring that to the attention of Washington."

She smiled ruefully. "You can bet I will just as soon as I expose these blackguards here in Savannah."

Max's smile faded. "You'll be careful, love?"

"Yes, Max. I'm no fool. One assault in a deserted warehouse is enough to teach me prudence." She sat up and pulled her work tablet back in front of her. "Besides, as you know, I am well guarded by Leo. I can't step out of this building without him."

She made a distressed sound. "I feel smothered, Max. I'll be glad when this series is done and I can resume a normal life."

"At least you've accepted the necessity for protection. My mind is relieved about that, I can tell you."

And Patrick's as well. She heard the thought as clearly as if Max had said the words. Although his name was never mentioned between them, she knew Patrick had collaborated with Max over this one aspect of her life. She had not seen Patrick since the night of the fire, and that was three weeks ago. He was honoring his promise. She was glad. Relieved. Lonely.

Max stood up and rubbed his hands together. "Here's an idea. Let's have dinner out tonight. We could try the country club. What do you say?"

"Yes, we'll do that." She didn't much care, but it was Lizzie and Leo's night to go to the cinema. Lizzie had mentioned it at breakfast, going on and on about Lily Pons's new picture show. The big house would be quiet without them. Too quiet.

She became aware that Max was watching her with concern. "Have you thought more about going back to New York?" he asked.

She rubbed her forehead. "Not really. I'm just not sure, Max."

He leaned closer, and with a finger beneath her chin, tipped her face up. "When you are ready, just say the word." His eyes searched hers. "Will you do that?"

She couldn't promise that. If she left Savannah and went anywhere, she would go alone. Her life was her own, her independence too important. To allow Max to take her away from Savannah and coddle and protect her was to put her destiny in his hands. Once before she had put her destiny in the hands of a man, and what a price she had paid for it.

No, she couldn't promise that.

"YOU'RE NOT GOING to leave Savannah ever, are you?"

Startled, Kathleen dropped her knife, and the clatter drew a number of curious looks from those dining in the country club's restrained atmosphere. "Why do you say that, Max? I told you this afternoon that I'm just not sure. I like Savannah even though..."

At her hesitation, he put down his own knife and fork and covered her hand. "Even though you're reminded of the other life you might have had when you think of Patrick O'Connor and his wife and child."

"Yes. Is that utterly insane, Max?" She studied him with a look of mystification.

Max picked up his knife and fork and took his time cutting into his steak before answering. "Where is it written that women have to be sane?"

"Max! That is such a typical male remark that I'm going to believe you meant it as a joke. Shame on you. What would Lily say?"

He sobered. "She would demand to know why I haven't offered you the job as editorial manager at the *Sentinel* before now."

"What?" Caught unaware, she simply looked at him.

"And I would have to admit to her that my reasons were selfish ones." He studied her untouched plate before looking almost apologetically into her eyes. "I knew if you took it, you would be committed to the job and to Savannah permanently and that...things would change."

"Max..."

"The truth is—" he smiled ruefully "—you're committed to your job and Savannah whether you have the position at the *Sentinel* or not. So..." He shrugged, a vulnerable, slightly sheepish movement that caught at her heart. "What do you think?"

She did love this man so much. And she owed him so much. She would have worked at the newspaper in any position he considered appropriate for her as long as it pleased him. Well, in any position within reason, said a tiny inner voice. Her smile began slowly and blossomed to a glow. Editorial manager. Freedom to choose issues. To provoke thought. To influence change. Oh, it was almost too much to take in all at once. She laughed.

Max leaned back, his gray eyes indulgent. "Hmm, that's better. I haven't heard the sound of your laughter enough lately." He picked up the wine bottle and held it poised near her glass. "So, shall I pour a celebratory toast?"

She picked up her glass. "Thank you, Max."

They drank the toast. If Max felt torn between pleasure for making her happy and fear that she had just taken another step away from him, he managed to hide it.

"Let's talk," she said, showing more enthusiasm than he'd seen since the night of the fire. "How is Edgar Jensen going to take this?"

The present manager was now indeed excess baggage. "What do you suggest?" Max asked.

"Reassign him to Financial. He's much more interested in the stock market than he is in social issues or current events. That's one reason there's been an increase in our readership since you arrived, Max. There's more verve and flair in the paper now."

"More controversy, you mean," Max said dryly. "And it's not me, it's you. But yes, Financial is where I thought Jensen would fit best. I'll tell him tomorrow."

"He wouldn't want to work for a woman, anyway," Kathleen said, glancing into Max's face just as he went still, looking beyond her at another table. "What? What is it, Max?"

Kathleen followed his gaze and her heart stopped. There, across the room, was Patrick. At the table with him were his wife and Jessy. She fought to bring the wild thumping of her heart under control. As she stared, he bent and whispered something to Jessy, who turned her small face up to his with a sweet smile. Such a perfect family picture they made. Her throat aching, Kathleen reached for her wineglass.

At that moment Patrick straightened and, still smiling faintly, glanced idly around the room. And then he saw her.

With her wineglass suspended halfway to her lips, Kathleen was trapped in the intense blue of his eyes. Around her the sounds of the restaurant ebbed and flowed—voices, the clink of china, the discordant kitchen noises—but she barely noticed. Her first thought was to run. Then Patrick nodded once, briefly, and she tore her gaze from his to find Max's gray eyes on her.

"Kathleen, we can go if you want."

Carefully, she set the wineglass down. "No, I can't run or swoon every time I see him, Max. It's cowardly." She touched her napkin to her mouth and then tucked it beneath the rim of her plate. "I think I'll visit the powder room."

He stood politely, wearing a stern look. "We can leave."

"No...no." Pushing away, she got to her feet and made her way through the maze of tables to the discreet doors at the back of the room and went inside. For a second, she felt like collapsing and giving way to a compelling urge to cry. But that would be incredibly stupid. And weak.

She went to the lavatory, laying her purse on the porcelain rim, then turned on the water. Savannah was not a large city, she reminded herself, watching the water run down the drain. From time to time, she was going to run into Patrick. It was to be expected. She would get over this insane craving to see him, to be with him. It would just take a little time. Already there were aspects of his life she found repugnant. He'd chosen wealth and power in his association with LelandFerguson over fairness and decency. She could not care for a man like that. Even though she'd turned to him so naturally the night Meggy had died in the fire. Even though it had felt so right to weep in his arms over the loss of their child. Even though... She would not care for a man like that. Then why this miserable feeling?

"Well, William Collins..." Soft and sarcastic, Caroline O'Connor's voice brought Kathleen to her senses quickly. "I do declare with all this murkiness about your identity, I wonder if you should be here in the ladies' powder room, honey?"

Taking a deep breath, Kathleen turned to face Patrick's wife. She nodded coolly. "Mrs. O'Connor. How are you?"

"Personally, I have nevah been bettah." Caroline brought a brimming cocktail to her mouth, her eyes crinkling from the smoke that curled up from a cigarette mounted in a jet holder. The dramatic bodice of her black gown revealed the full swell of her breasts. On any other woman, the dress would be scandalous, Kathleen thought.

Sipping gin, Caroline studied Kathleen over the rim of the cocktail. "If you'll pardon my sayin' so, honey, you look like you've been keepin' very late hours. That job of yours must be so...taxin'."

"Like any job, it requires some effort," Kathleen replied, irritated to find that the remark had stung.

"Well, as for a...job—" Caroline's lip curled "—I truly can't imagine such a thing."

"I know," Kathleen said dryly.

Caroline leaned close to the mirror, and with one long scarlet-tipped finger, meticulously removed a smudge at the corner of her mouth. "But then...Patrick takes such good care of me." Their eyes met in the mirror. "Aren't I the lucky one?"

Enough of this. Why was she standing here being tormented by this woman? Kathleen wondered, turning the water off. "I must get back," she said, and swept up her evening bag. No matter what, she could not speak the conventional phrases. Good to see you. Hope you enjoy your meal. Give my love to your family.

"My, my, what is that I see on your face, my deah?"

One step from escape, Kathleen paused and looked back. "I beg your pardon?"

Caroline laughed softly, a sly, feline jeer. "Envy, I do believe. Yes, that's it, all right. Envy." Her eyes glittered suddenly and all pretense fell away. "You do envy me my husband, don't you? You wish you had him, don't you? You, with your vulgar red hair and your even more vulgar newspaper job, do you honestly think you can compete with me for even a minute?" She made a contemptuous sound. "Just who do you think you are, you cheeky, jumped-up piece of Irish trash?"

"Mrs. O'Connor—"

"I'm not finished! Did he say he wanted a divorce?" With a superior smirk, she shook her head. "No? I thought not. Because he has some noble notion of holding our little family together. Is that what he told you? What a joke. He's so-o-o protective, Patrick is, lookin' out for his precious Jessygirl and my sick ol' daddy."

The woman's venom washed over Kathleen like acid. She breathed in defensively as Caroline came closer, glancing beyond Kathleen in a belated check for eavesdroppers. "Want to hear a secret, sweet li'l Kathleen? Jessy's not even his."

Her cruelty struck swiftly and painfully. *Oh, Patrick.*

"Shocked you with that, didn't I?" Caroline said with sly disgust. "Your heart's just been dyin' to love that sweet little innocent, hmm? Patrick's very own offspring?" She rolled her eyes, then her tone turned hard and cold. "Well, look all you want. But they're both mine, honey. Jessy and Patrick. Especially Patrick. Bought and paid for by my daddy, just for me."

Taking a draw from her cigarette, she studied the smoke lingering in the air between them. "It's sort of like the prize stallion in our stables, y'know? And that ol' hound Daddy paid a mint for the hunt. And my sweet li'l roadster, the Pierce Arrow? I think you get the picture. I wanted Patrick, so Daddy bought him." She looked straight into Kathleen's eyes. "And Patrick allowed himself to be bought."

Shouldering past Kathleen, she jerked the door open. Then, at the last second, she turned back. "Listen well, Irish slut. I keep what's mine and don't you forget it."

Kathleen's pale face and bloodless lips had Max starting from his chair before she waved him back into his seat. Sinking into a chair across from him, she tried to hide her trembling hands in the folds of the napkin. She would be sick if she looked at food.

Glancing back, Max saw O'Connor rising politely as Caroline O'Connor slipped into her chair. It took five seconds to surmise the source of Kathleen's distress. The two women had encountered each other in the powder room.

He rose without a word and put his hand beneath Kathleen's elbow, urging her to her feet. She was just dazed enough to allow it, and pulled the beaded shawl Lily had given her close against a bone-deep chill. It wasn't Caroline's words so much as the woman's personality that repelled Kathleen. How had Patrick chosen such a wife? The woman was evil. A shiver went through her and she moved closer to Max as they headed for the door.

They stepped out onto the sheltered portico of the building just as an ear-splitting boom of thunder split the sky. Max swore as the heavens opened in a torrential downpour. There would be little hope of getting to the car until the rain slackened.

With her teeth clenched, Kathleen closed her eyes and gave a soft, wry laugh as she felt Max's arm slip around her shoulders. "I'm all right, Max."

"I don't know what happened in there, but—"

"You wouldn't believe it." A streak of lightning lit up the whole world, and Kathleen moved closer, seeking more of his familiar strength and warmth. "Patrick's wife...I don't think I've ever met anyone quite like her."

"What did she say?" Another thunderous boom made him grimace and look up into the sky. "Maybe we'd better wait inside, love. It may be a while before this quits."

"No! We'll make a dash for it. I'd rather get a little wet than go back in there."

"Well..."

As the door opened behind them, they turned to look. Patrick, Caroline and Jessy stood backlit in the glow of the restaurant. For a second, Patrick hesitated, his features stern and unsmiling, looking directly into Kathleen's eyes. She wondered whether Caroline had mentioned their encounter in the powder room. Surely not. She could hardly repeat to Patrick what she had said. Or was theirs one of those modern marriages where each did as they pleased?

Jessy suddenly recognized her. "Miss Kathleen! Hi, Miss Kathleen!" Looking up at Patrick, her face shone in a happy smile. "Look, Daddy, it's Miss Kathleen." Breaking away, she ran over to Kathleen, who had frozen into place.

"I still have my Kewpie doll from the fair, Miss Kathleen. And my teddy bear, too. I sleep with him every night. Do you still have your teddy bear?"

Unable to resist, Kathleen touched the small, dark head and smiled at Jessy. Caroline shot a venomous look at Patrick, then drew in a deep breath as though controlling some violent impulse. Patrick's jaw might have been carved from granite.

"We were at the fair together, Mommy!" Jessy said, delighting in retelling the adventure. "We rode the Ferris wheel and got Kewpie dolls and cotton candy and a hot dog. Then the best thing, Daddy threw about a millyun baseballs and won two teddy bears for us. One for me and one for Miss Kathleen. It was fun!"

"And how about you, Mr. Rutledge?" Caroline asked icily. "Were you also with them havin' fun at the fair?"

"I'm afraid I missed it, Mrs. O'Connor."

"Hmm, let me see…" Looking at Patrick, she tapped her lips thoughtfully with a forefinger. "That would have been the last day of the fair, wouldn't it, sugah? You and Jessy begged and begged, but I had that prior commitment…"

She wrinkled her nose. "Oh, too bad. Seems I missed a very interestin' experience."

"Mommy, you didn't want to go, remember?"

She gave Jessy a hard look. "Don't talk when Mommy's talkin', sweetie."

"But—"

Patrick reached down and swung Jessy up into his arms. "Ready to make a dash for it, Cricket? You're not afraid of a little rain, are you?"

"No, Daddy." Her arms went trustingly around his neck. Watching, Kathleen felt an ache that went all the way to her soul. Then her eyes met Caroline's.

If looks could kill. The old adage leaped into her mind. Hatred burned in the woman's eyes. Without waiting for Max, Kathleen turned and stepped off the curb. Max's car was parked across the drive that wound up to the club entrance. The grass would be soaked and there was a small ditch between, but a drenching seemed little enough to pay to escape from Caroline's venom. With her shawl held over her head to shield her from the worst of the rain, Kathleen dashed out into it. Her flight had been so sudden that it was a moment before anyone at the curb reacted. With a curse, Max took a short step before noticing a parked car suddenly start up. As the onlookers watched in horror, the car accelerated to full throttle, then bore down directly on Kathleen as she ran, head down against the downpour.

Literally tossing Jessy to Max, Patrick leaped across the rain-drenched gutter in a desperate effort to reach her before it was too late. Unsuspecting, she had cleared a watery pothole and dashed a hand across her face just in time to see the front of a heavy, chrome-laden automobile rushing toward her.

"Kathle-e-e-en!" Patrick's cry was the embodiment of gut-deep fear.

As if caught in a time warp, Kathleen took in the sounds—the deadly swish of tires, the powerful roar of a straight-eight engine, a deafening crack and thunder—all seemingly happening in another world. And, finally, Patrick's anguished yell.

An instant before she was sideswiped by a ton of hurtling machinery, a strong arm closed hard around her waist and jerked her backward, then down into the mud and water. She cried out as her hip glanced painfully against the concrete curb. Cushioned beneath Patrick, she gasped as the speeding car passed so close that both were racked like debris in high wind. Then, with a mighty thrust of power, the car shot away into the night.

Heedless of the rain and the mud, Patrick cupped her chin, trying to see into her eyes. "Kathleen, my God, Kathleen..." His hand trembled violently.

"I'm...all right, Patrick. I...I think..." She shuddered suddenly, unable to manage any other words for the chattering of her teeth.

"Here, let me—" Shrugging out of his coat, he wrapped her in it, still on his knees. "Did it graze you?"

"No. No..."

His heart was booming in his chest. He felt such profound relief that he was dizzy. Closing his eyes, he waited for the world to settle. Only then was he able to run his hands over her limbs and shoulders and back and hips, into her beautiful hair and over her scalp to check for injury. He was only vaguely aware that Max had joined them.

"Is she...my God, tell me she's not—"

"She's all right, I think. Nothing's broken."

"I'm all right, Max," Kathleen said huskily, but her hip throbbed and burned where she'd struck the curb.

"We need to get her out of this storm." Patrick lifted her up into his arms, closing his eyes when her arms linked around his neck. He was filled with a fierce rush of love. "Where is your car?" he demanded, his features grim.

"Here. Over here." Hurrying, Max fished his keys out and with shaky hands managed to unlock it and swing the door open. "I have a blanket in the back. I'll get it."

Patrick settled Kathleen in the seat and, still unmindful of the rain, began smoothing her hair away from her face. "Do you hurt anywhere? I don't think anything's broken, but—" Closing his eyes, he swore again. "Kathleen, God, talk to me."

"Nothing's broken. The car missed me. I probably did most of the damage myself when I fell against the curb."

"Oh, God, I did that."

She touched his hand. "If you hadn't..."

Max reappeared. "Here's the blanket."

Patrick took it and tucked it snugly around her from neck to ankles before turning back to Max. "She's badly bruised. She needs to go directly to the hospital."

"Of course."

"I'd follow you, but—" For the first time, Patrick thought of his family. Through the rain, still falling in sheets, he could see a small group huddled at the club entrance, Caroline and Jessy among them. Even from here, he could tell that his wife stood stiff with disapproval.

"We don't need you," Max said brusquely. "You've done enough tonight."

"Max..." Kathleen spoke weakly, but in a tone that ended the exchange. "It was an accident."

"It was no accident," Patrick said.

Both Max and Kathleen looked at him. "That car was waiting on the edge of the macadam, engine running and no lights. When you broke free and darted in front of him, he grabbed his chance."

"Chance?" Shakily, Kathleen swallowed down rising hysteria. Holding on to the blanket with both hands, she asked, "To do what?"

"To silence you forever."

CHAPTER THIRTEEN

"WELL..." CAROLINE LIT a cigarette with a snick of her gold lighter and inhaled deeply. Taking her time, she watched Patrick closely through the veil of smoke. "I guess I know where Jessy and I stand now, don't I?"

After two stiff drinks, Patrick still had not managed to bring his emotions under control. The last thing he needed was a fight with Caroline.

Since he'd left the country club, his insides had been in turmoil. Rage and fear and sick relief warred with a landslide of unanswered questions. Who was trying to hurt Kathleen? Was it a warning or had it truly been a near-miss? Was someone trying to kill her outright? He shuddered and turned to kick at a log in the fireplace. What kind of people were they dealing with?

"Am I goin' to get an answer from you, Patrick? Or am I goin' to be ignored as I was most of the evenin'?"

He frowned, trying to recall her question. "You both stand exactly where you always have," he told her in an even tone. "You're my wife and Jessy is my daughter. My feelings haven't changed for either of you."

"Humph! I don't think I'll examine that remark, since I doubt your feelin's for me could hold up under close inspection."

"What do you want from me tonight, Caroline?"

She sauntered nearer until she was close enough to flick at the collar of his shirt. "Still damp, sugah. If you don't change, you might catch your death. Givin' your jacket to that poor creature that way.'' She sighed. ''Well, it was just too, too gentlemanly. Good thing I taught you to be a gentleman.''

''Considering how little you know about being a lady, it's amazing.''

Fire flashed in her eyes. Patrick had to be pushed mightily before he resorted to personal insults. ''You think you're so smart, don't you?''

''Tired, yes. Bored, yes. Smart? I wouldn't be trapped in this marriage if I was so smart, Caroline.''

''Oh, so now you want a divorce? Wait'll Daddy hears this.''

''Did I say anything about a divorce? You know as well as I what I've promised Wade.''

''And we can't renege on a promise made to a dyin' man, can we?''

''Wade is not dying. He's improving every day. If you'd go by the hospital once in a while, you'd know that.''

''Hospitals make me nervous. Sick people make me...'' She shuddered dramatically, drawing on her cigarette. ''Well, I just can't take it. Even for Daddy.''

''Then you should pray you never get sick yourself.''

She snatched the cigarette from her mouth. ''You'd love for me to get sick, wouldn't you? You'd love for me to die, wouldn't you? I'll bet you wished that was me tonight instead of your Irish slut nearly run down by that car. Well, how about this, Mr. Perfect Patrick? I wish that damn car *had* killed her. I wish she'd been hit square on. Good riddance to bad rubbish!''

''What is the point of this, Caroline? Why do you hate a woman you hardly even know? What has Kathleen Collins ever done to make you wish her dead?''

"She's tryin' to steal my husband, that's what! And she's tryin' to steal Jessy. Well, it won't work and I told her so. You should have seen her face when I told her—"

His eyes narrowed. "Told her what? When?"

She faced him defiantly. "Tonight, in the powder room. She's so pathetic. When I told her about Jessy, she—"

"You told her about Jessy?" He struggled to master an urge to shake her. "What about Jessy?"

"Oh, stop playin' games, Patrick. We've known each other too long. You know damn well Jessy isn't yours." She gave him a contemptuous look. "Do you honestly think I would have married someone like you if I hadn't been in a panic? Daddy made me do it, you fool!"

The fire crackled suddenly and the sound was like a gunshot. Patrick reached blindly for the mantel. "Jessy isn't my child?"

She propped a hand on her hips. "Did you think I was a virgin, for heaven's sake?"

No, he hadn't thought her a virgin. But he hadn't suspected she was pregnant, either. Blood and temper crescendoed in his head, making him dizzy. God, he was a fool. Ten times a fool. And Wade ... He'd known all along. That's why he ...

"He bought me."

"I don't believe I could have put it any better. In fact, that's exactly what I told your precious Kathleen." Her smirk faded abruptly when he turned and she saw the fierce look in his eyes. "My God, you didn't know, did you?"

He pushed past her, heading for the door.

"Where are you goin'?" she demanded shrilly. "I'm not finished talkin' about this, damn you! You made a fool of yourself tonight in front of all my friends when you went dashin' out in the rain like a crazy man to save that ... that woman! It looked peculiar, you riskin' everything like that while Jessy and me were left just standin' there stranded. Everybody could see you fawnin' all over a slut who's nothin' to us. Nothin', do you hear me?"

Grabbing a jacket from the coat tree in the foyer, Patrick didn't wait to put it on. With it bunched in his fist, he jerked the door open and had one foot over the threshold when Caroline stopped him with a clawlike hold on his shirtsleeve.

"Don't touch me, Caroline," he said in a dangerously soft tone. "Not tonight. Not ever."

Her grip eased as she stepped back sullenly. "Where... where are you goin'?"

"Not that it is any concern of yours, but I'm going to the hospital. Do you have any problem with that?"

"Daddy...Daddy isn't able to talk. He...I don't think you ought to say anythin' to him about this."

"What makes you think I'm going to see your father, Caroline?"

In two beats, her vulnerability vanished. "You're goin' to see that woman, aren't you?"

"What do you think? Maybe I've lived with you so long that I've picked up your habits."

"You bastard! You son of a bitch!" She drew back to strike him, but he caught her wrist. "I won't let you shame me by goin' to her. I'll have Daddy—"

"Shame you? Shame you?" His look was mockingly incredulous. "Who in hell do you think you are to mention shame to me? From the very first month of our marriage, you have been shameless. I don't owe you anything, Caroline. Do you hear me? I owe you nothing. In light of your revelation tonight, any debt I might have had is long since paid."

She gave a nervous laugh. "You're just bluffin'. You'll be back tomorrow, snugglin' all over Jessy and playin' the role of the wronged husband. I know you."

"No, you don't know me, Caroline. You never even bothered to try to know me."

"It's that woman! She's the cause of all this! She's cheap and easy and—"

In the middle of her tirade, he turned and left, slamming the door in her face.

Like a wounded animal, he headed to the hospital, driving with single-minded attention to the road. His head ached with rage and shock, but he dared not examine his thoughts, dared not think of Caroline's jeering confession. If he did, he wouldn't be responsible for what happened.

Kathleen. God, he wanted to see Kathleen. Tonight, when everything he'd built without her had been revealed for the sham it was, he burned to see Kathleen, but she wasn't his. He groaned. If he honored his promise to Wade, she would *never* be his.

Except in his heart. Staring at the rain-washed streets as he drove through the town of Savannah, he realized the truth. In his heart, Kathleen was his true wife. The vows they had exchanged before leaving Ireland bound them together forever. He was married to her as truly as though they had stood before a priest in the grandest cathedral in the land.

The hospital had long since been closed to visitors for the night, but he caught sight of the night nurse on Wade's ward and talked her into letting him in to see his father-in-law.

He slipped into the room and sat down on a chair at Wade's bedside. For a long time, he simply watched him sleep. Wade would probably be released soon. Leaning back, Patrick stared in misery at the ceiling. When it happened, he wasn't sure he, Patrick, would still be there.

The thoughts he had fought against churned in his mind. Jessy, his precious, sweet-faced Jessy, wasn't his child at all. She belonged to... Raking a hand over his face, he realized he hadn't even asked who had fathered Jessy.

He stood up, unable to sit still. In the gloom, with his back to Wade, he took stock. When Wade came along, it had seemed fated somehow. With his sights fixed on revenge, Patrick had made the most of the opportunity. Then he had married Caroline, but for the wrong reasons. He had known that at the time, but had told himself the end justified the means. How many individuals had embraced that flawed creed? Was that what this punishment was all about? Was he getting what he deserved? Had he taken the first wrong turn when Kathleen and the baby and their future together were taken from him? When revenge became his ruling passion? Had he lost his integrity when he lost his love?

No! His goal was good, worthy. And he was so close to realizing it. It had taken years, but a giant step forward had come when he was named to the board at LelandFerguson. He had already laid the groundwork with key board members. Tomorrow morning, he planned to leave for New York to meet with them. His suggestions meant radical change, and he needed the support of each man. He needed to know he could count on them all at the next quarterly. If he was successful, the men who had controlled the company for more than a dozen years would be ousted in one dramatic act.

Why was it that now, with the end finally in sight, he felt no triumph? No peace.

He had to see Kathleen. Rising and heading for the door, he told himself it was wrong, that he had no right. But just a few minutes to satisfy his craving, and then he would leave.

She was sleeping, her breathing deep and even. In the reflected moonlight from the window, her pale skin seemed even more translucent, contrasting dramatically with her fiery hair. With his heart beating hard, he looked his fill. She was so beautiful it stole his breath away.

From what he could see, there was a bruise and an ugly scrape on her arm, probably caused by the tumble into the curb. Her hip, he imagined, would be much worse. Closing his eyes, he reined in his rage with a few slow breaths. There would be time to seek out the one who'd done this and the ones who'd ordered it done. He would see to it. And there was one other task he was committed to for Kathleen's sake. He would take care of it when he went to New York.

Truth was like a searing brand in his chest. No one had hurt her as much as he had. He would have to live with that. Moving quietly, he took a seat in a chair in deep shadow to watch over her. Like Jessy, she no longer belonged to him, but in the deepest, darkest hours of that night, he pretended.

THROUGH A FOG-SHROUDED haze, she saw the boat. Pitching. Tossing. In trouble. The sea was a gray, turbulent beast with high-cresting waves slamming at the hull, washing over the decks with relentless, merciless force. From the disabled craft came the steady pulse of an SOS. It was an eerie, futile echo reaching far into the empty night. Panic filled her chest like a heavy hand crushing...smothering... At her side, her fingers twitched as she tried desperately to claw her way through the mist. She took a few sluggish steps, but more mist appeared, impeding her vision of the threatened vessel. Still she tried. She had to warn somebody. This time, she must tell...

"Patrick...Patrick..."

"I'm here, *mavourneen.*"

Oh, it was a dream. His deep, deep voice, the loving endearment. The reassurance of his touch. He couldn't be here, but she stubbornly clung to the fantasy. She needed to tell. Another tragedy. A boat this time. No, no. She had already dreamed that and Brigit had died. Licking her lips, she fought to open her eyes, but they were so heavy. Too heavy. Was she drugged? Yes, that was it. She had asked them not to, but they had insisted. Smiling, clucking, dismissing her pleas with Max's willing participation, they had insisted.

"Are you in pain, my darling?"

It was a dream, but a lovely one. To have Patrick near in the deep of the night. Seated in her room in the darkest corner watching over her. She didn't need to look. She knew it. At peace suddenly, she sighed and sank a little back into the mist-shrouded world.

Immediately the boat and angry sea materialized again. She tensed in renewed fear. "Patrick... don't go to sea again. Don't leave me."

"I won't ever leave you."

"There's a squall... the boat... It's in trouble."

"It's only a dream, love."

"Don't go to sea, Patrick. Promise me."

"I promise."

IT WASN'T A DREAM. Well, some of it wasn't. Patrick, of course, that was a dream. Wishful thinking. Staring out of the hospital window waiting for Lizzie, Kathleen frowned over the strangeness of it. He couldn't have spent the night beside her in this room, but the rest of it wasn't a dream. It was another visitation. A boat of some kind would be caught in a squall and there would be another tragedy. She knew it, but as usual, she didn't know enough.

She was struggling with frustration when someone tapped softly at her door. She turned. "Did you bring me a change of clothes, Lizzie?"

Lizzie held up a lacy cotton gown. "And what do you think this is? Your hairbrush and other personal things are all in here. Bertha supervised the packing, thinking she could do it better. If you don't like hospital food, just let her know and she'll fix whatever you want. And don't get too close to the other patients. You never know what they might have."

Kathleen smiled. "She's worried about me." Swinging her legs over the side of the bed, she braced against the sharp pain in her thigh and slowly managed to sit up.

"We're all worried."

Drawing in a deep breath, Kathleen stood up and waited for the whirling room to settle. Bracing a hand on the bed, she gritted her teeth at the pain in her hip. After a minute, she decided she could manage. "I don't want a gown, Lizzie. Did you bring any street clothes?"

With a cake of soap in one hand and house slippers in the other, Lizzie straightened and looked at her. "Whatever for? You're never telling me you think you're leaving this place, Kathleen."

"Then I won't tell you, but I need a dress." She went over to the opened case and began searching through it.

Lizzie opened her mouth to argue, but Kathleen forestalled her. "There's something I must do, Lizzie. I had a dream vision last night."

To the bottom of her Irish soul, Lizzie believed in Kathleen's clairvoyance. Although they never spoke of it, she accepted the wonder of it without question. She hesitated at the unpacking, clearly torn.

"Is Leo waiting?"

"To drive me home, not you," Lizzie snapped, her uncertainty making her short-tempered. "There's a policeman stationed in the hall to look after you."

"A policeman? Whatever for?"

"To keep somebody from finishing the job they started last night at the club, what do you think? Max demanded it, not that it took much pressure. Too many witnesses saw the whole thing."

Kathleen stood thinking in the middle of the room, one finger tapping her lips. "We need to get rid of him."

Lizzie crossed her arms and assumed a mulish look. "It would mean my job and Leo's, too, if anything happened to you, Kathleen. Max would not hesitate. Don't ask me to help you do something foolish. If you're determined to leave the hospital, then the only place I'm helping you get to is home to the house at Oglethorpe Square."

"Lizzie, you have to help me."

"Help you leave? I don't have to do any such thing. Now, if you would care to tell me what it is that's so important it's worth risking life and limb for, I might be persuaded to think up a way to help."

She fixed Kathleen with a challenging look.

"All right, then." With a wince, Kathleen sat on the side of the bed hoping to relieve the throbbing in her thigh. "Will you take a message to Patrick for me?"

"Patrick O'Connor?" Lizzie frowned her disapproval.

"Yes. I'll write a note, but I want it put in Patrick's hands, no one else's." She gave Lizzie a pleading look. "I know you don't approve, Lizzie, but it's important. It's a matter of life and death."

"You saw Patrick O'Connor in this dream?"

"No, I saw a ship caught in a squall. Or a yacht, maybe. I couldn't tell. Only one thing was certain—I felt danger and death, Lizzie."

"What does this have to do with Mr. O'Connor?"

"I don't know." She bent her head and rubbed her eyes wearily. "I just sensed the danger was linked to Patrick somehow."

Lizzie studied her at length. "It's odd that you never sense danger to yourself. This makes twice in the past few weeks that you've been hurt."

"I can't explain it, either." She looked up at Lizzie. "But that has nothing to do with here and now. The last time I had a message, I did nothing and Meggy died. Patrick runs a shipyard. I don't want him—I mean, I feel compelled to warn him. I can't go to his home, but you can. Please do this for me, Lizzie."

"If I do, will you get back in bed until the doctor says you can get up?"

Kathleen smiled weakly. "No, but I'll go home and rest until you and Max and Leo and Bertha say I'm fit again."

Lizzie began methodically repacking. "I suppose we can chain you to the bedpost if it comes to that."

"Thank you, Lizzie."

PATRICK WAS PACKED and ready to leave for the train station when he was told that Lizzie Stern was waiting downstairs to see him. Thinking instantly of Kathleen, he snatched up his coat and shouldered past the startled maid. Lizzie would never seek him out unless something was wrong with Kathleen.

God, he thought he'd taken care of it. To make sure, he had been at Maxwell Rutledge's door at the first hint of dawn, and he and the older man had discussed Kathleen's accident. The two had traded ideas, but the main thing they'd agreed on had been that Kathleen would have police protection until the situation was resolved. Hopefully his trip to New York would speed that up. Among other things.

So why was Lizzie here? If Kathleen had slipped away from that kind of security, he would have somebody's hide.

"Lizzie—"

"Hello, Patrick O'Connor. Kathleen sent me."

He looked at her, fighting the onslaught of panic, too fearful even to ask the question.

"She's safe, Patrick," Lizzie told him, watching as stark relief spread over his features. "She left the hospital. No, don't worry. Leo drove her home and there is a policeman wearing a furrow in the sidewalk in front of the house. Here, she sent this note to you."

Patrick took the envelope, ripping into it with hands that shook. Blinking a second to focus on the familiar scrawl, he read.

Patrick,
If you really meant it when you called my Dream Sight a gift rather than a curse, then please do not board a ship to travel by sea. Promise me.

Kathleen

He bent his head, thinking of the long night by Kathleen's bedside and what he'd imagined was a nightmare. It had been her clairvoyance. He looked at Lizzie. "She knew I was planning a trip?"

Lizzie frowned. "Are you?"

"Yes, I was just on my way to New York. Another thirty minutes and you would have missed me."

"You're never taking a boat, are you, Patrick?"

"No, the train." He pulled his watch from his pocket. "In fact, I need to hurry if I don't want to miss it."

"I'll need to tell Kathleen something," she reminded him, glancing pointedly at the note he'd refolded and was tucking into the inside pocket of his jacket. "She wants your promise, Patrick O'Connor."

"Tell her I promise I will not get on a boat of any kind." He glanced beyond her through the glass side panels of the front door. "Did Leo drive you?"

"And how else would I be here? I haven't mastered the art of driving the motorcar yet, nor do I intend to."

"Of course," he said, wondering at the fast friendship between two women as different as Lizzie and Kathleen. "I don't suppose I could catch a ride with you to the train station, could I? There's something I'd like to ask you, Lizzie."

She studied him silently. "Since we'll be passing right by the station on our way," she said slowly, "I think Leo could be persuaded to make a stop."

Patrick grinned. "I'll get my bag."

The drive to the train station from the big country house took twenty minutes. From the back seat, Patrick had a good view of the grim outline of Leo Stern's jaw. Did everyone in Kathleen's life despise him? he wondered miserably. It made the question he needed to ask Lizzie doubly difficult.

"So, Patrick O'Connor, what is the question you're so determined to ask?" Lizzie said suddenly as though picking up his thoughts.

He took a deep breath, hoping that this woman would see that his interest in Kathleen came from the heart. "Kathleen told me you were the first person she met at the Drummond mansion when she recovered after the shipwreck," he said.

"That's true."

"And you shared a room with her while you both worked there."

"Also true."

"Her pregnancy..." He cleared his throat, looking through the window at the dull, colorless November countryside. "I mean, not her pregnancy, but her labor. When she... When it was time for the..."

"I was there then, too," Lizzie said, as though taking pity on him.

He looked at her, needing to see her eyes, but she was facing straight ahead. "Lizzie, this is important."

She turned then, so that she could see him. "What is it you need to know about that black day, Patrick O'Connor? The baby is gone, and Kathleen has managed to bury her pain in a dark corner of her soul. So why must you drag it all up? The time for that was then. Where were you then, Patrick O'Connor?"

"I was in a dark, hopeless state myself, Lizzie. I thought Kathleen was drowned and I didn't particularly care about anything beyond that. But for my own peace of mind, I need to know these things. Did you actually see the baby when he was born?"

She frowned. "No, didn't Kathleen tell you? They sent me away at the last."

"I haven't talked to Kathleen about this. I don't want to hurt her any more. Why did they send you away? Was there a problem?"

Lizzie's gaze seemed to go hazy, as though focusing on the scene again. "Well, the baby presented in the breech position, but as the hours wore on—she was in labor two-and-a-half days—the midwife managed to turn him."

"Midwife? Do you think you can recall her name?"

"Muldoon, it was. Madge Muldoon. You know, I've often thought about this, Patrick. Kathleen's labor was hard, but then my own ma had given birth eight times, a few times with complications. I didn't sense that there was any real danger, just that the little one was stubborn and taking his time.''

"But they asked you to leave toward the last?"

"Yes. They insisted on drugging her and I said they shouldn't. Mrs. Parsons—the housekeeper, you know—didn't like any back talk from the staff, I can tell you. Then when it was over, they said the baby had died.''

"Then how did you know he was dark haired?" *That he looked like me?* As he had a thousand times, Patrick imagined the look of the son created in love with Kathleen, and it was like a shard of glass in his chest.

"I was told because I asked. They'd already taken him away when I was called back into the room to stay with Kathleen until she was herself again. She slept around the clock, so I didn't ever get to see the baby.''

"Was he buried?"

She bent her head for a moment before looking at him sadly. "Patrick, you don't want to know any more. Don't ask.''

"Was . . . he . . . buried?"

"I don't think so." When his eyes turned fierce, she added hurriedly. "Kathleen was a contract laborer with no money for a burial, and besides, she was unconscious and friendless except for me.''

"What are you saying?"

"I don't know. We, Kathleen and me, were never told what they did.''

When they dropped Patrick at the train station, Lizzie watched him shoulder his way through the milling crowd, her face thoughtful. He had planted the seed of an incredible possibility. She couldn't quite believe that she didn't dismiss it instantly. But it could be. It could be. She had had her own thoughts about that night, but... It was so long ago.

As in a dream, she heard the conductor's call to board. To perpetrate such a cruel deed—to steal a woman's baby! Why, even for the Parsons, it was beyond belief. And yet... all the pieces fit.

She watched Patrick swing up onto the boarding step of the train. Her first impression of him still held true. He didn't seem like a man who would shunt aside his responsibilities. With a burst of steam and a long, low whistle, the train began to pull away from the Savannah depot. Through the window, she saw Patrick find his seat and then look out. Grave faced, he saluted her, and she nodded in return. Then she finally settled back, content to leave everything in his hands.

CHAPTER FOURTEEN

ON THE SAME DAY that Patrick left for New York, a package was delivered to Max by special courier. When he opened it and read the list of names, he leaned back in his chair, deeply shocked. It wasn't often his judgment of a man's character went awry. He was angry, not only at fate and a consortium of rogues, but at Patrick O'Connor.

Especially Patrick O'Connor. They had talked just that morning in Max's office. Before he left, he had extracted a promise from Max to tighten the security around Kathleen. He had seemed genuinely concerned about her. In fact, he had looked like a man who was close to the edge. He had appeared strained and red eyed, as though he hadn't slept much. He hadn't said so directly, but Max felt that Patrick knew more than he was ready to reveal about who might be behind the assaults on Kathleen. Now that he had the list in his hand and Patrick's name was on it, Max didn't know what to think. His protective behavior seemed odd if he was mixed up with this investor group.

As he got up and shrugged into his coat, he wondered if there was any way he could keep the list from Kathleen or possibly give her all the names except Patrick's, at least until the man had a chance to explain. If he *could* explain. But no, Kathleen was too good a journalist, too professional to be coddled. Right this minute, instead of resting and taking some time off after coming dangerously close to dying, she was probably working at home on the series. There had never been a chance that she could be talked out of seeing it through to the end. She had come this far. He didn't have the right to withhold from her the missing link.

Just as Max expected, she was on the patio, diligently scribbling in her notebook. "Here, you'll probably find this interesting, Kathleen."

Something in Max's tone brought her head up sharply. "About the investment group?" Since she had promised to stay indoors a day or two, Max had agreed to take her notes and research and see if he had more luck than she in finding names. From the look on his face, he'd found something. She never failed to get a thrill when the pieces of a story began to come together. She lay aside her notebook and took the sheaf of papers from him.

Glancing at it, she said, "I was just working on the series, Max. It's pretty strong. I've linked the group to the woolen mill that burned as well as a couple of sweatshops in the Mill Street district. Everyone knows they employ underage females to do cutwork, but with the economy in dire straits, people have turned a blind eye." She looked up excitedly. "But this is more far-reaching than Savannah. This group also owns textile mills in North Carolina. This is what I think they're doing—they manufacture textiles at their own mills, ship it to Savannah, then use near-slave labor to cut and finish. Savannah is a perfect distribution center. From here, they can ship anywhere in the U.S., or the world, for that matter, and their overhead is cheap. All nice and tidy, but undoubtedly illegal."

"Very clever," he murmured dryly.

"Unless, of course, you're a teenage girl like Meggy. Those girls are being taken advantage of, Max. I'm determined to expose the people responsible."

Max sighed. "Kathleen, take a look at those papers."

She focused on the print again even though her thoughts were still on the content of her series. "I don't care who these men are, Max, they shouldn't be allowed to victimize their workers. Actually, I'm not sure which laws they're violating. I still need to do some re...search..." Frowning, she reread a line, then, concentrating fiercely on the print, began to read rapidly.

Beside her, Max wore a grim look as he watched her reaction to the list. After another minute, she finished and closed her eyes briefly, then straightened the papers neatly and tucked them into the folder with the rest of the material she'd collected for the series.

"How did you get this, Max?"

"I called in a few markers."

"So it's solid?"

"I've no reason to doubt it, Kathleen."

"I suppose I shouldn't be shocked," she said, looking beyond Max to the big magnolia tree. "But Patrick!" Her eyes filled with tears.

"I was shocked, too," he said. "And puzzled. I can't see O'Connor being party to any group terrorizing a woman. Until I saw his name on that list, I was convinced the man was honorable."

He was! He is! How else could I have loved him so? How else could I still care so much? "Besides Patrick, do you know any of the others?" she asked quietly.

"A couple of men on the Leland board back in New York, and one of Wade Ferguson's right-hand men here at the shipyard, Ben Sculley." He shrugged. "The rest are solid citizens in Savannah."

"Solid citizens!" She flung the papers aside in disgust and rose from her chair. Still stiff and sore, she couldn't walk off her disappointment and pain, but she couldn't sit still either. "They won't be when I get through with them."

"Kathleen..." Max cautioned. "Twice now these people have tried to hurt you. Be careful."

She looked at him. "Not Patrick," she whispered bleakly. "You don't think he—"

"No, I don't," Max said firmly. "In fact..."

"What is it?"

"I get very uncomfortable when facts just don't square, Kathleen. My instincts as a newsman tell me that we haven't sniffed out everything that's going on here. And somehow Patrick O'Connor is involved. Things may not necessarily be the way they appear."

"In what way? What things?"

"If I could answer that, Kathleen, I wouldn't be feeling uncomfortable, now, would I?"

She pulled the incriminating documents from the folder and scanned them again. Then, with an impatient sound, she looked at Max. "Oh, nothing you're saying makes any sense, Max." She shook the papers at him. "This does. The names are here in black and white. It's the information I was waiting for. I'm going ahead. The first column will be ready a week from Sunday."

"O'Connor's in New York," Max told her. "He left this morning. Don't you want to wait and hear what he has to say?"

Kathleen rubbed at her throbbing hipbone. She did want to give him a chance to explain, though it was a chance he probably didn't deserve if he was in business with the investors' group. That made him as bad as they were. He would be ruined. Unless... What was she doing! She shouldn't be rationalizing like this. She was a journalist and facts were facts. Why did she care if Patrick's name was tarnished along with all the rest when the story broke?

Max walked to her and put an arm around her shoulders. "I think we should reserve judgment until he can defend himself, Kathleen. A week from Sunday, you said. That's ten days. A lot can happen between now and then.''

PATRICK HAD A DEMANDING schedule of appointments in New York. Forcing his conversation with Lizzie out of his mind, he made his contacts at Leland, carefully picking and choosing which individuals on the board would be most open to change, and spent several days generally advancing his plan for LelandFerguson. He would need the support of several key men at the upcoming quarterly meeting, which he had persuaded them to hold in Savannah. A couple of the board members had already bought summer homes off the Georgia coast on Jekyll Island. The others agreed readily to the change.

But for the first time since he had set his sights on bringing Leland down, he was distracted from his goal. He felt edgy and impatient to get on with more important personal business. Finally, on the afternoon of his third day in New York, he made it to the Drummond mansion.

Edward Drummond was clearly puzzled by his visit. After Patrick had declined brandy and a cigar, Drummond leaned back with his hands resting on his considerable girth and studied him through a cloud of smoke. "You say you're a friend of Maxwell Rutledge?"

Patrick had decided against using Kathleen's name before getting in to see Drummond. Bitterly he guessed nobody in the mansion would enjoy being reminded of the pretty, pregnant, unmarried Irish girl or the circumstances that had driven her into Rutledge's protection.

"Yes," he said. "Max mentioned that you might be able to help me out with a problem."

"A problem?" Drummond removed his cigar.

"A problem. Do you still employ Amelia Parsons as your housekeeper?"

"Mrs. Parsons? Of course, but I don't see—"

"And Herbert Parsons. Is he still driving for you?"

"Well, yes, but..." He took a puff of his cigar. "I've been a bit disappointed in Herbert, don't you know? He seemed very promising a few years back as my garage man. Then it appears things grew rather more than he could manage without— I say, this is very unusual. What interest could you possibly have in my domestic staff, Mr. O'Connor?"

Patrick looked him in the eye. "Bear with me, Mr. Drummond. Please. For personal reasons, I'd appreciate having a chat with both of them. Do you think that would be possible?"

"Well..."

"Max felt sure you'd cooperate."

"Well, of course, of course. To oblige Rutledge. In Georgia now, isn't he?"

"Savannah."

"Your area, too, I take it."

"Yes, I'm with LelandFerguson there."

"Patrick O'Connor. It's coming to me now. Been named recently to their board of directors, isn't that right?"

"It is. About the Parsons..."

"Yes, yes, I'll just call them in." Rising, he went to the door of his study.

The Parsons, mother and son, were about what Patrick expected. They sidled into Drummond's office, clearly as puzzled as their employer at being summoned by a stranger. Black emotion rose in Patrick just looking at them. The grievous wrongs done to Kathleen by these two people defied human understanding. He barely managed to sound civil as he greeted them.

The moment she heard his name, Amelia Parsons's manner became tinged with caution.

"A friend of mine once worked here under your supervision, Mrs. Parsons," he said, getting right to the point. Glancing at Herbert, he added, "Both of you probably remember Kathleen Collins."

Kathleen's name froze them both. "I see that you do remember," he said dryly.

"That was a long time ago," Mrs. Parsons said. "Over six years."

Herbert spoke up suddenly. "She didn't know a good thing when she had it. She quit without notice, just left without a by your leave, didn't she, Ma? Over a year left on her labor contract, too."

"Herbert—"

With a rush of fury, Patrick interrupted. "Why exactly did she leave, Parsons?" he asked in a dangerously soft tone.

Drummond gave him a startled look. "I hadn't anticipated anything quite like this when you asked to see my staff, Mr. O'Connor. Perhaps we should talk privately first."

And take a chance that Parsons and his mother might disappear? Patrick shook his head. "I'll bet there is a lot about your staff that you haven't anticipated, Mr. Drummond."

"That may be," Drummond said quietly, "but I do know about Kathleen Collins. To my regret, she was treated unfairly here, and without my knowledge, I might add. But I know it to be a fact that she was happy and well-treated once Max and Lily Rutledge took her in."

Patrick grunted, reluctant to grant Drummond any credit. "I'm here about things that happened to Kathleen before she sought refuge with Max," he said, his eyes on Herbert Parsons. The man was sickly pale and fidgeting. It pleased Patrick that a simple inquiry about Kathleen's abrupt departure from the mansion disturbed him. Both mother and son were cold-blooded, evil criminals, and Patrick was going to enjoy exposing them.

"In fact," he said, deliberately focusing on Herbert Parsons, "I came here to ask some questions about Kathleen's baby."

"Baby?" Drummond was clearly dumbfounded.

"This is ridiculous!" Amelia Parsons stood up.

"What's her bastard got to do with anything?" Herbert Parsons demanded. "She was nothing but a tart and—"

He yelped as Patrick lunged from his chair and grabbed a fistful of his shirt. "Watch your mouth, you spineless sap! I don't ever want you to even speak Kathleen's name again. Do you hear me?" Shaking him like a dirty rag, he slammed him back into the chair with enough force to stun him.

"Here now!" Drummond was on his feet.

Patrick took a turn around the room, rubbing the back of his neck while he forced himself to calm down. He was not finished yet. He wouldn't get anything out of the SOB if he scared the hell out of him. "I've talked to Madge Muldoon," Patrick said shortly. He saw Amelia Parsons put a hand to her heart. Good, he thought. She was rattled, too.

She began, "I don't know any—"

"Don't lie!" Patrick stalked across Drummond's study to the window, not trusting himself to stand too close to either one of them. They were scum. *Scum!* What made people sink so low?

"I know Kathleen's baby was not stillborn," he said through his teeth. "Madge admitted everything. However, she didn't know the name of the family you sold the baby to."

Edward Drummond made a shocked sound. "This is preposterous!" he sputtered. "Herbert, Mrs. Parsons, tell this man that we don't engage in such scurrilous goings-on in my household. Really, Mr. O'Connor. Max Rutledge notwithstanding, I can't allow you to—"

"I apologize for being the bearer of such news, Drummond." He looked at Amelia Parsons. "Would you like me to dig further into your closet for a few more skeletons, Mrs. Parsons? Or are you prepared to give me the name of the family who bought my child?"

"Your child?"

"Yes, my child. Kathleen was my fiancé." He flicked a disgusted glance at Herbert. "Your son recognized my name immediately, didn't you, Herbert? You made certain Kathleen would have nobody to turn to when she was finally able to check the rolls of the Leland Company looking for me. She was beautiful and young and smart and without friends. You wanted her." Patrick's chest swelled with anger and his own remorse. "But you didn't want her baby."

"Mrs. Parsons...Herbert..." Drummond looked from one to the other, scowling. "Is this true?"

"Think carefully," Patrick said quickly. "Before you deny everything, you should know that Madge keeps surprisingly good records of all births she attends. My son's birth—a live birth—was duly recorded on November 7, 1927. Incredibly, my name is on the certificate because, during her long labor, Kathleen called for me." He mastered the thickness in his throat after a second and went on. "Madge cared nothing about what you did with the baby after she delivered it, but she's a canny old crone and she knows how to look out for herself."

"I repeat," Drummond insisted. "Is this true?"

"All I want is a name," Patrick said. "I don't intend to have the two of you arrested, even though Kathleen and I have every right." He glanced at Drummond. "I'll leave it to you to discipline these two in your own fashion, provided I get what I need. Push me and your own negligence could come to light along with everything else. All I want is a name and I will walk out of here."

"I...I...don't know what to say," Drummond blustered.

"Rutherford," Amelia Parsons muttered.

Patrick's heart leaped. "A full name, if you please, and an address."

She ignored the squawk that came from Herbert. "The Charles I. Rutherfords. They live on Long Island."

Without a word, Patrick turned on his heel and left.

IT TOOK ONLY HALF A DAY to locate the Rutherfords. But he had to wait almost two days to catch a glimpse of the boy. As in Kathleen's dream, tall wrought-iron gates protected the privacy of the mansion. A large, nearly impregnable prison. In the hours he waited to see his son, Patrick worked out a plan.

In the end, it was surprisingly easy.

There was a governess. She was a kind-faced woman who held the hand of the dark-haired boy from the moment they got out of the long, black, chauffeur-driven Cadillac until they were safely in the confines of a park about two miles from the Rutherford estate.

Charles Rutherford and his wife were deceased, Patrick had learned. Both had died in Africa a year earlier from cholera when on safari. They'd been exposed along with a party of British friends. Deep in the wilds, only two of six had survived. Ironically, Patrick remembered reading about it.

Survived by their five-year-old son, Cameron.

No, not their son. My son. Kathleen's son. Our stolen baby. God, dear God.

Closing the car door with a slam, Patrick crossed the road that wound through the park and took a seat on the same bench as the governess. Looking up from her knitting, the woman smiled politely when he gave her a nod. Not too friendly, but not too distant, he reminded himself. With the chauffeur not fifty feet away, she had no reason to feel uneasy. Patrick shook out his newspaper and pretended to read.

A minute passed.

"Doby, Doby, watch me!"

Patrick tilted the corner of the newspaper and watched his son swing wildly with a sized-down baseball bat.

"Yes, you're very good, Cam," the governess said, smiling. "But mind you don't dirty the knees of those knickers."

"I'm going to play for the Yankees someday!"

Patrick chuckled, praying that it sounded natural. "We might have the next Babe Ruth there," he said to "Doby."

The woman seemed willing to chat. "Oh, today it's baseball, tomorrow he'll be a fireman, the next day a policeman. I've never known a child with such zest for living."

"His parents must be very proud of him."

"Now, that is one of life's sad misfortunes," she said, shaking her head. "The sweet lad is an orphan. Both parents gone overnight in a foreign land. One of those safari hunts, it was. Poof! An exotic disease takes them both to heaven."

"Very sad," Patrick murmured, thanking God for the governess's chatty, unsuspecting nature. With the Lindbergh kidnapping in all the papers, he would have understood if she'd bundled the boy back into the limousine and hightailed it.

"Unlucky, that's what it was. And the boy with no other living relatives. He's a ward of his great-uncle now."

"Doby!" Cameron called impatiently. "Come pitch me a few balls. I need help."

Patrick folded his paper and set it aside. "I'll pitch a few for him." He gave her a friendly look. "That is, with your permission."

"Oh, he'll love it. He doesn't have the company of grown men enough. Cam!" she called. "This gentleman is going to play with you." Out in the field, Cameron's exuberance faded to shy caution as he watched the tall stranger coming toward him. Patrick walked slowly, his heart thrumming, thinking of Kathleen and love and loss. Up close, father and son studied each other curiously.

He was tall for a six-year-old, Patrick thought proudly, and straight and strong as a sapling. His hair, as dark as Patrick's own, hiked up at the crown in a cowlick, and he had a sprinkle of freckles across his nose. Mastering his shyness, the boy looked up at Patrick with eyes of clear green. As green as Kathleen's. As green as Ireland.

Swallowing the tightness in his throat, Patrick put out his hand. Cameron grinned and trustingly stuck out his own.

"Hello, I'm Cameron."

Patrick felt a jolt that went all the way to his soul. "Hello, Cameron."

WITHIN AN HOUR of leaving his son, Patrick had booked a ticket on a night train back to Savannah. His first order of business once he got home would be a visit to his lawyer. With the Rutherfords out of the picture, and armed with a copy of Cameron's birth certificate, he hoped to build a case in which a court would be sympathetic to Kathleen's claim for their son.

As the train hurtled through the night, he tried to think, to come to terms with the upheaval in his life. Until he had spoken with the lawyer, he was uncertain about telling Kathleen anything. Still, he was bursting with the news. It would be all he could do when the train finally pulled in not to rush straight to the house on Oglethorpe Square to tell Kathleen that their son was alive and well and bright and beautiful.

But that would have to wait. Mixed with his elation at having found Cameron was the pain of discovering Jessy did not belong to him. Caroline's betrayal had left him feeling nothing for her except a deep, abiding bitterness. He probably should despise Wade, too, but he'd been motivated by a father's concern. In Savannah, a woman pregnant out of wedlock would be ruined, even a woman who moved in the Fergusons' social circle. Wade must have been desperate to spare her that. Unlucky Kathleen for having nobody to come to her defense as Wade had for Caroline.

And Jessy. For the first time since he learned the truth, Patrick looked at his feelings for Jessy. He pictured her big, dark eyes and small pixie face, so solemn so much of the time, and felt a melting tenderness. No matter what Caroline had done, he realized, watching the dark eastern coast flash by, no matter who had truly fathered Jessy, she would always be his little girl. With that thought, a measure of peace came to him finally. Jessy was his and he loved her. When the train pulled into Savannah, his heart was lighter than it had been in days.

His spirits sagged somewhat as his taxi came up the lane leading to the big house Wade had built to Caroline's specifications. He never felt particularly good coming back here, he realized with a frown. He had never really belonged here. But he forgot his gloomy mood as he spotted a couple of strange people on the wide veranda. And then he noticed the police cars.

He got out of the taxicab, still frowning, then hurried up the steps to the front door. Before he touched it, the housekeeper opened it, murmuring his name thankfully. "Oh,

Mr. Patrick, thank God you're home. We didn't know when your train was—"

"What's wrong?" he demanded, looking beyond her to two grave-faced policemen. One he recognized. "Mc-Pherson, what's going on here?"

As Emma stepped aside, McPherson twirled his cap, having a hard time looking him in the eye. "Mr. O'Connor, sir. I'm afraid we have bad news. You might want to come over here and have a seat first."

Alarm streaked through Patrick like a bullet. *Jessy.* God, don't let it be Jessy.

"Tell me, for God's sake!"

"It's your wife, sir."

"Caroline?" Patrick looked from McPherson to the other officer. "What about her?"

"She's..." He cleared his throat. "Ah, I'm afraid it's bad, sir. The worst. There was a squall at sea. The yacht...ah..." McPherson stared at Patrick's chin. "Duncan Wheeler's yacht, you know..."

With the force of squall winds, Kathleen's warning screamed across his mind. "What is the worst, McPherson?"

"Your wife has drowned, sir. She's dead."

November 26, 1932
Caroline O'Connor was buried today, her reputation in shreds. What could she have been thinking? Drowned while frolicking with her lover on his yacht. Of course I know now the message of my Dream Sight. It was not Patrick who was endangered, but his wife.

It was a day without sunshine, cold and bleak, drizzling rain. Still, the cream of Savannah's elite turned out en masse for the ceremony along with many other vulgar curiosity seekers. My heart ached for Patrick.

*With Wade Ferguson still hospitalized, he was alone
except for the little girl. His face ravaged, he stood stiff
as stone, coming alive only when Jessy touched him.
Was I the only one who saw his bitterness?*

*The graveside ceremony was mercifully brief. At a
signal from the minister, Patrick placed a red rose on
the casket. And then it was Jessy's turn. He bent and
said something to her. She nodded and leaned over to
place another red rose, just as Patrick had done. Everyone was touched, even the cynics. My throat clogged
with tears when with a grim face he swung the little girl
up into his arms and held her tight against his heart.
Over the top of Jessy's head, his eyes met mine, but
there was nothing there. He seemed a man damned by
fate.*

KATHLEEN CAME SLOWLY awake as the clock on the mantel
was striking two in the morning. Patrick was her first
thought, filling her mind and her senses. It was as though
every atom of her being was saturated with Patrick, his
thoughts, his feelings, his need. He was as real as he had
seemed the night she had imagined him at her bedside in the
hospital. She lay still for a moment, letting her senses direct
her. Misunderstandings, suspicions, death, dishonor, all
faded to nothing as his need rose like a strong tide, pulling
her...

Rising slowly, she slipped out of bed.

Not bothering with a light, she moved as in a dream,
walking to her closet and taking out her coat. Her movements were slow but purposeful, as though choreographed
to silent music. She drew the coat on over her long white
nightgown, rubbing her cheek against the soft silver fox
collar. Dropping to her knees, she found a pair of satin

slippers and put them on, though the night was cold and damp. Turning her face toward the window where the clouds had cleared and a full moon now frosted the night with silver, she spoke to Patrick.

I'm coming.

A whisper only. A silent promise.

WHAT DID IT MEAN? Patrick stared into the swirling depths of his glass before tossing back a stiff shot of Irish whiskey. Two times now the sea had claimed the women in his life. Was he cursed? Shuddering, he poured himself another drink and went over to the window to stare out into the moonlit night.

Kathleen. He had never needed her as much as he needed her tonight. And it had never been more impossible to see her, now that his wife lay in a cold, wet grave. He felt numb. Empty. Rage would have been understandable, even welcome. Or embarrassment because the world now knew their marriage had been a farce. Or worry over how he would ever put the pieces of his life together again.

But he felt nothing.

Except for this aching, soul-deep need for Kathleen.

Just then, light winked through the trees that flanked the winding drive to the house. Slowly, Patrick lowered the glass in his hand. As he watched, a slow-moving car appeared, headlights sweeping over the lawn and house and windows, fading off as the car stopped.

With his heart pounding in breathless, glad disbelief, he saw Kathleen slip from the car and make her way toward the house like a silver angel in the moonlight. Suddenly emotion too tangled to fathom swirled through him in a hot, rushing tide. Like a frozen limb renewed with circulation, he came fiercely alive.

At the door, she did not pause, but came inside as though pulled by invisible strings, and started up the stairs in the big, dark, still house. Was that why he had not locked the door? Had he known in his heart that she would come because he needed her so desperately tonight? Standing in frozen wonder, his back to the window, he waited for her.

At the top of the stairs, Kathleen turned unerringly in the direction that would take her to Patrick. Trailing a hand along the exposed balcony, she made her way to the room where he waited.

At the door, she looked directly across the room into his eyes. No lights burned. She needed no light to see into the heart of the only man she had ever loved. Shedding her coat, she dropped it negligently on the floor and walked across the room to him.

Without words, they spent one long moment simply looking. In his face she saw his wonder, but she had dismissed the right or wrong of it when she had come to him. She had always been helpless in her love for Patrick. Now, looking into his eyes, she felt his need as a fierce living thing. He was ready for bed, wearing nothing except a dark robe that hung unbelted from his broad shoulders. In the sheen of the silvery moon, his bare chest had the look of marble, cleanly muscled, beautifully male, utterly captivating.

He drew in a deep, shuddering breath. "Kathleen... everything is turned upside down. My life...Jessy... There are things..."

She put her fingers on his mouth.

"I need you, Kathleen."

"I know. I woke up and...heard you." She saw him swallow, saw the movement of his throat. There was no misinterpreting what she offered tonight. He came a little closer, drawn as surely to her as he'd ever been, helpless to resist her.

He watched as if in a dream as her fingers went to the tiny buttons at the bodice of her nightgown. She freed them, one by one, and then, her eyes still fixed on his, slipped out of the sleeves and pushed the gown down. Past her waist, her hips, her sleek belly, her mons in its auburn nest, her thighs and legs, to her feet, pale and bare. When she stood before him in the moonlight, he caught his breath. She was beautiful, far more beautiful than the girl of seventeen who had claimed his heart and soul forever a lifetime ago.

He reached out and touched her hair, a wild, fiery tangle. "The world would be scandalized," he said softly, lovingly.

"I have known scandal before."

He closed his eyes briefly, his fingers clenching in her hair. "Because of me. Because of me then, and now, too." His voice broke. "Kathleen, I never meant to hurt you. I would cut out my heart before hurting you."

"This will not hurt me, Patrick," she said, reaching to push his robe off his shoulders, letting it go the way of her nightgown. "Tonight is . . . my choice."

Hurt? How could such pleasure hurt? They came together with all the hunger and yearning that had been building between them. They kissed deeply and tenderly while hands explored and caressed. He went to her like a man starved, as truly he was. Kathleen yielded joyfully, opening to him with the same sure sensuality that had come to them so easily years before. She wrapped her arms around him, bringing them close like two pieces finally fitted to make a whole. With her face held fast between his palms, Patrick reacquainted himself with the taste of her, his mouth skimming over every inch until he found her mouth. His tongue plunged into the sweetness, and Kathleen went soft and pliant, loving the taste of him, the rampant carnality of his loving. Standing fused together, mouth to mouth, body to body, they assumed an erotic rhythm, falling easily into a rocking, earthy simulation, hardness against softness, until they both moaned with gratification. But it wasn't enough.

With a groan, he tore his mouth from hers and swept her up in his arms. The world tipped crazily, but Kathleen curled into his strength, held safe against his pounding heart until he lowered her onto the bed. With her arms tight around his neck, she smiled and nuzzled the musky, warm skin beneath his chin. Opening her mouth against the rough, abrasive night growth on his jaw, she tasted and licked and nipped him, indiscriminately loving every bit of him she could reach.

And then he was covering her, his limbs hard and warm, a pleasurable, sensual weight that ignited more heat and want and need deep within her. Their mouths sealed again, the planes and angles of his body adjusted to her softness. The hot insistence of his kiss was like heady wine, leaving her breathless when he shifted and began making his way down her body, coasting openmouthed over her breasts and belly and beyond.

Even though they had loved all those years ago, she realized she knew little about loving between a man and woman. Now Patrick loved her in ways that were new to her, kissed her in places he had not years before. Her head spun dizzily, then, opening to him, she reveled in the sensations washing through her, over her, drowning her in a sweet, slow flood tide. She wanted to savor it all. She wanted to feel it and hold it in her heart to warm her when he would no longer be in her life.

Knowing what she did about him, there could only be this one time.

There were no words between them, only sighs and murmurs, soft cries and low moans. With desire finally built to fever pitch, Patrick braced on both elbows and swiftly and surely thrust into her. Curling her legs around him, she let him take her away, moving to an intimate rhythm that was more natural than breathing.

Suddenly they were at the edge. Now he spoke, but she heard no words except for her name. Still, she understood the language of his desire because it was hers. Burying her face in the heated flesh of his neck, she murmured his name, over and over, as though, after suppressing it so long, her tongue and her heart simply ran away with the sound of it.

She sensed he fought for control, but she was impatient now, urgently seeking that sweet remembered release. He was dark and driven, heaving with passion, demanding as he surged closer to completion. Finally, sweeping his hands beneath her hips, he thrust himself deep. She shuddered once, twice, as small, exquisite explosions burst within her. With a glad cry, Patrick threw his head back and together they both fell madly into the abyss.

She did not sleep afterward and neither did Patrick. They lay together in a tangle of arms and legs, faces close, kissing, touching, savoring the joy of being together without the crushing weight of guilt or shame. Lovingly, Kathleen stroked him, rediscovering, her hands delighting in his smooth, hard muscles, his warmth.

"Another scar," she said, finding a small imperfection on his shoulder.

"A cable snapped on the job."

"Which job?"

"Leland in New York."

She leaned close and kissed it and he sighed softly. Reaching up, she smoothed the hair on his forehead, smiling as it sprang right back. Stubborn. Like Patrick himself.

"That's how I met Wade," he said in the quiet.

"In New York? At Leland?"

"Yeah, he walked under an overloaded platform just as it gave way. Missed him by a hair."

"Missed . . . thanks to you?"

"I was the one who happened to be close by."

"And so he offered you a job?"

"He felt obligated."

"And you grabbed it."

"I had no reason to stay in New York." His jaw tensed. "Or so I thought."

Kathleen withdrew her hand. "Is that the day you met Caroline?"

He curled his palm around her neck, not letting her withdraw, and rested his forehead against hers. "No, that was later."

"Why did you marry her?"

There was a moment of silence. "Wade . . . wanted it."

"Why?"

He moved, lying back again with his hands beneath his head, his eyes fixed on the ceiling. "I know why now, but I didn't at the time." From the back of his throat came a bitter sound. "She was pregnant and the baby needed a name."

When she said nothing, he turned and found her propped on an elbow looking at him. "You don't appear surprised," he said, trying to see her face. "She threw it up to me that she'd told you. I couldn't believe she would do something like that. We had a terrific row over it." He frowned in the dark. "Those were the last words we ever spoke. I left to go to New York the next morning and she left to go to her lover."

After a moment of silence, she said, "I'm sorry."

"Was I the only one who didn't know that Jessy wasn't my child?" His tone was anguished.

"She only told me to shock and hurt me," Kathleen offered. "It's not something she would want the world to know. Besides—" she leaned close and pressed a kiss to his jaw "—you love Jessy in spite of everything, don't you?"

"Yeah, I do."

"And you're very lucky to have her. I just wish..." Her words trailed off as her hand on his chest moved idly back and forth.

Patrick knew she was thinking about their baby. What were her memories? Not memories, because she had never seen him. She had only secondhand information to feed her hunger. A tiny body, a cap of black hair, a small heartbeat that was forever stilled.

He ached to tell her, but too much could go wrong and she would be hurt again. What if a court ruled against them? It would be a miracle if Cameron was simply handed over to them after all these years. The last thing he wanted was to bring her any more pain.

Suddenly there was a commotion down the hall, the nanny's soft voice and Jessy whimpering, calling his name. With a groan, Patrick threw the covers aside and reached for his robe. Standing by the bed, he looked at her. "Jessy is probably having a bad dream. The nanny is..."

"The nanny is not her daddy."

And she no longer has a mother. "She needs you, Patrick."

"I'll just be a little while." His heart swelled with love for her. Shrugging reluctantly into his robe, he said, "It was an upsetting day for her."

"I know. Go, it's all right."

As soon as the door closed behind him, Kathleen slipped out of bed. Her gown was a white cloud near the window. Scooping it up, she shook it out and put it on. Pushing back her hair, she buttoned the tiny buttons and smoothed her hands over her body. She was still flushed and tingling. Standing still, she felt the unfamiliar throb between her legs with a rush of emotion. She had done an impulsive, wildly irresponsible thing. And she felt no remorse.

Her coat was exactly where she had dropped it. Bending, she picked it up and put it on, then slipped her feet into the satin slippers. She listened a moment for the sound of Patrick's voice, but there was nothing in the dark, empty house.

Except Caroline's ghost.

CHAPTER FIFTEEN

PATRICK PARKED WITH a screech of brakes and climbed out of his car in front of the *Sentinel* offices. Three days. He'd been trying to see Kathleen for three days and all he'd gotten was a lot of interference from Maxwell Rutledge's flunkies. He couldn't figure it out. For the first time since setting foot off the ship from Ireland, his life was finally on a straight course, but only if Kathleen could share it. There would be things to work out, but it was meant for them to be together. Why was she avoiding him after giving him a glimpse of heaven?

That was how he thought of the hours they spent together on the night after Caroline's funeral. Eaten up with guilt, filled with a sense of failure, he had regarded it as the darkest time of his life. And then Kathleen had come.

Why wouldn't she talk to him?

Kathleen had managed to elude him, but Rutledge would find it a damn sight harder. With a scowl in place, Patrick approached the young woman at the front desk. "Where is Rutledge's office? I need to see him."

She stood, eyeing him warily. "Do you have an appointment, sir?"

"No. Look, just tell him it's O'Connor and he's not dodging me this time. It won't take long. I'm not leaving this building until I have a few words with him."

"Well—"

"I mean it," he said, but he tempered the hostility in his tone. "Max knows me." He forced a smile, but it felt as alien as all his attempts to smile lately.

"Wait here."

He didn't. The instant she disappeared through a door, he followed her, determined not to be put off again.

"I can't hold him off any longer, Kathleen," Max said, closing the door behind the receptionst. "He's not the kind of man who will tolerate it. Have you decided what you're going to do?"

"About what?"

Max looked at her silently before taking a seat on the chair in front of her desk. "You know what, Kathleen. About the series. About Patrick's involvement in the investors' group."

She bent her head, rubbing a spot between her eyes wearily. "I thought we had already covered this. I'm going to go ahead with the series, Max. Next Sunday. As we planned. What did you think I would do?"

"Exactly that." He shook his head, looking troubled. "But at such a price... I'm thinking of you and your happiness, Kathleen. This will probably destroy him, at least in Savannah. I was thinking that you might consider turning your notes over to another journalist here at the paper. Let someone else—"

"Do the dirty work? Max, I can't. I've come this far. I intend—"

The door flew open suddenly and they stared at Patrick. Ignoring Max, he looked directly at Kathleen.

"So, we can finally talk," he said, shoving the door closed behind him. His eyes locked with hers. "We can speak privately or we can speak in front of Max, but we *will* talk, Kathleen."

"Patrick." She stood up slowly.

"O'Connor." Max put his hand out in a futile attempt to ward him off. "Why don't you come to my office? We can talk there."

"Not on your life." Patrick blocked the closed door. "I'll be happy to talk to you later, in fact—I'd planned to. But first, Kathleen owes me . . ."

"I don't owe you anything!"

". . . an explanation. What's it to be, *mavourneen*? Our differences aired before Max or a few minutes in private? It's up to you."

He waited, tall and intense. Kathleen took in the sight of him with a hunger that could never be satisfied, waiting for her heartbeat to settle. With his white shirt unbuttoned and his tie askew, he looked as unlike the southern gentlemen who normally frequented her office as a panther was unlike a house cat. His black hair was just a little too long, his skin a little too tanned, his eyes . . . oh, his eyes.

"Now, O'Connor, there's no call to take that attitude. Remember, Kathleen's been through a lot lately."

Patrick stared at Max. "And it could easily have happened again. Damn it, Rutledge! You were supposed to be looking out for her."

Max instantly bridled. "I have been looking out for her. Leo is with her every instant she's out of the house or this office. And I'm—"

"Every instant?" Patrick's tone was too quiet suddenly, almost silken.

"Patrick—" Kathleen held out her hand to stop him.

"Yes, every instant," Max stated emphatically.

"And three nights ago? Was Leo in the back seat when she drove to my house then?"

"Drove? To your house?" Max looked at Kathleen.

"Patrick, say one more word and I will turn and walk out of this office and never speak to you again." Kathleen's voice was chilling in its intensity.

The look Patrick gave her was bleak and angry and helpless. With a deep groan, he turned from them both and walked to the window. "What are you trying to do to me, Kathleen?" he asked in a tone so full of anguish that Max frowned, looking first at Patrick, then at Kathleen.

"I feel as though we're in a play here and I'm the only one without a script," Max said, studying Patrick.

Kathleen twisted the pencil in her hand. "Patrick shouldn't have spoken, Max."

"Did you drive to his house in the middle of the night?"

"Yes."

"After two attempts on your life?" he asked incredulously.

She shrugged. "He's right, Max. This is something Patrick and I need to talk about."

"I can stay, Kathleen. Just say the word."

"She's safe, Rutledge." Patrick's tone had a subtle edge. "You have *my* word."

Max gave Kathleen a measuring look. "Kathleen?"

She tossed her pencil on her desk and sat back down with a sigh. "It's all right, Max. Please."

As the door closed very softly behind Max, Kathleen gestured to the chair he'd vacated. "Have a seat," she said coolly. After a second or two, Patrick folded himself into the chair and crossed his legs, one ankle on the opposite knee. He leaned back, his blue, blue eyes penetrating, as though trying to figure out a particularly difficult puzzle. Kathleen was the one who looked away first.

"Why, Kathleen?" he asked.

"Why have I been avoiding you?"

"Yes. And why did you give yourself if you didn't mean it? Why did you slip away like a thief in the night? I'm driving myself crazy trying to figure out the answers." He straightened suddenly, pushing out of the chair to pace back and forth in front of her desk. "God, Kathleen, you came to me just when I needed you most. It was like a dream come true. I thought we... I thought it meant we could begin again, that we had finally—"

"I had no right," she said softly. "Your wife was in her grave only six hours and I was in your bed. I should never have done what I did."

And why did I? she cried silently, her eyes clinging to his. Knowing the kind of man you've become, how could I? I knew then you had betrayed every good and decent principle we once held sacred. What does that say about my own principles?

Her gaze fell to her hands. "It was wrong."

"Don't say that, Kathleen! It was right! It was the most perfect, right thing that could happen between two people. I love you and—"

"Don't!" Kathleen stood up, looking fiercely into his eyes.

"What?"

"There is something I need to say." She picked up the papers strewn over the top of her desk and straightened them. Then, looking down, closing her eyes, she drew in a breath. "I know everything, Patrick."

When she lifted her eyes, he was simply looking at her... waiting.

"I know about the people you're in partnership with. About the way you do business—opting for huge profits while employees work their hearts out and sometimes even lose their lives in your obscene lust for more profits." She turned away. "I know everything."

"Kathleen—"

"My research is complete. The series is almost written. The first article will appear in Sunday's paper."

Looking at her, he wondered what he could say. This was Thursday. The board meeting was set for next Tuesday morning. Only two days' difference between the success of all his plotting and planning and...disaster. Her story would be dynamite when it hit the papers and everything would be lost as his targets scrambled madly to cover their rears.

She looked at him expectantly. "Well, Patrick?"

She was a journalist. His coup, if all went according to plan, meant far-reaching change for LelandFerguson, from Savannah all the way to New York. It was a major story, one that would further enhance the reputation of William Collins. He studied her intently for a moment. Could he afford to trust her? God, there was so much at stake. "Things are not always the way they appear, Kathleen," he said.

"Oh?" She rattled the papers in front of him. "This is my research, Patrick! It's all here in black and white. You're involved with these...these jackals! I can't imagine that you thought I wouldn't find out. Oh, I took a lot of wrong turns. The people you've chosen to do business with are some of the wiliest I've ever stumbled across. But the facts were there. I just kept on until I had the whole picture."

"Facts, research, the whole picture..." His eyes met hers. "Just words, Kathleen. So far, you haven't said anything that means much."

She slapped the papers down on her desk. "Is this enough for you?" She pointed to a page. "This is a sweatshop on River Street that hires young girls. More than half the work force is under fourteen. And this! A warehouse for illegal liquor, although it doesn't seem that the law enforcement people care very much," she said bitterly. "A fact that is understandable since this—'' she turned a page and pointed to a list of names ''—tells me that two of the investors are a judge and a policeman.''

She looked up, her expression clearly condemning, but Patrick remained silent.

"Still unimpressed? Well, you may be beyond shame, Patrick, but when I saw that one of the holdings of the investors' group was the woolen mill that burned—the one where Meggy was killed—then I freely admit I was shocked . . . and ashamed for you.''

If she'd expected a denial, she didn't get one. But there was a tight look to his mouth, and his hands were clenched. She knew him well enough to know his thoughts were in turmoil.

"One thing puzzled me," she said. "Your future was made at LelandFerguson. You could have stayed within the corporate structure there and never ventured beyond to these . . . these illegal dealings. LelandFerguson's holdings are vast. There are no threats to their shipbuilding and shipping interests or to their market share of ocean liner travel. Why branch out into these other . . . sidelines. Why, Patrick?''

She watched his profile as he stared out the window. His jaw was like granite. Her eyes narrowed as he swallowed once, hard.

"Don't you have anything to say?" she demanded in a sharp tone. And why did she feel like crying? She was a weak-willed fool where this man was concerned.

He turned and looked her fully in the eye. "I'm impressed. I see how you've become so successful as a journalist.''

She stared at him for a long minute. "Is that it?''

"No. I have one request. Please delay the first article." At her astonished look, he added, "For just a few days. Wednesday would be good."

"Wednesday would be good."

He held her gaze doggedly. "The following Sunday would be better."

"Why should I do that, Patrick? To give you and your cronies time to regroup? To protect their investments? It won't work. No matter what you or they do at this point, the damage is done. The facts are out and their heyday in Savannah—in this state!—is over."

"Would it help if I promised you that there would probably be an even bigger story breaking and you could get an exclusive on it?"

"You are amazing," she said incredulously. "Do you expect me to believe that? Didn't you hear anything I just said? This series will expose these people for what they are. You're one of them, Patrick. You haven't denied it. No, I won't hold up awhile, and no, I won't pass for something bigger just on your word. I can't believe you have the nerve to even ask."

His jaw clenched at the lash of her words, even though he knew that from her view, from everything she'd put together, he appeared as dirty as every other man on the list. He couldn't explain. He couldn't take the chance.

"Maybe it's you I'm thinking about," he said grimly. "Have you forgotten that you're dealing with very dangerous people here?"

"What are you suggesting, Patrick? That I stop reporting? That I stop inciting unrest among Savannah's disadvantaged? Forget it. I'm never going to pull my punches just because I've been threatened by thugs. The series comes out in Sunday's paper."

"Goddamn it!" His control suddenly snapped. "I'm trying to reason with you here! Do you think I'll just step aside meekly and let you have your head like some...some wild-eyed Carrie Nation! What if the people you're naming in that precious article take it into their heads to silence you forever? I lost you once, Kathleen, through a crazy twist of fate. I'm not allowing—"

"Allowing!" His temper ignited her own. She was on her feet, glaring at him over her desk. "You don't allow or disallow anything, Patrick. I've been making my decisions independently for years—since I left my father's house in Kilkenny, to be exact. I'm not handing over my independence to any man, not even you!"

"Just what the hell is that supposed to mean? Why not to me? I—"

"I don't need a protector!" she cried. "And don't you dare try to twist this around. We were talking about my journalism, not my choices as a woman. As a journalist I will never skirt controversial issues, no matter what the consequences. And if I offend the powers at Leland-Ferguson, then so be it."

"Listen to you!" he bellowed. "You're talking like a fool! Your politics can get you killed, Kathleen, and I'm perfectly within my rights to try and protect you. No wife of mine—"

"I'm not your wife, Patrick!"

Silence descended as the truth of her words settled, stark and undeniable.

"Aren't you?" he asked quietly, after a moment. "When you accepted my ring on that night in Ireland before I left, didn't you become my wife?"

She raised her chin and looked at him through the tears gathering in her eyes. "That was before I learned that you had turned your back on honor and integrity."

"And you slept with me, anyway?"

She lowered her eyes before the look on his face.

"If you're telling the truth, then I've been used. There's a word for that," he told her in a hard tone, "and it's not flattering."

She looked up quickly. "No! It wasn't like that. I—"

"Yes, it was exactly like that. And if you can't believe in me, can't trust me to be the man I *tell* you I am, the man I *show* you, time and again, that I am, then, yes, you used me."

She studied her hands again, clenching them together when she saw that they were trembling. "I never meant—"

"I have only one more question," he said grimly. "How long have you known this?"

"Have long have I…" She blinked, shaking her head. "A few days…" She shrugged. "The day of Caroline's accident. When you were in New York."

"And believing me to be beyond redemption, why did you come to me that night after her funeral?"

"I told you, I don't know exactly," she said, faltering. "You needed me, I felt it. It seemed the most important thing at the time."

He studied her intently for a moment and then his expression gentled. "Following your heart," he said softly. At her mute look, he reached out and cupped her jaw. "Maybe you should consider doing that one more time."

"Are you saying you aren't involved with these people?"

"I'm saying that you can trust me, Kathleen. You have always been able to trust me."

"How can I? Why should I?"

Her lips trembled and Patrick could not bear it. With a muttered oath, he bent quickly and kissed her. It began tenderly, rife with the emotion that was locked inside him.

A low moan escaped her, then was dissolved against his mouth.

Kathleen shuddered at the rush of sensation, an almost painful joy. For a few moments, she savored the pleasure that melted her limbs and heated her blood. But in the next instant, she jerked free. "No, I won't let you do this, Patrick! Not again. Not until you explain." Stepping back, she wrapped her arms around herself. What was she doing! A few words from Patrick, a soft kiss, and she turned into a shameless, spineless shadow of herself.

Looking at him, she almost cried out at the expression on his face. But she would not let her love for Patrick rob her of her principles. He had already robbed her of her heart. She would never love another man the way she loved Patrick, but she had managed to live a good life without him once before and she could do it again.

Lying in bed that night, she faced the truth. For a little while that afternoon, she had actually considered Patrick's request that she pull the series. If he had offered *any* explanation, if he had made any denial or attempted to defend his association with the investors' group, maybe she would have...

Groaning, she turned over in her bed and angrily punched her pillow. Here she was making excuses even now, trying to find a loophole to explain away his perfidy. She touched the ring threaded through a silk ribbon that lay against her breast. As always, it felt warm and good and oh, so right. She wondered how long it took for love to die.

It was later that she awoke with a start, her heart pounding. Outside, the sun was barely up. Early birdsong mixed in her head with sounds echoing from her dream. Voices. Strange voices... No, not all of them strange. One deep and familiar. And filled with pleasure, joyous and hopeful.

A woman moved across a winter lawn. There were no flowers, no green leaves; everything was dull and brown. She sat on a bench with a baby—the baby from Kathleen's previous dream—and then a man was there. He reached for the baby, but suddenly...Kathleen drew her breath in sharply. It was Patrick! He was smiling, and her heart turned over. Then he reached for the child and it was a baby no longer, but a little boy.

A little boy. And Patrick held him by the hand. They looked at each other, the boy all wide eyes and wonder. The blood rushed from Kathleen's face, leaving her weak and stunned. Why was she so affected by this dream? There was no evil here. No portent of doom. Just Patrick and a little boy. And a name echoing in her mind.

What did it mean?

She shed her nightgown, then hurried to her closet and took out the first dress her hand touched. Trembling, her thoughts in chaos, she put it on, and a few minutes later, she was rushing down the stairs to find Leo.

"KATHLEEN! MY GOD, what's happened?" At the top of the stairs, Patrick stood half dressed, unshaven, his black hair still damp from his shower. He started down to meet her, moving fast, his fingers working at the buttons on his shirt.

"Patrick, who is Cameron?"

He stopped dead. The color drained from his face and he blinked once, twice, and swallowed. Then he moved again, taking the stairs slowly this time.

"Who told you? Was it Lizzie?"

She frowned. "Lizzie? What does Lizzie—"

"How did she know his name? I haven't mentioned this to another living soul, Kathleen. I swear I would kave—"

"Mentioned what?" she cried. "I don't know what you're talking about, Patrick. I came here to talk to you about my dream."

"Your dream?"

"Yes, the dream I told you about. The baby. Don't you remember?"

"Yes, I remember," Patrick said slowly, his gaze resting on her face. "Why did you ask about Cameron?"

"I don't know." She bent her head, rubbing a spot between her eyes. "In the dream, I kept hearing voices... voices." She looked up at him suddenly. "Your voice, Patrick. And then there was a little boy. Not a baby anymore. And a woman. At a park or something. You were there talking with the boy."

He looked at her mouth, watched it tremble, then dragged his gaze back to her eyes. "My God, Kathleen, this is..."

"What is it, Patrick? What does it mean? Who is Cameron?"

He took a step and pulled her into his arms, holding her close. "Kathleen, Kathleen... I didn't think you should know until—"

She pushed against his chest, tilting her face to see him. "Know what, Patrick?"

He glanced beyond her. "How did you get here?" he asked sharply. "You didn't come alone again, did you?"

"Leo brought me," she said impatiently. "But never mind that."

Holding on to her arm, he spoke to Ezra, standing by the open door, watching curiously. "Go and tell Leo that he can drive on home. I'll take Miss Kathleen later in my car." As Ezra left, Patrick closed the door behind him and took Kathleen's hand. "Come upstairs with me where we can have some privacy."

He pulled her up the first few steps, then, as though impatient to have her alone, he swept her into his arms and took the remaining stairs two at a time, laughing as her arms clung around his neck. When they were in his room with the door closed, he looked at her with an expression that made Kathleen catch her breath. "I have such a story to tell you, Kathleen." He picked up her hand and placed a kiss on her palm. "Think, my darling. Don't you know, in your heart of hearts, who Cameron is?"

A rush of emotion burst in her. For a second or two, she was dizzily afraid that she would faint. With her eyes wide, she whispered, "Is he my baby?"

"Our baby, *mavourneen*," Patrick said softly. "Cameron is the child of our love."

"Not dead," she whispered hoarsely, her lips barely moving. "He was not stillborn."

"No, my love. He was born strong and healthy, and he is still that way today."

She burst into tears.

With a groan, Patrick hauled her into his lap, murmured words and endearments and apologies and promises while she shuddered in an excess of joy and grief and wonder. Laughing softly, aching with his own joy, Patrick held her, kissing her temples and the tear-wet corners of her eyes, giving heartfelt thanks that even with all that was wrong between them, he was privileged to share this moment with her.

When the storm had passed, Kathleen was too shaken, too drained, to move from the haven of Patrick's arms. "My baby didn't die, Patrick," she said, her voice catching. "I can't believe it."

"It's true. Incredible and remarkable, but true."

"A miracle," she breathed softly.

He kissed the corner of her mouth. "Definitely a miracle."

"Tell me everything."

"There's much to tell, darling. You were victimized from the moment you were pulled from New York harbor until the day Maxwell Rutledge took you away. It was the Parsons."

"Amelia Parsons? Herbert?"

"Both. After you were drugged, the midwife delivered our baby, a healthy boy. But Herbert Parsons wanted you without the nuisance of a child, so he made arrangements to get rid of it. There are always people who want healthy babies, and they're willing to pay money for them. His mother went along with it."

"He always referred to my baby as a brat," she murmured.

"Yes, but I'm convinced he won't be guilty of that again," Patrick said grimly, thinking of the satisfaction he'd felt as his fist slammed into Herbert's horsey teeth. He knew, too, that Edward Drummond had dismissed the Parsons, mother and son. They had both gotten what they deserved, even though it had taken more than six years.

Sitting on the bed within the circle of Patrick's arms, Kathleen listened as Patrick told her the whole story.

"You suspected this when I told you my dream."

"It was so incredible that I wouldn't allow myself to hope," Patrick said quietly. "After thinking it over, I became more and more convinced. Something told me... Anyway, the only person I could think of who might help was Lizzie."

"Lizzie?" Kathleen repeated. "She never said a word."

"So, you see—" Patrick tipped her face up so that he could look into her eyes "—your clairvoyance is truly a gift.

Without the dream that has been with you since the birth of our son, we never would have found him."

She was silent for a long moment, thinking. "I want to see him. Is it possible?"

Patrick nodded. "Yes, but I don't think we should, Kathleen, not just yet. I've hired a lawyer. Let's wait until he sorts through all the legal odds and ends."

"I don't want to wait."

He tucked her beneath his arm and kissed the top of her head. "I know, darling. But if you stop and think a minute, you'll see this isn't something that can be pushed, no matter how much we long to see Cameron. We'll probably have more success if we act through a lawyer."

"They stole my baby, Patrick. They don't have any rights as far as I can see, lawyer or not."

"I understand your feelings, but we don't want to stampede them into taking the boy somewhere and—"

She jerked back to look at him. "Do you think they might do that?"

"No, no. I'm only thinking of things that might happen. Since we don't know these people, I honestly believe we should proceed carefully." He touched her cheek. "Besides, I don't want you to go to New York without me and I have something very urgent scheduled for today. Afterward I plan to devote every minute to getting our son back."

She settled against him again. "What did he look like, Patrick? Describe him. Is he...oh, I know he looks like you. I know it."

With a smile, Patrick pictured the boy. "He does have the look of the O'Connors, but his eyes are as green as your own."

"Dark hair and a stubborn chin?"

He chuckled. "Just like his mother's."

"His father's, you mean!"

"Then we'll share the blame for that trait, *mavourneen*," he said, stroking her back. "At any rate, he is a wonderful boy and I can't wait for the two of you to meet."

"Thank you," she said, nuzzling against his chest.

"Thank *you*." With a smile, he lay back on the bed, taking her with him. Shifting, he turned her so that they faced each other, their legs entwined. For a long minute, he looked his fill. "I've dreamed of this," he said, tangling his fingers in her hair. "Just the two of us, together in the morning."

"Patrick—" She wanted to tell him no. She should tell him no. But he was pulling her close, and his mouth settled on hers.

Closing her eyes, Kathleen absorbed the sweetness of it. Her lips softened and opened beneath his, and as their tongues joined, the heat and pleasure grew, spreading through her limbs, washing through her mind. Drawing back, Patrick smiled into her eyes and then he was kissing her again, slow, wet, erotic kisses that could not be mistaken for anything except the preliminaries to the act of love.

Even as her senses were awash in desire, her thoughts churned with uncertainty. Could she find the strength to leave Savannah and Patrick? Surely there was no other way that she could live her life with any semblance of honor. And now there was the added complication of their child. Her determination firmed at thoughts of Cameron. She would have her child. No judge in the land could tell her otherwise. She still struggled with her decision to leave Patrick, but she would have Cameron.

Oh, but now...yes, now there was this moment. This hour. With a sigh, she wrapped her arms around Patrick and loved him.

CHAPTER SIXTEEN

PATRICK CAST A SIDEWAYS glance at Kathleen and frowned. He ought to be feeling good, jumping-over-the-moon happy; instead he felt downright uneasy. There was something about the look of her as she sat next to him in the car. Was she feeling guilty about the hour they had just spent together? No, how could she? It was right and good for them to love each other. He only wished he could have prolonged their time together, spent the rest of the day making slow, sweet love with her. But today of all days, it was impossible. Once he got her to Max and safety, he had dark, urgent business in front of him. He had managed to reach the board members and reschedule the meeting for today. At last, the moment he'd waited for, plotted for, dreamed about, was here. His life would be changed forever.

And Kathleen's, too, if things went the way he planned. It had been a long, hard road they both had traveled to finally come to this point, but they were destined for each other. He believed that with all his heart. It would soon be over, with a bit of luck.

He stole another look at her. She seemed sad, almost. Resigned. Resigned to what?

Her lack of faith in him hurt, yet how could he blame her? After all, trust worked both ways. He was guilty of the same thing, but soon he could tell her everything. It would be interesting to see her reaction when she learned exactly what he'd been up to for almost six years.

"Why are we stopping here?" Kathleen frowned as Patrick turned the Packard into the gates of the shipyard and headed toward his office.

"I'm late for the appointment I mentioned," he told her. "I need to let them know. It'll only take a minute, then I'll drop you at the *Sentinel*."

"You shouldn't have sent Leo home. He would have waited."

"And wondered what kept you for two hours?"

"I wouldn't have stayed two hours then."

"Oh?"

She flushed uncomfortably, remembering his remark about using him. "Patrick—"

"Forget it," he growled, pushing the door open. "Stay here, and, damn it, I mean stay! Don't get out and wander around or open the door to a single soul. I'll be less than two minutes. I just need to let them know everything's still going as planned. Now that it's showdown time, I don't want anybody thinking I'm—" He stopped abruptly. "Just wait right here."

"As if I have a choice," Kathleen muttered to his backside as she watched him walk to the door of his small office.

Showdown time? What did that mean? As she was puzzling over it, she became interested in the activity around her. In spite of the depressed times, there seemed to be work at the shipyard. Beyond the small office complex, she could see the keel being laid for the construction of another navy PT boat. Men were everywhere, going about the business of shipbuilding. Again, she wondered at Patrick's decision to throw his lot in with rogues when he seemed to have carved out a secure future for himself here. She didn't think she would ever understand.

Idly, she watched two men approaching the door to Patrick's office. One was well dressed in a suit and tie and hat. Was he here for the "showdown"? she wondered. The other was a tradesman in overalls, a thick brown sweater and knitted cap. With the observant eye of a reporter, Kathleen noticed the two were in an intense conversation. Actually they were arguing, she decided, watching them a little closer. She could hear their voices. The big one sounded mean and somehow familiar. That was odd.... Just then, Patrick came out and, as though some signal passed between the two men, their argument ended. The tradesman sidled off as Patrick greeted the man in the suit.

For some reason, Kathleen watched the tradesman turn the corner of the office and begin to walk away. There was something about him from the rear... Frowning, she watched as he pulled a large handkerchief from his pocket and removed his cap to mop his head.

Her thoughts scattered like chickens before a hungry fox. He was bald! He was big and thick shouldered, raspy voiced. No wonder she had found him vaguely familiar. He was the man who had attacked and threatened her in the empty warehouse!

Without thinking, she pushed the door open and started after him.

"Kathleen!" Patrick's sharp tone stopped her.

The man beside him looked at her curiously.

"Kathleen, we're leaving now," Patrick said in a tone that seemed to convey a message, but she wasn't thinking about that. She was intent only on pursuing the bald man. "Kathleen!" he repeated harshly.

"In a minute, Patrick," she said, giving him an impatient wave with her fingers, her eyes on the tradesman. He had ducked behind huge spools of steel cable. Just before she darted behind the first one in pursuit, Patrick's hand closed on her arm.

"I told you to stay in the car, damn it!" he said through clenched teeth.

She jerked, trying to pull free. "It's him, Patrick! It's the bald-headed man who attacked me in the warehouse!"

"Will you shut up, for crissake!" he muttered for her ears only.

She hesitated. "What?"

With his hand still wrapped tightly around her upper arm, Patrick spoke to the man in the brown suit, who had watched everything with intense interest. "I'm going to drive Miss Collins to her office, Sculley. Go on in to the meeting. I don't plan to be longer than half an hour. Russ Whitley is handling things until I get back."

"Do you have Wade's proxy votes?" Sculley asked stonily.

"Yes." Patrick looked him straight in the eye. "Do you have a problem with that?"

There was a short, hostile silence, then Sculley's lips curled. "You think you're a real hotshot, don't you, O'Connor?" Without waiting for Patrick's response, Sculley gave Kathleen an assessing look, nodded curtly, then turned on his heel and went into the building.

"He hates you!" Kathleen said, distracted from her own quest for a second.

"I know, and with good reason. I'm going to hang him out to dry today."

"Who is he?"

"Ben Sculley."

She recognized the name as one of the investors on the list. Another rogue cohort of Patrick's. But hardly a friend, it seemed.

"Sculley was formerly Wade's right-hand man," Patrick volunteered. "But long before Wade's stroke, he had come to have second thoughts about his integrity, among other things."

"Oh, I see." And she did. A woman scorned was dangerous, but so was a man. And if she was any judge, Ben Sculley was enraged. She forgot Sculley as Patrick gave her arm a little shake.

"I told you to stay in the car, Kathleen. What possessed you to go haring off across the yard like that?"

"I told you, I recognized the bald man."

"And you were going to chase him down for an interview," he said sarcastically.

"Well, I was going to chase him down," she admitted. "What could he do to me in full view of hundreds of people?"

Patrick stared at the sky before heaving a sigh. "You'll be the death of us all yet, woman." He hustled her to the Packard none too gently and urged her into the passenger seat. "I'm asking you once more to have some faith in me, just for a day. If I don't erase your doubts and restore your belief in me by the end of this day, I swear you can walk out of my life and I'll let you go without lifting a finger to stop you."

She studied him intently. "You're just going to ignore what I said...that the bald man is the one who attacked me in the warehouse?"

"I'm not ignoring it. I suspected it."

"And you're not even calling the police?"

"Not yet."

"Does it have something to do with Ben Sculley?"

His dark brows drew together. "Why do you ask that?"

"They were arguing just before you came out of your office."

He closed the car door, then walked around it and climbed in behind the wheel. "Part of trusting me is that you don't ask me any more questions until I can answer them all."

"I didn't promise to trust you."

"Yes you did."

"When?"

"Six years ago," he said flatly. "And I'm holding you to it."

After Patrick dropped her off at the office of the *Sentinel*, Kathleen forced to the back of her mind the heart-stopping discovery that her child was alive—and the memory of the time she'd spent in Patrick's bed. Both were enough to destroy anyone's peace of mind. So she did what had always worked for her. Calling on the discipline necessary to all good newspeople, she polished and edited the first in the series of her articles. Finally satisfied, she read it through and then, reluctantly, handed it to the copyboy.

Sealing the fate of the man I love, she thought unhappily. *Destroying his reputation as an honorable and respected man.*

Standing suddenly, she went to the window and stared outside. Why couldn't she shake this strange, uneasy feeling? What had happened to her belief in the series? She had hard, solid evidence for every fact she'd written, but was she about to make a terrible mistake? On the sidewalk below, Leo was chatting with an acquaintance as he waited for her. Following orders, Patrick's orders. Not to keep her imprisoned or to threaten her independence, but to protect her from harm.

Was that the behavior of a corrupt man?

He had traveled to New York and found their child. He had kept it from her so that she wouldn't be hurt if there was no hope that they could ever have him.

Was that the behavior of an uncaring man?

He was a loving father to Jessy and indulgent with his sick father-in-law, even though Wade Ferguson had manipulated him into a loveless marriage.

Was that the behavior of a man without integrity?

He had remained faithful to his vows for years even though his wife had thrown her own promiscuity in his face since the early days of their marriage.

Was that the behavior of a man without honor?

On and on her thoughts chased one another, like a cat running after its own tail. If she was so convinced that Patrick was guilty of bad things, then why was she so drawn to him? Could she love a man if she believed he was without honor and integrity and concern for his fellowman? Staring into the pale light of the day, she knew she could not.

Then how to explain the list? There was something going on, and somehow Patrick was involved. With all her interviews and research, with her famous nose for news, she hadn't unearthed it. But whatever it was, something that explained everything was going on right this moment in Patrick's office at the shipyard. She had let him hustle her away when Sculley and the thug had appeared. If she had stayed, she probably wouldn't be asking herself these questions or agonizing over loving a rogue. Or a man who appeared to be a rogue.

That's what it was, she decided, hurriedly slipping into her coat. Smoke and mirrors. Somehow, for some reason, Patrick had set an elaborate plot into motion and today was the day his plan came to fruition. Today was the showdown. Whatever that meant.

"Going someplace?"

"Max..." She gave him what she knew was a limp smile.

He took a closer look at her. "Now, that's a serious face for somebody who has just turned in a piece of journalism that any newspaper would be proud to run."

She shrugged diffidently. "Did you like it that much?"

"I did. It was fine work. If the rest of the articles are as good, we may have an award-winning series."

"If we aren't sued first."

"Uh-oh." He came inside, pushing the door closed behind him. "Those are ominous words, not even to be spoken in jest. Why sued? Are we saying anything libelous? Don't we have proof for everything you allege?"

"More or less."

He sat down carefully. "Smile when you say that, Kathleen."

She waved away his concern and began to pace. "I don't really mean it, I suppose. And it's probably nothing to be concerned about. It's just that—"

Max's eyebrows went up. "Just that . . . ?"

She stopped in front of him. "Today when Patrick drove me here, he went into your office, Max. What did the two of you talk about?"

"Your safety," Max said promptly.

"Why talk to you about it? Why not talk to me directly?"

"He's old-fashioned enough to think that a man is responsible for the safety and protection of the woman he loves." Max smiled gently. "He knows I love you almost as much as he does."

"It's more than that, Max."

He gave her a long, thoughtful look and then seemed to reach a decision. "We discussed a number of things. Another was your child in New York. He was worried that you might disregard his advice and board a train for New York if his business today wasn't cleared up as quickly as he'd led you to think. He begged me to try and keep you from doing it."

"Patrick doesn't beg."

"He does for the woman he loves."

She sat against the edge of her desk. "I suppose he knows me pretty well. I do want to go to New York. My baby was taken from me and I won't rest until I have him with me. But I promised I would let the lawyers handle it and I will. Still..." She bent her head, rubbing a finger between her brows. "I have to decide about Patrick."

"Decide what, love?"

"Whether to believe him, whether to believe *in* him, in spite of everything." She stood up suddenly. "Oh, Max, he can't have done those things! He can't be in league with those men. Patrick wouldn't. I know him too well. A man doesn't change that drastically."

Max smiled as though he knew a secret. "You're sure of that?"

"Yes," she said finally. "I'm sure of that. I'm sure of Patrick." With the words, a burden fell from her heart and she was suddenly infused with the absolute certainty that she was right.

Max relaxed and crossed his legs. "So what now?"

"First of all, hold my series for the time being. I have a gut feeling that if we run it, we'll be sorry. Meantime—" she went to the door and pulled it open "—I'm going to find Patrick. He's going to talk to me if I have to lock him in a room and throw away the key."

She left to the sound of Max chuckling.

PATRICK PULLED UP in front of the *Sentinel* office for the second time that day just as Leo was helping Kathleen into the back seat of the big Hudson. When she saw him, her face lit up with a smile. With a word to Leo, her eyes still fixed on Patrick, she got out of the car and headed straight to him.

"Hello," she said huskily. "I didn't expect to see you so soon." He didn't return her smile, nor did he look like a man whose mission had been successful. Her own smile faded slightly. "Your meeting didn't go well?"

"It went fine," he answered coolly. Then he glanced at Leo standing by the Hudson. "Looks like you're headed somewhere."

"Yes, I—"

"The train station?"

"The train? No. Actually, I was headed for the ship-yard."

He flicked a look at Leo as though to confirm it.

"It's true, Patrick. I was coming to see you to ask you—"

"Ah, more questions," he said. "I see."

She stamped her foot. "No, you don't see! I was coming to tell you that I don't believe your name belongs on that list."

"What list?"

"The list of businessmen in Savannah who are connected with the sweatshops and mills using underage and slave-wage labor, bootlegging whiskey, using illegal shipping practices... Want me to go on?"

"No, I've been treated to a review of your series before, remember? What made you decide I wasn't involved?"

With her decision made to trust him, Kathleen had flown down the stairs from her office eager to find him and tell him so. Where was his relief and joy? Her buoyancy faded in the face of his aloofness.

"Well? How is it I'm not a corrupt scoundrel any-more?"

"Faith," she said.

"Faith?"

"And trust."

"Faith and trust."

"Yes, Patrick," she said, exasperated. "Although you make it very hard to have both, the way you play your cards so close to your chest."

"Are you sure you weren't influenced by the press release?"

"Press release?" She shook her head. "I haven't seen any press release."

He glanced again at Leo, who was studying his feet. Beyond him, standing in the door of the *Sentinel,* was Max Rutledge. In his hand was a typewritten paper. He waved it with a lift of both eyebrows. Kathleen looked confused.

Patrick reached for her arm. Looking intently into her eyes, he said, "Are you telling me Max didn't show you the press release I sent over here an hour ago? You don't know that I..." His words faltered at the bewildered look on her face.

"I haven't seen anything from you, Patrick. Since leaving you this morning, I've spent most of the day coming to terms with loving you."

"In spite of the evidence you've collected over the past weeks damning me?"

"Yes, in spite of that."

"And what about that evidence, *mavourneen?*" he asked softly, his hand now caressing.

She searched his face, her eyes wide and loving. "I just don't believe it." She shrugged ruefully. "I can't explain it, but I just don't believe you could be anything but good and honora..."

She was silenced by his mouth claiming hers in a swift, hard kiss. Oblivious to the amusement of Max and Leo or the curious looks from passersby, Patrick wrapped his arms tightly around her and plundered her sweetness. The kiss lengthened as traffic honked and drivers hooted.

When Patrick finally ended the kiss, Kathleen was left breathless and as bewildered as ever. But happy. Leaning back to look at him, she saw every trace of aloofness had disappeared, and her own joy was restored. They exchanged a smile, rife with promise.

Patrick drew in a deep sigh. "I was afraid that you would never believe in me again," he said, resting his forehead against hers.

She closed her eyes and smiled. "Well, now that I do, will you please explain everything?"

"First things first." He gave her a quick kiss and opened the door of his car. "Get in. We're going home. I'll explain on the way."

"Home?"

With his hand on the door, he stopped. "For right now, my place in the country." He searched her eyes with concern. "Is that all right?"

"Anyplace with you is all right, Patrick."

He looked at her intently, then snapped his fingers and headed to the office door where Max still stood. He took the paper and, with a grin and a wave, jogged to the Packard.

"Here, read that," he told Kathleen when they were seated behind the wheel. Then, with a squeal of tires, he drove off.

As Patrick pulled into the curved drive of the big white-columned house, Kathleen dropped the press release into her lap. "You've reorganized LelandFerguson," she said, stunned. "You're named as the new president."

He stopped the car. "Uh-huh," he said, looking extremely pleased with himself.

She scanned the page again. "Several board members ousted, including John Leland himself."

"Well, ousted may be too harsh a word for Leland's fate," Patrick said, draping an elbow over the steering wheel. "But he's been persuaded to accept retirement. Since he's almost eighty, I don't think he'll complain."

"Some of these people were on my list."

"Ah, yes. The infamous list."

"They're gone, too."

"With full disclosure of their sordid business practices. Savannah is only small potatoes for them. Their influence has been wide all along the eastern seaboard. They quickly realized the money to be made with underpaid and underage labor, bootlegging, illegal shipping—everything you unearthed in your series."

"I didn't unearth how you were involved," she said quietly.

"No, but then I've been very careful to cover my tracks. It's easier to keep a secret when you tell nobody."

"Not a soul knew of your plan?" she asked.

"Wade knew, but only recently."

"He'll be glad to know you succeeded," she said as they got out of the car. "How did you manage it, Patrick? It seems incredible."

He ushered her in the front door of the house. "Control of the company slipped away from John Leland about ten years ago. That's when the shoddy stuff began—poor construction of Leland ships, poor maintenance, overbooking passenger liners, especially when immigrants were involved."

"The *Irish Queen*," Kathleen murmured.

"Yes, the *Irish Queen*. When I thought you were drowned, I vowed to bring the company down. It was an ambitious undertaking. Only a raw, inexperienced lad would have even entertained the notion. When Wade Ferguson offered me a job, it seemed fated. Eventually a full-fledged merger with Leland came about.''

"It was your association with that investment group that bothered me the most," Kathleen said. "Why did you do that?"

"The key players in that group were Leland people. I had a better chance of exposing them from the inside." His expression darkened. "Ben Sculley was the ringleader there. Your editorials were causing some of the group to want out. He recruited Art Shoemaker, the bald thug you recognized this morning, to scare you."

"Was he the driver of the car that nearly ran me down at the restaurant?" she asked, shuddering at the memory.

Patrick pulled her close, locking his arms tight around her. "I suspect he was, but we probably will never be able to prove it. At any rate, Sculley is gone from Savannah. As soon as he saw the direction the board was headed, he lit out. I heard he caught the noon train. The sheriff arrested Sculley. He'll serve time," Patrick said grimly. "Count on it."

Then, taking her by the hand, he went with her up the stairs, turning at the top and heading down the hall. "Where are we going?" she asked breathlessly.

"To the only place where we can be assured of privacy— my bedroom." He stopped and looked at her. "Will you?"

With her hands against his chest, she smiled at him. "What do you have in mind?"

He chuckled softly, stroking her back.

"This." He drew her up until their mouths met, then gave her a lingering kiss. His lips were warm and musky with the taste of him. Her mouth blossomed beneath his, and she sighed with the pleasure of it.

There would be a time—years—for loving. Just now, it was enough to know that at last they were together, really together. That they would share the rest of their lives. That it would be good. That before the world and God, the promise of that first, innocent love was at last fulfilled.

EPILOGUE

March 15, 1933

Today God granted my deepest wish. Patrick and I took the train to New York. We were to meet with a lawyer, so Patrick said. I was more nervous than the day I boarded the ship to sail to America. More nervous than the day—only a week ago—that I stood beside Patrick and took my marriage vows. I knew that something different was at hand. I can always tell with Patrick. Instead of driving to Manhattan and meeting with a lawyer at the top of a skyscraper, we went to Long Island to a neighborhood park! I recognized it instantly from my Dream Sight. My heart began beating like a wild thing. Across the park grounds, a young boy was waiting beside an elderly gentleman. Both looked at Patrick and me as we made our way through fallen leaves from the trees lying on the frozen ground. For the rest of my life, I will think of that moment. We walked right up to them, the old man and the young boy. Then Patrick turned to me with tears in his eyes. "My darling Kathleen, here is Cameron." The boy stuck out his small hand, and with my knees quaking, for the first time ever, I touched my son.

THERE WAS SILENCE in the garden as Kathleen finished reading the last entry in the journal. The air was laden with the smell of roses. She looked up as her granddaughter approached, but her eyes were misty as her innermost thoughts remained fixed on a distant place.

Shannon's own throat was tight with withheld tears. She dropped her gaze to Kathleen's aged hands, which were clutching a worn and faded ribbon. Once it had been sky blue. The blue of Patrick O'Connor's eyes? Shannon wondered. She knew her guess was right when she caught a glint of gold. It was the ring with which Patrick had sealed the promise made the night the two young lovers said goodbye.

Shannon turned and slipped quietly away, leaving Kathleen with her memories.

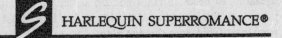

HARLEQUIN SUPERROMANCE®

WOMEN WHO DARE
They take chances, make changes
and follow their hearts

#615 GONE WITH THE WEST by Dawn Stewardson

Paranormalist Alanna DeRain got more than she'd bargained
for when she arrived in the old ghost town of Chester City,
Nevada! She hadn't counted on having two money-grubbing
thugs for company. Nor had she expected to fall in love with
1880s cowboy John McCulley, who insisted he was quite alive.
But how could that be? If John wasn't a ghost, what was he
doing in the year 2014?

**AVAILABLE IN OCTOBER, WHEREVER
HARLEQUIN BOOKS ARE SOLD.**

WWD94-2

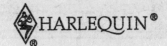

THE VENGEFUL GROOM
Sara Wood

Legend has it that those married in Eternity's chapel are destined for a lifetime of happiness. But happiness isn't what Giovanni wants from marriage—it's revenge!

Ten years ago, Tina's testimony sent Gio to prison—for a crime he didn't commit. *Now* he's back in Eternity and looking for a bride. *Now* Tina is about to learn just how ruthless and disturbingly sensual Gio's brand of vengeance can be.

THE VENGEFUL GROOM, available in October from Harlequin Presents, is the fifth book in Harlequin's new cross-line series, **WEDDINGS, INC.** Be sure to look for the sixth book, **EDGE OF ETERNITY,** by Jasmine Cresswell (Harlequin Intrigue #298), coming in November.

WED5

This summer, come cruising with Harlequin Books!

PORTS OF CALL

In July, August and September, excitement, danger and, of course, romance can be found in Lynn Leslie's exciting new miniseries PORTS OF CALL. Not only can you cruise the South Pacific, the Caribbean and the Nile, your journey will also take you to Harlequin Superromance®, Harlequin Intrigue® and Harlequin American Romance®.

- ◆ In July, cruise the South Pacific with SINGAPORE FLING, a Harlequin Superromance
- ◆ NIGHT OF THE NILE from Harlequin Intrigue will heat up your August
- ◆ September is the perfect month for CRUISIN' MR. DIAMOND from Harlequin American Romance

So, cruise through the summer with LYNN LESLIE and HARLEQUIN BOOKS!

CRUISE

HARLEQUIN®

Don't miss these Harlequin favorites by some of our most distinguished authors!
And now you can receive a discount by ordering two or more titles!

HT #25525	THE PERFECT HUSBAND by Kristine Rolofson	$2.99	☐
HT #25554	LOVERS' SECRETS by Glenda Sanders	$2.99	☐
HP #11577	THE STONE PRINCESS by Robyn Donald	$2.99	☐
HP #11554	SECRET ADMIRER by Susan Napier	$2.99	☐
HR #03277	THE LADY AND THE TOMCAT by Bethany Campbell	$2.99	☐
HR #03283	FOREIGN AFFAIR by Eva Rutland	$2.99	☐
HS #70529	KEEPING CHRISTMAS by Marisa Carroll	$3.39	☐
HS #70578	THE LAST BUCCANEER by Lynn Erickson	$3.50	☐
HI #22256	THRICE FAMILIAR by Caroline Burnes	$2.99	☐
HI #22238	PRESUMED GUILTY by Tess Gerritsen	$2.99	☐
HAR #16496	OH, YOU BEAUTIFUL DOLL by Judith Arnold	$3.50	☐
HAR #16510	WED AGAIN by Elda Minger	$3.50	☐
HH #28719	RACHEL by Lynda Trent	$3.99	☐
HH #28795	PIECES OF SKY by Marianne Willman	$3.99	☐

Harlequin Promotional Titles

#97122	LINGERING SHADOWS by Penny Jordan	$5.99	☐
	(limited quantities available on certain titles)		

	AMOUNT	$
DEDUCT:	10% DISCOUNT FOR 2+ BOOKS	$
	POSTAGE & HANDLING	$
	($1.00 for one book, 50¢ for each additional)	
	APPLICABLE TAXES*	$
	TOTAL PAYABLE	$
	(check or money order—please do not send cash)	

To order, complete this form and send it, along with a check or money order for the total above, payable to Harlequin Books, to: **In the U.S.:** 3010 Walden Avenue, P.O. Box 9047, Buffalo, NY 14269-9047; **In Canada:** P.O. Box 613, Fort Erie, Ontario, L2A 5X3.

Name: _____

Address:_____City: _____

State/Prov.: _____ Zip/Postal Code: _____

*New York residents remit applicable sales taxes.
 Canadian residents remit applicable GST and provincial taxes..

HBACK-JS